# THE SPARK

*A Carolina Connections Novel - Book 2*

## SYLVIE STEWART

Rolling Hearts Press

# ALSO BY SYLVIE STEWART

*The Carolina Connection Series:*

**The Fix** *(Carolina Connections, Book 1)*

**The Lucky One** *(Carolina Connections Book 3)*

**The Game** *(Carolina Connections Book 4)*

**The Way You Are** *(Carolina Connections Book 5)*

**The Nerd Next Door** *(Carolina Kisses, Book 1)*

**Then Again**

**Happy New You**

**Game Changer** *(July 2019)*

**About That**

**Full-On Clinger**

**Between a Rock and a Royal** *(Kings of Carolina, Book 1*

**Blue Bloods and Backroads** *(Kings of Carolina, Book 2)*

# COPYRIGHT

First Print Edition: 2016
Copyright © 2018 Sylvie Stewart
Edited by Heather Mann

ISBN: 978-0-9989260-7-0

*"Though she be but little, she is fierce!"*
- William Shakespeare, *A Midsummer Night's Dream*

*Chapter One*

# LUCKY

**F**IONA

"You must be so proud," yet another couple gushed while their eyes tracked me. Not that they were speaking to me, but everyone's eyes were always directed my way at these events. I was a bug under a microscope—a well-dressed and polished bug, but a bug nonetheless. I stood dutifully by as my parents received the compliment and my mother doled out air kisses to the couple decked out in expensive but understated formalwear.

Ugh.

We wouldn't want to go crazy and wear peek-a-boo lace or down-to-there necklines or, well, a color that actually stood a chance at catching someone's eye, now would we?

How inappropriate.

I didn't know how I was going to make it through another one of these yawn fests without at least something sparkly to look at. Come on, people! It was as if the invitations had read "Attire:

Funereal Chic." My gaze swept the room—black, black, black—
ooh, charcoal! Wait, *red*! Oh, just the exit sign—my bad.

I was stuck in this receiving line of sorts with nary a glass of
champagne to keep me entertained. My only small act of rebellion
was wearing the sexiest, skimpiest pair of lilac lace panties I could
find, but they were completely hidden under my (modest, of
course) black sheath Dior gown. I had forgone the delicious red
patent leather Manolos—the poor things were stuck at home in my
closet, probably happy they didn't have to endure this evening's
event.

*"Shut up, Fiona! Positive thoughts, please,"* my inner voice,
Guilt, reprimanded.

Oh, right. *Sorry.*

So right now, you might be curious as to why I was the reluctant center of attention at this function, and you may even sympa-
thize with me for having to stand here sans champagne and bored
out of my mind (sexy panties aside). But in a minute, you're going
to agree with Guilt and think I'm a bitch.

You see, when all these people approach my parents and say,
"You must be so proud," what some of them really mean is,
"You're so goddamn lucky and a tiny part of me resents the shit
out of you." But it would be unseemly to actually say that so they
always go with the former comment.

Regardless of etiquette, behind their eyes I can always see the
envy along with the effort it takes to not let it show. They would
give anything, and I mean *anything*, to have a daughter like me.

I know, what a bitch, right?

But it's the God's honest truth. Many of these couples would
trade their very lives to have what my parents have—a daughter
who survived childhood cancer and lived to tell about it.

"I thought that went exceptionally well, didn't you?" my mother asked as she perched on the sofa next to me, her makeup still flawless and her blond up-do as elegant as it had been five hours earlier.

"Definitely," I agreed, removing my shoes to massage my sore feet. I mean, I may not have gotten to wear the Manolos but I wasn't a heathen or anything—I had still worn a pair of stilettos. At five-feet and a quarter (you bet your ass I'm including that extra quarter inch), I always wear heels—the higher the better.

Fact: adults don't take short people seriously. So I do anything I can to even the playing field. If I had a nickel for every time I'd been patted on the head by some patronizing asshole, I'd be—well, I'm already rich, so let's just say I'd be *disgustingly* rich.

To be fair, I, myself, am not actually rich, but my parents are. And they both evidently got straight As in preschool because they are awesome at sharing.

We have this odd relationship where I just exist and they are so tickled that they throw money at me. That, in and of itself, would be pretty pathetic, but along with the money, they also throw unwavering love, affection, and support in my direction and I hope I do a halfway decent job of returning the same to them. Lots of people say they have the best parents in the whole world, but I actually do. And that, in short, is why I can never say no when they ask for my help with The Foundation. That and my ever-present companion Guilt, of course.

"Ah, there are my beautiful girls!" my father said as he entered my parents' massive living room. He'd loosened his bow-tie and removed his tux jacket and was now looking between us and the screen of his smartphone. "Guess how much we netted? Just take a guess!" From his excitement, the answer was clearly a good one.

"$350,000?" my mother guessed.

"Um, $375,000 and Barbara Rogers' hotel keycard—I hear 80 is the new 40," I said, earning a nudge from my mother.

My dad looked at me with the most serious expression he could muster. "Fiona, you know I won't go older than 75—at that point they're more housecat than cougar."

I giggled—what can I say? I'm a daddy's girl. Did I mention how awesome my dad is?

"So, drum-roll please," he said and my mother and I dutifully tapped our respective sofa arms. "$432,350!"

Mom and I enthused appropriately and my dad went to the kitchen to fetch a bottle of champagne—finally, I was going to get some bubbly!

"Totally exhausting, but so worth it," my mother sighed as she let herself relax back into the cushions of the stylish gray sofa, her formal gown somehow remaining completely un-rumpled. I propped my stockinged feet on the designer coffee table and pretended not to see the chastising glance aimed at me. "This is going to make such a difference—I think this may put us over the top to get the new MRI for Children's."

We speak in shorthand around here where medical terminology, facilities, and organizations are so ingrained in our everyday dialogue that I often wonder if we need complete words at all. We're like a depressing version of a teenage text exchange.

Everything is "WBC," "ALL," "SCT," "Children's," and "County" to name just a few. And it's a good thing because if we used all the actual terms, we wouldn't ever have time to finish a conversation. For instance, saying "ALL" is a lot easier than saying "acute lymphocytic leukemia," which just happens to be the disease that has defined and redefined our lives over and over.

All right, so here's the 4-1-1: When I was nine years old I was diagnosed with ALL, and because of a series of unlucky test results and poor response to treatment, it was revealed that my chances were quite shitty. Undaunted, my parents used every resource available to them and refused to let the poor prognosis stick. It took three hospitals, a clinical trial, every alternative form of treatment my mother could find on the internet, and finally a stem-cell transplant to put me in remission. When I tell you that acupuncture was the highlight of my treatment plan, you understand how much the rest of it sucked donkey balls. And anybody who tells you acupuncture is "fabulous" or "so rejuvenating" is a big, fat, lying whore. Just so you know.

Where was I? Oh, right.

Needless to say, we were all elated when we got the good news that my leukemia was in remission and we would finally be able to return to normal life. The only problem? There was no "normal" to go back to.

Suddenly, our whole family was grappling with a host of conflicting emotions. For the two years we'd been fighting the disease, we'd assumed the finish line was remission. Instead, we were almost paralyzed by the simultaneous onslaught of not just the joy, but also fear, guilt, and sadness. What if it comes back? Why did we reach remission when so many others didn't? What comes next? And what happened to the sense of innocence an eleven-year-old is entitled to?

It was at this point in my life that Guilt moved into my consciousness and made herself comfortable. As far as I can tell, she spends her days tsk-ing disapprovingly at the cobwebs in my head and honing her skills as the most spectacularly annoying backseat driver ever. I would not recommend her as a house guest.

After a few weeks, I attempted to return to the life of a typical eleven-year-old, but everything was so different and awkward. My brain didn't seem to want to work the same anymore, and things that had previously come easily to me were suddenly overwhelming. I was having trouble remembering things, and my academic performance, which had always been stellar, began a downward spiral, with tests and homework becoming a huge struggle.

There were also physical implications from the disease and its treatment, the most noticeable of which was my development, or more specifically my lack thereof. While other girls my age were shooting up like beanstalks and wearing training bras, I was still essentially living in the body of a nine-year-old, with stunted growth and hormonal issues, neither of which would ever fully resolve—much to my dismay (see previous short-person rant).

In addition to all these issues, and possibly even because of them, my social life was a mess. My friends, classmates, and teachers treated me either like glass or like I didn't exist, their discomfort achingly obvious—which was all particularly hurtful to a young girl who had spent her childhood as a total people-person, embracing the world with complete exuberance and in the girliest manner possible.

I longed to return to the ease of my pre-cancer life but knew that I should just be happy to be alive. To ease the situation for everyone, I resolved to plaster a smile on my face so no one would think me ungrateful or worry about me. It was a habit I still maintained much of the time.

Meanwhile, out of a combined sense of gratefulness and contrition, my parents dove headlong into establishing a foundation for cancer research and childhood cancer facilities. To this day, it sometimes seems my mother's entire reason for existence is to spare other families the devastation wreaked by cancer. Other times, I'm reminded that about forty percent of her existence is actually reserved for worrying about me and trying to smother me —with love and attention. Although it often feels like plain old-fashioned smothering—you know, like with a pillow.

Obviously, my father is also very involved in what we call "The Foundation." But somebody has to bring in the big bucks, so he also runs the family's tech firm in Raleigh while my mom holds the reigns of The Foundation and I pitch in when called upon.

Then about four years ago, when I had reached my nine-year anniversary of remission, I decided to leave the nest—you know, the one full of pillows—and move to Greensboro to branch out on my own. I was twenty and finding it very difficult to find direction, so I figured becoming more independent might help me out.

My parents naturally fought it at first, but they eventually relented and bought me a gorgeous condo in a downtown high-rise with amazing floor-to-ceiling windows and two balconies. I freaking love it! They wanted to buy me a house, but I am way too much of a girly-girl to be responsible for my own appliances and grass and stuff. No thanks. I did mention the heels, right? Well, there is a whole designer wardrobe to go along with those heels and not a single pair of overalls in it. They also wanted to buy me a Mercedes, but I talked them down to a Prius with a mere mention of environmental effects and carcinogens.

So, I had my own place and my own life in Greensboro, and it was only an hour and a half to Raleigh so my parents could still hover enough to keep them relatively content. The one thing I still didn't have, though, was direction. It apparently didn't come with the new life and new condo like a gift-with-purchase at Nordstrom. I've spent the last four years floating from job to job trying to figure out what I want to do with my life and having very little luck.

The floating around has, however, provided a couple of amazing benefits—some really hilarious and awesome experiences, and some really hilarious and awesome friends. The greatest of these is, of course, my best friend in the whole wide world, Laney.

She and I met when I was doing a brief stint as a receptionist at the same company she was temping for. At the time, Laney had been raising a baby, going to college, and working a part-time job.

Needless to say, Laney rocks, and I am in complete awe of her most of the time. She is a single mom to a five-year-old little heartbreaker named Rocco (Oh, excuse me, he now demands that I say he is five-and-three-quarters) and she almost ties my mom for being the best mom in the world. However, Laney's inability to wear stilettos or any article of clothing made from a material other than cotton will eventually result in Rocco growing up to marry a girl with similarly bad taste—and that's just irresponsible. Therefore, she rates second in the best mom competition.

What my best friend lacks in fashion sense, though, she makes up for in her taste in men. She recently scored herself one seriously hot man in the form of an adorably doting construction god named Nate. I often want to cry tears of joy at his love and dedication to Laney and Rocco—well that and his tight ass.

*What? Laney doesn't care that I ogle him. Sometimes we even do it together. It's a bonding thing.*

Laney has not had the easiest time since she accidentally got knocked up her freshman year of college and the douchebag dad essentially skipped the scene. So seeing her and Rocco with such a great guy does things to my heart. It almost makes me wonder if that's something I could want for myself. Almost.

But I have my condo and my various jobs and my flitting back and forth to Raleigh, not to mention Guilt to keep me company, so I'm good.

My phone vibrated on the coffee table next to my empty crystal flute, sending me reminders I'd need for the morning. This particular night of flitting to Raleigh was thankfully over and had ended just as I preferred—with a drink and the people I love. Celebratory champagne consumed and the night's events adequately dissected, my parents and I doled out goodnight kisses and decided it was time for bed.

The thought of driving back to Greensboro so late was unappealing at best, and with the bubbly coursing through me, would have been idiotic. I am not the most responsible person on a good day—Guilt can attest—and I have a healthy respect for my own limits, so driving would just be begging for trouble. Instead, I crashed in my old bedroom. This happens often enough that I keep a small wardrobe and stash of beauty supplies at my parents' house for just such times. I consulted my phone on the next day's plans and slipped into my nightgown. As soon as my head hit the pillow, I was out.

Thank God for champagne.

Oh right, and for letting me be alive.

*Can I go to sleep now, Guilt?*

*Chapter Two*

## GO TEAM!

**M**ARK

Maybe if I just opened one eye it wouldn't be so bad.

I slowly lifted my left eyelid but quickly snapped it shut again as the morning light seared through my eyeball on a direct path to my brain.

*Ow*.

Last night had not been one of my better ideas.

Time to man up. I gradually opened both eyes and then blinked rapidly, finally registering the unfamiliar light fixture above me. The bed shifted slightly and I stilled every muscle. Shit!

I tried to recall last night's events, but things were a bit fuzzy past the numerous shots at the bar. Everything I knew about myself promised that my bedmate was at least of the female variety, but any other details were up for grabs. I was extremely confident in my sexuality, but I was equally confident in the power of Jack Daniels.

Ever so slowly, I looked to my side. Okay, lots of dark hair on the pillow—long dark hair—this was good. I could resume breathing.

Wait, not too fast. I didn't want to wake her up.

I carefully rose onto an elbow to have a look around. My brain throbbed painfully in my skull.

So, not my bedroom. And definitely not my sheets. These had a bunch of colorful girly shit on them. Was that…were those fucking unicorns? It was then I realized I was naked—naked on a shitload of unicorns.

Oh, God, please tell me I did not just spend the night with a teenager! How could this happen? I was at a bar last night, not a high school party! I looked around frantically for some evidence that this was, in fact, an adult's room and not that of an underaged girl. *Sweet Jesus, what had I done?!*

A pink lava lamp on the bedside table—*Shit!*

A stuffed rabbit on a chair in the corner—*Shit! Shit! Shit!*

And the rabbit was holding a baby bunny in its fluffy rabbit paws.

*Fuck me—I was going to jail.*

I was too pretty to go to jail, and I definitely didn't want to be anyone's bitch. My mom always told me my smile would get me in trouble one day, and here it was. That day had arrived. My perfect smile was going to land me in a twelve-by-twelve cell with a roommate named Attila who would probably want to call me *his* baby bunny.

"Oh goody, you're awake!" a high-pitched voice came from the pillow next to mine. My head swiveled around and I got my first sober look at the girl who would be the cause of my incarceration. Okay, well, Jack had a partial share in the responsibility, but whatever.

She did indeed have long dark hair that was currently in a rat's nest around her head, and she had one of those little pug noses that can sometimes be cute, but when faced with a future in the state penitentiary, I wasn't finding anything cute.

She offered me an extremely wide smile and almost bounced in the bed while remaining horizontal. She was very cheerful. And young.

Cheerful and young…and bouncy…cheerful and young? And bouncy?

Wait one minute—it was coming back to me! I sprang up in bed, ignoring my complete nudity, and searched the floor—and there it was. A goddamn cheerleading uniform.

*Nooooooo!*

"Baby, what's the matter?" the little jailbait asked.

"You're a cheerleader," was all I could say. Or whimper.

"Duh," she perked up. "Remember? Goooooooo Mark!"

I cringed and then looked back at her. In the midst of her cheer she had lost the top half of the sheet and her plump breasts were on display. I lunged for the sheet to cover her up but she obviously misunderstood my intent.

"Oh, yay, are we playing lion and lion-tamer again?! Rawr!"

"No!" I yelled at her. "No more playing! I need to get out of here. Oh my God." I put my head in my hands and tried to fight off the giant migraine that was forming so I could come up with a plan. A plan that did not involve a three-hundred-pound man feeding me, *ahem*, carrots.

"Oh, okay," she chirped. I chanced a glance at her again to see her shrug and then climb out of bed buck-ass naked.

I was not only going to jail, I was also going to hell.

"I have to go to class anyway. Leave your number if you want —maybe I'll call you sometime. Thanks for the fun night!" She slipped on a robe, blew me a kiss, and opened the bedroom door, grabbing a shower caddy on her way out.

Thank my lucky motherfucking stars—I was in a college dorm.

"Why does all the awesome stuff always happen to you?!" Brett asked as he slapped the table in frustration and then took a gulp of his beer.

What I was doing at a bar again was beyond me, but I was still freaked out by my near miss from the night before and I didn't feel like hanging out at my place alone. I took a sip of my soda and gave him a look that I hoped communicated exactly how stupid I found him. "Did you not just hear that story?" I looked around the table at the other two guys sitting with us, but they didn't seem to think Brett's comment was anything less than spot-on.

"Dude, you spent the night in a women's college dormitory with a fucking cheerleader. How old are you? Twenty-eight? Twenty-nine? That doesn't happen. And not only did you bang the cheerleading co-ed, she then invited you to come back again and bang her some more. This is like the foundation for every teenage boy's spank bank. Scratch that—every male on earth, not just the teenagers," said Brett.

"I have to say, I'm definitely filing it away," said Gavin, a friend from work. Gavin's sister, Laney, was dating my buddy Nate, who also happened to be my sort-of boss. Yeah, confusing, but we'll get to that later.

"I might be sporting wood right now thinking about it," said Trey, as he raised a handful of peanuts to his mouth.

We all looked at him with a good measure of revulsion.

"Dude, keep it to yourself or just go home," said Gavin.

"You know those nuts have been touched by probably a hundred guys who didn't wash their hands after taking a leak, right?" Brett pointed to the peanuts and Trey dropped them on the table.

"Whatever," I said, sweeping the mess of nuts aside. "You guys don't fully understand the feeling I had when I woke up and thought for just those few moments that I had crossed that uncrossable line. It was…it was…indescribable. I mean, I was scared shitless and I completely loathed myself. It was awful." I suppressed a shudder just thinking about it.

"Okay." Gavin raised a hand like he was asking permission to speak. "Let's assume for a moment that this was really as bad as you say." I nodded and he went on. "What if you, I don't know, stopped drinking to the point where you black out and bang a complete stranger who may or may not have a daddy waiting down the hall with a loaded shotgun?" He shrugged. "Just an idea."

Huh. It was possible he could have a point.

"Nah," said Trey. "I say you go back next weekend. I'll be happy to be your wingman. I used to play football in high school—I'm feeling the need to hear someone cheering my name again—Trey, Trey, Trey!" He raised his beer in a toast and simulated humping under the table. Why did I hang out with this guy again?

Oh yeah, because I did stupid shit like that too.

God, I was a mess.

Today was going to be a new day. I was going to clean up my behavior and start acting responsibly—well *more* responsibly at least. It was, after all, completely moronic to drink so much that (a) I couldn't remember who I'd screwed, (b) I couldn't be one hundred percent certain I'd used a condom—*I know. Just don't, okay?*—, and (c) I could have conceivably broken the law as well as about two hundred moral codes. I'd never envisioned myself as such a douchebag.

In general, I'd say I am a pretty dependable guy. I have a good job working for a construction company called Built by Murphy, and I'm well thought of there, as far as I know. My friend Nate's family owns the company and they've been really good to me. I started out working there after high school while I took night classes at community college, and over the years I've worked my way up to foreman and then, more recently, taken on responsibilities on the administrative side. I get paid well, I work hard, and I enjoy the job and the people I work with.

In fact, out of all the guys I know in their late twenties, I'm probably the most responsible among us—in theory, at least. I don't own a home, but I rent a house and I keep it furnished with nice stuff that I take care of. I know what it's like to live in shit and I don't reckon I'd like to revisit that experience, so I'm generally careful with my things and my work. I have a truck that may not be the latest model, but it does the trick. I've worked hard for my success, which is another reason I was so pissed at myself for losing sight of that and acting like an idiot.

After the night out with the guys, I'd had a hard time sleeping and couldn't seem to shut my mind off. It could have been the caffeine from the soda, but I had a suspicion it was more than likely a guilty conscience. *Yes, even I have a conscience.* Most of my brain wanted to blame my bonehead behavior on the Jack, but there was that one part telling me that maybe I was getting too old to be such a manwhore. Or not. It was too painful to think anymore.

I ended up getting out of bed at five and going for a run before hitting the gym. I gave a chin lift to Blaine, one of the trainers, on my way out of the locker room. The gym was practically empty at this time on a Sunday morning, with only a few of my fellow die-hards present. I threw my towel on one of the benches and began to stack the weights for my first set of reps.

The gym is my zen place. I don't like to brag—okay, that's not true, I totally like to brag—but I'm a super fit guy. I work out reli-giously and love to challenge myself and push my limits. I do an hour of cardio six days a week and I do weight training five days a week, rotating areas of the body to achieve maximum results. And I definitely achieve the desired results if the looks I get from women are anything to go by. And then there's that smile my mom was always talking about, so you do the math.

I don't have to try too hard to get a girl into my bed when I want one. Which, I'll be honest, is pretty often. I like all kinds of women—curvy, thin, short, tall, blond, brunette. As long as it's not the same girl twice, I'm game.

I don't do repeats. It's too much hassle—feelings get involved and then I have to try to avoid the girl and it's just a headache I don't need. Instead, I'm always upfront and tell every girl I'm with that all I'm looking for is a good time. One night of fun and then we part as friends. Or not precisely friends—in fact, the exact opposite. We part as strangers—just how it was meant to be.

So, the fly in the ointment must have been the alcohol because my fuck-and-run policy was certainly not the problem. It had always worked perfectly for me and I was getting too old to drink like that anyway. I was just going to have to cut down on the booze, just like Gavin had suggested. Awesome plan.

*See, I told you the gym was my zen place.*

Problem solved.

"Why are these girls so fucking boring?" I asked Nate for the third time that night as I returned to our table.

"Maybe because you're sober as a judge and you're not blocking out their voices while mentally undressing them?" he returned.

No, that wasn't it. I was definitely mentally undressing them. They were just boring as shit.

Gavin had recruited Nate to help clean up my act—you had to admire his youthful energy and optimism. Somehow they had talked me into going to happy hour after work on Friday to hone my new technique. Ha!

Their plan was for me to attempt to meet an "appropriate" girl without the aid of alcohol and then—*choke*—simply engage her in conversation instead of seducing her and taking her home. What was the fun in that? What were we, high school virgins?

*Oh right*, now I remembered the reason for this little intervention. I decided to placate them and give it a try, but I didn't really see the point.

"How do you ever expect to meet the right girl if you can't have a conversation with her before you whip it out?" asked Nate as he checked his phone. Probably looking for messages from Laney—he was so pussy whipped I was almost embarrassed for him. He'd turned into a fuckmuppet.

"I meet the 'right girl' all the time," I told him. "I think you and I have different definitions of the 'right girl.' My definition involves the girl who's right for my dick on that particular night." I fist bumped Gavin as Nate's eyes lifted from his phone and he gave me a look you'd give a dog who'd just eaten its own shit.

"What?!" I demanded.

"For the moment, let's set aside the issues of possible incarceration and diseases that make your dick fall off. Do you want to be 'that guy'?" Nate asked.

"You'll have to elaborate—my mind is still numb from the conversation I just had with that girl at the bar. She wouldn't shut up about her pet cockatoo, and I wasn't even allowed to make any awesome jokes about it."

Nate hastily dropped his phone on the table and threw his hand out in exasperation. "The pathetic guy who's in his mid-thirties and still trolling for college chicks while his friends are starting families and not having to spare any thoughts for STDs and psycho one-night-stands!"

"That was only once, and how was I supposed to know she'd just gotten out of rehab?!" I pointed my finger in his face and then grabbed my drink, forgetting for a moment that it contained no alcohol. "Since when did you get so old and boring?!" I demanded and slammed my glass down. "This sucks!" I may have whined a bit.

"Tell that to my cockatoo," Gavin snorted and then ducked as my fist almost connected with the side of his head. I wasn't going to actually hit him but I wouldn't have been too sad if he'd at least fallen off his stool, the asshole. Nothing was going my way tonight.

"Okay," Gavin said once he'd stopped laughing and deemed it safe to resume his position on his stool. "Let's do a little math here." He spared Nate a glance. "I'm not sure I'm with you a hundred percent on this one, Nate." His gaze turned back to me. "How old are you?"

"Twenty-nine."

"So, half plus seven—that gives us twenty-one and a half—let's be safe and go with twenty-two. It's not socially acceptable for you to date or bone anyone under the age of twenty-two… which makes last weekend pretty fucked up." As if I didn't know that already.

"We've established that, thank you, Dr. Drew," said Nate. Why in the hell was *he* so agitated? That was *my* gig tonight—he needed to get in line.

"So, all I'm saying is you don't have to be all domestic like dickless wonder over here—" He gestured to Nate who opened his mouth to object. Gavin's hand shot out to intercept. "Don't even try it—you're dating my sister. It is my God-given right to consider you a eunuch." Gavin then looked back at me. "Maybe you can at least take a girl out to dinner first—wouldn't hurt to try. Hell, I'm a lot younger than you and even I take a girl out—well, most of the time."

Well, shit, now I'd been slut-shamed and kind of felt like a cross between a lecher and Charlie Sheen—wait, was that redundant? Not important. Instead, I made a mental note to go get tested on Monday.

Nate turned to Gavin with a half-awed, half-amused expression. "I kind of want to take a video of your little speech and show Laney—you sound so grown up I think she would cry."

Gavin just responded by flipping him off, making the whole point completely moot.

I felt my phone vibrate in my pocket and pulled it out to see who was calling, hoping for a distraction.

Shit. My mom.

I was not in the right head space to talk to her right now, although she did provide further evidence of why romantic relationships are way more trouble than they're worth. I noted the time —8:15. I'd only be here a bit longer and then I'd call on my way home to check on her.

"So," Nate continued, fidgeting on his stool, "I've gotta get over to Laney's soon, but if you're both done striking out with all the girls in this bar, I need your help with something."

"Anything to get off this topic," I offered.

He paused and folded and unfolded the bar napkin in front of him. He looked weird. Was he gonna puke?

"Dude, do I need to hold your hair back or something? You look like you're gonna puke," said Gavin, echoing my thoughts.

"No, I'm not going to puke!" Nate bellowed as the napkin tore in two.

"Well, you look like it. Oh wait, do you have the shits? Do you need me to walk out behind you? If that's it, you're going to owe me big-time!" Gavin grumbled.

"I don't have the shits—Jesus, Gavin—I'm going to ask your sister to marry me!" He looked dumbstruck that those words had escaped his mouth, and he face-planted on the table.

"Fuck," was all I could say.

"Dude," Gavin said, and then promptly fell off his stool.

Huh, look at that—something finally went my way.

## Chapter Three

# MY FAVORITE RIVER IN EGYPT

**F**IONA

"Oh my God. I think I just had a tiny orgasm," Laney whispered under her breath, closing her eyes and licking her lips to retrieve any stray remnants of sauce she may have left behind. "You are more than welcome to work your culinary magic in my kitchen anytime," she said as if she'd forgotten that I cook at her house at least once a week as it is.

"Why, thank you. The pleasure's apparently all yours," I laughed at her. I love cooking for other people—it's depressing cooking for one. And leftovers suck, unless of course it's Chinese takeout.

"Wasn't that awesome, Nate?" Laney asked her hot-ass boyfriend who was silently staring at her mouth with his fork stock-still in midair. His dark hair was in need of a cut, but it did nothing to detract from his general hotness.

I snapped my fingers in front of his perfect scruffy face and he suddenly came to. "Oh no, lover boy—no dirty thoughts allowed at the dinner table. I have to eat here too and I don't need mental images of you two going to pound town on this table."

"Tell her to stop moaning and maybe I can accommodate you," Nate addressed me but his eyes were still glued to my best friend.

Okay, this was just getting gross. It was time to either stage an intervention or get laid myself *very* soon.

Laney blushed on her side of the table and put a finger to her mouth to shush us as her other hand gestured to the living room where her son Rocco was playing. He'd started the dinner with us, but it would seem my pork tenderloin masterpiece had missed the mark for him if the number of rolls he'd consumed was any indication. He'd been let off the hook early.

As if he'd been summoned, the little guy yelled from the other room, "I have dirty thoughts all the time, Aunt Fiona!"

We all stilled and Laney glared at us in a manner that would give Anna Wintour a run for her money.

"POOOOOOP!"

"Rocco!" Laney scolded.

"What?" he asked. "I think about poop a lot. What's dirtier than that?"

She shook her head and Anna Wintoured us again.

"What?" Nate and I asked simultaneously.

"Soooo, this is a new development," I said to Laney as she and I sat on her couch having a glass of wine after dinner. Nate had taken Rocco to get ready for bed without any assistance required from Laney. "I knew Rocco liked it when Nate read to him, but the whole routine? I'm impressed."

"I know," she said with that annoying dreamy look on her face.

Okay, it wasn't annoying—it was frickin' adorable. "Aside from his freakishly organized living habits and maybe his obsession with Notre Dame, I can't find a thing wrong with him."

"Go Tar Heels!" We erupted simultaneously. Enough said.

"Is he finally going to move in?" I asked. He'd been having "sleepovers" at Laney's since the holidays and it was March now, so I didn't see what the hold-up was.

Laney's brow creased and the dreamy look disappeared. Uh oh. "I thought he was. I mean, we've talked about it and it just seems like the next natural step." She gestured toward the hallway. "Rocco absolutely worships him and I know Nate loves us. But he's been acting a bit...*off* these last couple weeks." Her hand rose to her cheek and she rubbed it—this being her habit whenever she gets stressed or uncomfortable.

"It's probably just work." I waved her off, hoping I was right. "And besides, I was moments away from excusing myself at the dinner table so you two could go ahead and play hide-the-pork-tenderloin in private—I wouldn't be too concerned."

She smacked my arm and I almost spilled my wine.

"Hey! Watch it," I scolded her. "I just bought this blouse and I don't want to soak it in red wine if you don't mind. It's not like I could borrow anything from *your* closet to wear home—how embarrassing," I teased and then shielded myself from further assault.

I love giving her a hard time about her uber-casual wardrobe—I mean the girl wears athletic shoes to work, for Christ's sake (oh, and I'm not referring to Jesus with that expression—"Christ" is just my pet name for Christian Dior). But as long as she lets me dress her up like my own personal Barbie now and then, I'm usually content.

Laney is one of those women who should have lived in the

fifties, although she would never have survived as a stereotypical housewife type considering her closets are those of a hoarder and her idea of a home-cooked meal is frozen pizza. However, she has boobs and booty for *days* and I love dressing her up and showing off her, ahem, *assets*. She is also a good five inches taller than me (sigh) and has thick, glossy hair that hangs in a dark sheath halfway down her back. I try to buy her clothes all the time but she has very strict boundaries, which I can respect even if I don't totally understand. A sweater from a local boutique is okay, but a nightie from La Perla is sent right back—it's not like I could wear it. Please, my whole body could fit in her bra cup, sadly.

"Whatever." She blew me off, as usual. "So, on to *your* love life…any hot dates lined up?"

"Unfortunately, no. My muffin will remain unbuttered this weekend. No pork tenderloin in sight." I stuck my lower lip out in a pout. I was in a dry spell, as in the Sahara, and I was in desperate need with no prospects on the horizon—only mirages where my vibrator then had to play stand-in-stud.

"Why don't you call Terrence?" Laney asked so quietly I almost didn't hear her. She was hiding her face behind her dark hair.

"Um, excuse me?"

She faced me fully again. "I know—you don't want a relation-ship, but we love Terrence," she pleaded.

"*You* love Terrence. *I* love Terrence's man parts."

"God, you're such a guy," she said in disgust.

"Love and commitment are perfect and dreamy for you and Nate, and that's awesome—for you. I'm just not wired that way, and you know I don't feel that way about Terrence. We had a perfect arrangement and then he screwed it up by asking for more. I'm sure his 'more' girl is out there, but she is not me."

It was Laney's turn to pull out the pouty lower lip.

"As much as I love you, Laney, I'm not getting into a relationship just so we can double date and have a Brady Brides wedding. Although, if that were to somehow happen in an alternate universe, you know I'd be Marcia, right? I mean, just admit it. She was always the better dresser."

"Fine," she conceded, to which part I wasn't sure, but I was relieved to have the subject closed.

On my drive home, I was distracted by thoughts of our conversation and of Terrence. Thinking about him always made me alternately mad and nostalgic. Thinking about my love life in general usually conjured conflicting emotions.

Terrence and I had met a little over a year ago when I had been traveling to one of The Foundation's events to stand in for my mother. I was flying to DC and found myself killing time in the Ambassador's lounge, waiting for my delayed flight, when an extremely handsome pilot strode into the room. He was tall with short cropped hair and dark brown skin, his face bright with a smile.

I remember wondering who elicited such a response and feeling a flash of jealousy—or maybe just longing—to be a person who could provoke that kind of joy. I kept watch out of the corner of my eye as he flirted with a flight attendant, and I was all but captivated by his laugh. I don't know how to describe it, but it just made me feel happy and weirdly carefree.

After the flight attendant left, the man who later introduced himself as Terrence Dunbar seated himself across from me. I surreptitiously assessed him from my seat—and was evidently not as subtle as I'd intended to be because it was only moments before he struck up a conversation with me. His slightly crooked but utterly charming smile was almost as captivating as his laugh, and he had an uncanny talent for making me feel like I was the most important thing in the world to him at that moment.

We ended up talking and laughing for an hour before I had to rush to my gate. I only found out later that he'd intended to stop in the lounge for a mere five minutes but had stayed just to talk to me. I'd given him my number and he'd promised to call the next time he was in town.

Thus began our friends-with-bennies arrangement. It was perfect—neither of us wanted the entanglements of a relationship, and we both happened to find each other attractive and fun to be around.

And the sex was hot.

H-O-T.

But, just as I'd known they would, things came to an end. Terrence came to Greensboro one weekend for one of our sex-a-thons and declared that he wanted to move things to the "next level." I'm ashamed to admit I became a bit enraged and I'm sure I completely overreacted, but I was pissed that he had taken what I found to be a perfect arrangement and ruined it. I told him what he could do with his "next level" and hadn't spoken with him since.

Harsh, I know.

But it's for his own good. I promise. There is something broken in me. Or more accurately, there are a lot of things broken in me.

Terrence deserves better. He deserves a woman who will adore him and who he can adore in return—one who will give him babies with his gorgeous skin and crooked smile, and that woman will wake up every morning confident that she is the center of his world.

I know Laney was disappointed that Terrence and I were unable to, in the immortal words of Tim Gunn, "make it work," but I knew deep down that I'd done the right thing by breaking it off. He had certainly lit up many parts of me, and the things he could do with his—well, I digress. Suffice it to say, as much as he lit up my lady bits he never lit up my heart, and once it had become clear that he wanted to involve that organ, as opposed to just the one below his belt, I knew it was time to move on.

So, if I had to pretend to be glib about it to avoid talking about my "issues," so be it. Denial is not just a river in Egypt, as you well know.

## Chapter Four
# ET TU, PA?

**F**IONA

"Dr. Brandon is ready to see you, Fiona," said Darcy, one of my favorite PAs in the oncology department. Tearing my attention from my phone, I smiled and followed her, chatting about her kids and what had been happening in both our lives in the year since we'd seen each other.

I was there for my annual "make sure the bitch isn't back" appointment—my thirteenth such visit, so I was very familiar with the routine. For those of you lucky enough to be unschooled in the world of cancer, an annual visit to one's *pediatric* oncologist after thirteen years of remission is not exactly normal. However, in the world of my overprotective mother, it's required—unless I want to look into her tear-filled eyes and try to explain why I don't need to go. Yeah, not gonna happen. And despite the lack of any suspicious symptoms to suggest a possible illness, I still get chills running up my spine every time I approach Dr. Brandon's door.

"Fiona," Dr. Brandon said as he came out from behind his desk and wrapped me in a bear hug. "How are you, sweetheart?" He is a tall barrel-chested man in his sixties and has a neatly trimmed beard that has grayed over the years. His reading glasses are an ever-present decoration around his neck, and his tie is permanently askew. It was nice to see that nothing had changed in the last year.

"I'm good," I told him, hugging him back. I love this guy. He'd been my knight in shining armor when I'd been a petrified nine-year-old and he'd held my hand and told me we'd slay the mean old leukemia dragon together. And to this day I hold on to some of that old hero worship. I can't help it—he's like Santa Claus and Pa from *Little House* combined into one awesome guy.

"Where are you working these days?" he asked, knowing my penchant for drifting from job to job. I released him, and he walked back to the chair behind his giant oak desk, a smirk on his face. Did I say Santa Claus? Maybe not.

"Haha," I responded, but really had no good comeback. I had only been at my current job for two months after quitting my last one where I'd been working as a gofer for a promotions company and getting a skeevy vibe from my boss. Can you blame me for quitting? Well, technically I was fired, but who's keeping track? My new job wasn't anything glamorous, but at least my boss was cool and he didn't hit on me. "I'm working for a landscaping company answering phones and filing and stuff," I answered, knowing just how unexciting it sounded.

"Do you like it?" he asked, genuinely interested, I knew.

Ugh. I felt like I was disappointing him. "Yeah!" I said cheerfully, hoping to move on to the next topic. My job was only slightly more interesting than watching golf on TV, but I didn't mind. It was stress-free and it didn't hurt my brain.

"Hmph." He let out a small sound, communicating just how unconvincing I'd been. "All right. I'll let you off the hook and get down to business." He raised his glasses to his eyes and opened the file sitting on his desk.

My heart rate suddenly skyrocketed and I had the distinct sensation that I might actually faint. What was wrong with me? My breathing picked up. Surely he wouldn't have been so nice and casual if there was bad news to deliver. Pa Ingalls would never do that!

*Breathe, Fiona. It's been thirteen years.*

"Your blood tests look great."

Mini heart attack averted. Whoa, Nelly.

*See what I did there? Nelly from Little House?*

*No? Okay, whatever. I was nervous—you can't expect perfection.*

My hand went to my chest where my heart was still working overtime. "Wow, I didn't expect to feel this anxious after all this time. I mean, I know you only see me because my mother hounds you," I noted with the best grin I could muster.

"You know I look forward to our visits, sweetheart. And your smiling face always brightens my day." I knew what he meant without him having to explain. We share an unshakable affection for one another, but he is a pediatric oncologist and doesn't get to deliver tons of good news on a daily basis.

"As do I," I told him. "Kind of." I smiled.

He gave a low chuckle. "Okay, lab work aside, I also got the results back from your cardiologist and things look good on that front as well. Have you noticed any changes either physically or mentally that I should be aware of?" he asked.

Ugh. "Not really. My memory is still a bit screwy, as usual, and my cycle is practically nonexistent. I'm still waiting for that growth spurt I know is coming any day for sure, though," I joked, trying to keep things light. I even threw in a cheesy smile and a thumbs-up.

"Are you able to keep a handle on it?" he asked, ignoring my lame attempts at humor.

"Pretty much." I held up my phone. "That's why I have a phone that's smart—so I don't have to be," I tried to joke again but he was having none of it. I took in his chastising expression and thought about trying again—*I'll tell you, doc, the damn thing vibrates so much it almost eliminates the need for a date!*

Maybe not.

Quick! Change of topic!

"So how are your kids?" I blurted out.

Dr. Brandon has three grown children and is amassing a collection of grandkids that seems to grow like a rabbit colony every year. It's as if the women in his family are in competition with the Duggars to see whose uterus will fall out of her body first. Perhaps that was a bit hostile—I expected my wine to taste a tad sour this evening.

"Wonderful, as usual—Jenny and Isaac just opened a spa in High Point—did I tell you that?" he asked, already knowing he hadn't, but proud of his daughter and needing to brag on her a bit. "And three new grandkids since I saw you last." He pointed to a corkboard on his wall that was crammed with photo after photo of cute little kids (and some not so cute, but I oohed and aahed anyway). "What about you?" he asked.

I was momentarily shocked as I wondered what would possess him to ask such an insensitive question—until I noticed his pose. He was leaned into his desk with his hands folded perfectly in front of him and his head lowered just enough that he could look over his glasses.

Oh no. Lecture pose.

*Retreat!*

"What about me?" I laughed lightly, fooling no one.

"When are you going to find a nice guy and settle down?"

I waved him off. "Doc, I'm only twenty-four. What's the hurry?"

"Uh-huh, I know, but that's been your excuse the last four times I've asked and I know for a fact you haven't had a single boyfriend."

I inhaled sharply. "How do you know that?!"

"How do you think I know that?" His left eyebrow quirked.

*Damn meddling mother! Damn HIPPA—I sign away my privacy way too quickly.*

Crap!

Dr. Brandon is a close friend of my parents, as they've worked together on many projects with The Foundation since he became my oncologist years ago. He has offices in Raleigh and Greensboro, and I swear his presence in this city was one of the reasons my mother relented when I wanted to move here. Additionally, I unfailingly sign my stupid HIPPA paperwork every year, allowing the good doctor to discuss my medical information with my mother and father at will. Unfortunately, my mother doesn't seem to find it inappropriate to reciprocate by sharing my dating history with him! *Dammit!*

"I'm disowning her," I declared.

He laughed. "She's just worried about you."

"Well, she'll be a lot more worried when I disappear to Fiji and stop speaking to her."

"Fiona." He looked at me over his glasses again.

I couldn't help it. I hung my head and folded my hands in my lap. "What?"

"What you're feeling is not at all abnormal. Lots of survivors have a hard time forging personal and intimate relationships. I just don't want you to miss out on the good stuff in life because of fear. You may not believe it but you're one of the toughest people I know and I—*we*—want you to be happy and fulfilled. Moving from job to job and guy to guy without establishing any roots? Is this making you happy?"

I started to tear up because he wasn't telling me anything I didn't already know. But I'm usually great at putting on a happy face and shoving the truth down deep where I don't have to acknowledge it.

"I know it's not as simple as I'm making it sound and I don't want to upset you, but I wouldn't feel as if I were doing a good job as both your doctor and your friend if I didn't at least bring it up. Please, Fiona, give it some more thought and, for God's sake, pick up the phone and call me if you want to talk. I'm always here." He stood. His glasses went back around his neck, settling over his crooked tie, and he opened his arms for another hug.

Damn Pa! I went to him like Laura after someone pulled on her braids.

## Chapter Five

# I'LL TAKE HELL IF PURGATORY IS ANYTHING LIKE THIS

*M*ARK

"This is ridiculous!" I thought to myself. The woman sitting two seats over got up and switched to a seat across the room from me. So maybe I hadn't said it to myself after all.

I dropped my head down, elbows on my knees, as I waited for my mother to reappear from behind the closed double doors of the emergency room. My hand scrubbed at my short hair in a futile attempt to release some of my frustration.

Why did they have to make these waiting room seats so uncomfortable? And what was with this reading material? The least they could do was give me *Men's Health* or even *Car and Driver*, but all they had were chick magazines. And I already knew how to bring a girl to orgasm in less than five minutes, thank you very much. That thought brought the first smile to cross my face all day.

It was the Friday after Nate's momentous announcement, and

the mental replay of Gavin falling off his barstool had kept me entertained all week.

*What? I'm easily amused.*

We'd been of absolutely no help in coming up with a good proposal plan, but Nate should have known better. He needed to talk to his sister, Bailey, if he wanted advice that didn't include a reenactment of Justin Timberlake and Andy Samberg's famous "Dick in a Box" skit. Pretty sure the answer would be a right hook if he took guidance from us. Although come to think of it, Bailey would probably give even worse advice so he was pretty much screwed.

I'd been behaving myself all week, not drinking and not even going out to the bars to scope out the talent. And what was my reward? A phone call from my mom at four this morning begging for a ride to the ER. Let me tell you, that is not a call any son wants to get, early morning or any damn time.

Luckily, she was not the one who'd been injured.

No, as if the Fates were punishing me for my bad behavior with the co-ed, it had been my dad who'd landed himself in the ER —my piece-of-shit dad whom I hadn't seen in eight years and whom I'd hoped to never see again. Thus the reason I was going out of my mind in the waiting room while my mom was somewhere back in the ER with the dirty son-of-a-bitch.

Why? I had no damn clue.

When I'd picked up the phone this morning, I hadn't been able to understand a word my mother was saying, but I did finally catch something about a hospital. Once I'd calmed her down a bit, she'd been able to explain.

"It's your father," she'd said, sniffling.

"What the hell do you mean?" I'd asked, still half asleep but relieved to hear she wasn't hurt.

"The hospital just called and said that your father was brought in late last night by ambulance and he was unconscious and b-b-beaten." She started to cry again.

What. The. Fuck?

"Mom, calm down. Everything's gonna be okay."

This was bullshit. That asshole had ditched her thirteen years ago and now he was calling her from the hospital in the middle of the night?

"Sweetie, I need you to drive me to the hospital. I'm too upset to drive. I'll get in an accident."

"I don't mean to be insensitive or anything, Mom, but why did he call you?"

"He didn't," she said. "The hospital did. He's unconscious and I guess I'm still his emergency contact."

Note to self: When he wakes up, knock him out again.

So here I was at the hospital on a Friday morning—instead of working like I should be—wishing I were anywhere else for any other reason. Getting a prostate exam? Sure—lube up that glove and bring it on. Nothing could be worse than this. I couldn't for the life of me figure out why my mom gave the tiniest shit about what happened to my dad.

Had I been the emergency contact, the conversation with the nurse would have been a short one: "What's that? My dad's been beaten and he's unconscious? Good. Tell him I hope it hurts." Click.

How could she still care about him? Let him make her cry? He'd caused enough tears when he'd been around, I would have thought she'd want nothing to do with him after all this time. I guess I was wrong.

Growing up in my family had not been a picnic. While we didn't live in a trailer park or starve, we didn't have a whole lot.

My dad had a hard time holding onto a job, mostly due to the fact that he was the laziest human being to ever walk the earth. His exceptional talent for shifting responsibility off himself and onto absolutely anyone else didn't hurt either. He'd once blamed the family dog for losing a job because he claimed the dog "distracted" him and made him forget he was on shift.

He would constantly do idiotic things like using his unsteady paychecks to buy dozens of scratch-off tickets instead of milk or peanut butter. Or he'd get fired from a job and then get the brilliant idea to come home with fifty dollars' worth of takeout for dinner. My older brother, Jake, and I were luckily pretty good at making friends, so we spent a lot of time at other families' dinner tables.

Most nights, our father would come home after a day of work or hanging out with other deadbeats and proceed to tell my mom everything that was wrong with her. Or me. Or Jake. He had a brilliant knack for undermining and belittling and for finding just the right vulnerability to poke at.

For Jake, it was his natural charisma and his less-than-stellar performance at school. For me, as paradoxical as it sounds, it was my better-than-average success at school—and also my scrawny-ness. I was only slightly less awkward than a drunk newborn giraffe. And for our mom, it was just about anything she did or sometimes simply the fact that she existed.

I'd spent many sleepless nights conjuring up confrontations the adult Mark would someday have with my dad, meticulously outlining all his faults and putting him in his place, never comprehending that a man like him would never be swayed in his stubborn perception of his own superiority.

Despite his general surliness and his miserable treatment of our family, he never got physical with any of us—apart from the occasional smack to the back of the head.

"I don't understand how any man could lay a hand on a woman," had been a phrase I'd heard him utter many times.

We were, after all, a God-fearing family, and hitting your wife would have been a grave sin. However, he didn't find verbally and emotionally abusing his family or failing to provide for them to be frowned upon by God, so he went whole-hog and developed quite the talent for those pursuits.

When we were little, my mom worked the night shift as a cashier at a convenience store so there would always be an adult around to care for us in the event my father found himself employed. On nights when my dad was too drunk or too busy being a deadbeat to feed us, the older lady on the other side of our duplex would usher Jake and me to her kitchen.

Her name was Mrs. Finley and she was a widow whose husband had died in the Korean War. We knew this because every time we came over she told us the same story about how kind he'd been to her dying mother right before he'd left for the war and she only hoped someone had been as kind to him before he died. Being the young kid I was, the sadness of that didn't register until much later.

Mrs. Finley was a petite woman with short silver hair, and she wore a variety of housecoats that zipped up the front. Her house smelled like roses, despite there never being any fresh flowers in sight, and she made gingersnap cookies that were so spicy they burned our taste buds. For some reason, this made them even more appealing to Jake and me, so she baked them constantly.

The other thing I knew about Mrs. Finley, besides the fact that her husband was dead and she baked strange cookies, was that she *did not* like my father. Not one bit.

With my mom working nights, there was always some money coming in, just never quite enough. Looking back, I'll never understand how my mother managed to take care of us during the day and still get enough sleep to make it through her night shift, but she somehow did it. Mrs. Finley pitched in when she could, but it was mostly just my mom.

As time passed, though, it became apparent that the home environment my dad created was taking its toll on our mother. There would be many times when I'd hear her crying through her bedroom door or days when we'd come home from school and find that she'd just been sitting on the couch and staring at the TV all day instead of eating and getting some much-needed sleep to make it through her night shifts.

Although Jake and I had inklings that this wasn't quite normal, it was all we knew so we didn't think to question it much. Once we were a bit older I think we finally recognized our mom's tendency toward depressive behavior, and as the years progressed she became more and more "delicate." Not sure if that was the right word to capture the nature of it, but it seemed to fit.

Then two things happened.

First, Jake graduated from high school and signed up for the Marines the same day. I was fourteen and was suddenly alone with a depressed mother and a deadbeat father. By that point, my mom had moved to a better-paying job as a waitress, but there were a lot of times when she couldn't get out of bed and I worried she'd get fired. I got a part-time job as a busser at a local pizza place—the owner knew I wasn't sixteen when I lied about my age, but he hired me anyway and paid me under the table until I was legally allowed to work. We ate a lot of pizza at the Beckett household in those days.

Needless to say, I was more than a little resentful toward my brother for ditching us.

The second thing that happened was better than the first,

although I may have been the only one to see it that way. About a week before my sixteenth birthday I awoke to the sound of my mother crying, which wasn't unusual, I'm sad to say. I found her at the wobbly kitchen table holding a piece of paper. Tears streaked her cheeks and her eyes were puffy and red. I took the paper from her and read the words written in my dad's messy scrawl.

*I can't let you drag me down anymore—I deserve better.*

That was how my dad chose to leave our family. If his departure hadn't wounded my mom so sharply I would have thrown a fucking party in celebration. I was certain Mrs. Finley would have pitched in with decorations and ginger snaps, but sadly she'd died the previous summer.

It had happened peacefully in her sleep, and I remember thinking at the time that I hoped I'd been especially kind to her the last time I'd seen her. Although she wasn't there to celebrate with me, I was sure Mrs. Finley was whooping it up in heaven that the bastard had finally flown the coop.

That was thirteen years ago, and apart from a visit from him in my early twenties—where he asked me for money—I hadn't laid eyes on the old man since.

As far back as I can remember, I've thought of it as my job to worry about my mom and to this day I constantly wish to be a better son. I should have taken better care of her. Maybe if I had, she wouldn't be in an ER crying over a guy who never deserved her tears.

I rubbed my hands over my face as I mentally cursed him one more time. How much longer was this thing going to take? My ass was falling asleep and I needed a caffeine fix. I approached the main desk and asked the nurse if there was anywhere close by to get a coffee. She informed me that the hospital actually had its own Starbucks.

Of course it did.

I stumbled in the direction she pointed and sniffed the air for the scent of a caffeine trail. After a couple wrong turns, I finally approached the ubiquitous green and white sign and got in line.

I was completely zoned out so it took me a moment to realize that someone was staring at me from a few feet over.

Sitting at a small table in the corner was a tiny shift of a girl I'd encountered once before.

The encounter had not gone well.

I'd tried to hit on her and she'd not only rebuffed me, but she'd insulted me repeatedly and without reason. It was just my luck to run into Fiona Pierce on what happened to be one of the shittiest mornings I'd had in a long while (the cheerleading incident notwithstanding).

Unable to cease being a member of the male species, I looked her over and, despite her diminutive size and overall insulting tone, I still found her to be physically appealing. What can I say? I own a penis.

She has delicate features but huge green eyes and light blond hair that falls around her shoulders and sweeps over her forehead. It's almost as if a breeze accompanies her wherever she goes, causing her hair to float around her face in constant motion. There was just…something about her, some hint of fire I'd noticed the very first time I'd spotted her across Laney's backyard. It was the very thing that had propelled me toward the deck where she'd been standing, where I'd then proceeded to bomb in a most spectacular fashion. That had been the day after Thanksgiving and I hadn't seen her in the months since.

Until today of all days.

She wore a light jacket and a knee-length skirt and sat with her legs crossed, one leg bouncing and showcasing some strappy heels.

For a brief moment, my mind wandered and I imagined those heels biting into my back as her legs wrapped around my waist—and then I remembered what a harpy she was and forced my mind back to coffee.

I'm sure I looked like shit, and that had to be the cause of the small smirk on her face. I didn't think I was up to the challenge of sparring with the little spitfire, but the fact that she kept her eyes on me told me I wasn't going to have much choice in the matter.

It was all a little baffling to me. She was Laney's best friend and—according to Nate—was really sweet, smiled a lot, and was funny as hell. He had mentioned that she had a bit of a temper, but that was no news flash to me. I simply couldn't reconcile the two versions of this girl in my mind.

It was my turn at the counter so I looked away from her to place my order. A moment later a voice came from my side.

"Care to join me?"

I turned to see Fiona standing next to me, coffee cup in hand, wide innocent-looking eyes peering up at me. Hmm.

The top of her head barely reached my chin even with the heels. How short was this girl? I bent down in an overly exaggerated manner.

"I'm sorry, can you say that again? I couldn't quite hear you from way down there." I was determined to fire the first shot over her bow. And it seemed my aim was impeccable.

Her cheeks pinked immediately and her mouth got tight. "I was *trying* to be nice, but I'm obviously wasting my time," she hissed and spun around to stalk back to her table, her hair swinging gloriously around her.

Okay, so maybe I'd completely misread this situation.

But she'd totally blindsided me with her bitchiness at our last encounter and I must have still been harboring a bit of resentment.

After all, if memory served, she'd called me a "meat-head," a "moron," and had suggested I "go eat a bag of dicks," all within the span of sixty seconds. If it hadn't been aimed at me I might have found it impressive. And all I'd done was say hello—and I might have called her "Tinkerbell" and directed her to the kids' table—that part was a little fuzzy.

Since I couldn't afford any more bad karma, I decided to go apologize once I got my coffee. I took my first sip to steel myself for what promised to be a delightful exchange.

"Hello, Fiona." I approached and she pretended not to hear me as her thumbs typed away on her phone—probably texting Laney about what an utter dick I was.

I sagged into the seat across from her. "I'm sorry for what I said. It's been a shitty morning and, based on our last meeting, I wasn't prepared for civility."

She set her phone on the table and eyed me speculatively for what seemed like an eternity. Finally, she spoke. "I suppose I can understand that." She tossed her hair and sipped her coffee. "I accept your apology."

We were both silent.

Her leg bounced.

I spun my coffee cup around in circles.

We both pretended to find the décor of this particular Starbucks to be fascinating.

It was awkward as shit.

I almost wished I were back in the waiting room.

Or at the proctologist's office—yes, it was almost that bad.

## Chapter Six

# MYSTERY SOLVED: TONY SOPRANO IS ALIVE AND LIVING IN NORTH CAROLINA

## FIONA

Shit, this was awkward. Why wasn't he saying anything? I was the last one to speak, and according to the common rules of conversation, it was his turn, dammit!

*Fine.*

"So…" I said. *I know—brilliant.*

"So…" Mark replied.

*Seriously?*

We were a match made in heaven—the dumb blonde and the dumber jock.

Had his neck gotten thicker since the last time I'd seen him? I just didn't understand the point to all these muscles—it was all a bit excessive.

Don't get me wrong. I love the solidity of a guy who works out and takes care of himself, and I wouldn't turn my nose up at a nice set of abs and biceps—or a nice ass, of course—but this guy was like a walking ad for steroids. Okay, well, maybe that was a bit harsh, but he was just so…so…bulky. I mean, his boobs were ten times bigger than mine and there was something exceedingly wrong about that.

Aside from his overly-muscled physique, though, I had to admit he's kind of a babe. He has a great smile, not that I'd seen it yet today, but I remembered it from our last encounter. And I usually don't care for the whole buzz-cut thing, but it so works on him. His eyes are also a rich deep brown and—holy eyelashes—how was that fair? All the mighty forces of Sephora couldn't produce lashes that nice! Oh well, it wasn't as if a nice smile and some eyelashes could make up for the fact that he is completely insufferable.

He finally spoke. "What brings you here at—" he checked his watch, "ten-twenty-four on a Friday morning?"

"Just a check-up," I answered. I certainly wasn't going to elaborate on my visit with Dr. Brandon. "How about you? You mentioned a shitty morning." I sipped my coffee and hoped I had successfully transferred the focus to him.

He must not have been lying about his crap-tastic day because he looked like he hadn't slept at all last night. His brow held what looked like a permanent crease big enough that I could potentially store my eyeliner pencil in there, and the area under his eyes had a greenish-gray cast that even those lashes couldn't disguise.

"Yeah, you could say that. Just some family stuff—had to come in early this morning to the ER." He scrubbed a hand over his light brown hair.

Before I had time to think about it, I covered his other hand with my own. "Oh God, is everything okay? Who got hurt?" My heart pounded and I suddenly regretted any of my negative thoughts toward him. *Muscles are great! And who needs a silly old neck anyway?*

He waved me off. "Nobody." He stared at my hand on his and I couldn't read his expression. I removed my hand as nonchalantly as possible and used it to grab my coffee—super casual-like. *Ugh.*

Mark leaned back in his chair and sighed. "Well, somebody, but he's nobody important. My mom wanted to come in to see him so I drove her—that's all."

I let out a breath I hadn't realized I'd been holding, although I was a bit confused by his comment. "Oh, well that's a relief I suppose."

"Yeah, I guess," he said distractedly.

Clearly there was something going on that I was not privy to—and why should I be? I didn't even know this guy. Apart from sharing a few insults and a cup of coffee we were virtual strangers. Our only connection was some mutual friends and that didn't necessarily amount to anything much in the grand scheme of things.

"Listen, I'd better get back to the waiting room. I don't want my mom coming out and wondering where I am." He stood from the chair. "I guess I'll see you around, what with Nate and Laney and Gavin…" he trailed off.

He stood still for a moment, looking oddly pathetic in an old threadbare t-shirt and track pants. I don't know what possessed me, but out it came. "Would you like some company while you wait?"

His head snapped up, almost as if he'd forgotten I was there. Then he blinked a few times and I saw the crease in his brow release a bit. "Actually, that would be nice."

I had never realized before how uncomfortable the chairs were in the ER waiting room. Back in the day, I'd spent many a night waiting in similar rooms, but I had usually been too nauseous or in too much pain to care about the hard chairs. I made a mental note to ask my mom to add new chairs to the ever-growing list of fundraising efforts. Not that is was that important, but sometimes it's the little things that can make a difference.

I was flipping through my texts and trying not to laugh out loud at something Laney had texted about Rocco—totally inappropriate to laugh in an ER waiting room, I know, but that kid cracks me up! I don't have to deal with him on a daily basis, however, so I'm allowed to find his antics funny.

Rocco is an exhibitionist of sorts, always preferring to hang out in his underwear and absolutely nothing else.

Am I the only one who finds tiny boxer briefs to be completely adorable?

Anyway, according to Laney's frantic text, Rocco had accidentally seen Nate naked and kept asking when his wiener would be big like Nate's. She then caught Rocco walking around the house wearing Nate's boxer briefs with a belt cinched around his tummy to hold them up. If I hadn't been sitting next to a very seriously brooding Mark, I definitely would have laughed my ass off.

*Laney: I'm worried this has scarred him for life!*

*Fiona: Shut up. This is hilarious. These are the moments you store in your memory only to be brought up at his rehearsal dinner when he gets married. Please tell me you took pictures of the belted underwear!*

*Laney: No way! Now Nate is never going to move in! He's worried CPS is going to come and arrest him for letting Rocco see him naked!*

*Fiona: Calm down. He didn't "let" him. It was an accident. Plenty of little kids see their parents naked. How many times has Rocco walked in on you naked?*

*Laney: But Nate is NOT his parent.*

*Fiona: Seriously?*

*Laney: What??!!*

*Fiona: Don't be ridiculous. You know you're going to get married and have more beautiful babies and Nate will be a father to all of them.*

*Fiona: Your silence speaks volumes. Stop worrying.*

*Laney: I love you.*

*Fiona: I love you too.*

*Laney: Oh my God—I am a horrible friend! I totally forgot! How was your appointment?*

*Fiona: All GOOD!*

*Laney: Yay! I'm so happy!*

*Fiona: Me too.*

Too bad my heart didn't quite agree with my text. Damn Pa and his thought-provoking nuggets of wisdom.

*What was wrong with me?* I'd just gotten good news and I was sitting next to a guy who, while claiming this ER visit was no big deal, was obviously grappling with something monumental.

Guilt shook her finger at me. Yes, Guilt is a woman because women are better at head weaving and finger shaking so it's more effective. If Guilt were a guy he'd just shrug his shoulders and say, "Eh, just rub some dirt on it."

I pushed the negative thoughts aside and peeked over at Mark. We'd been sitting in a somewhat companionable silence for the last half hour, but it was clear he was getting restless. We had both finished our coffees and he sat with his hands clenched over his knees while I had been occupying myself with my phone. I quickly glanced at my calendar one more time before putting the phone back in my purse and turning my body toward Mark.

"How are you holding up?" I asked.

"What do you mean? I'm just waiting for my mom," he scoffed.

"You are quite possibly the worst liar I've ever met in my life," I informed him with a smile.

"Not possible. I'm awesome at poker." He turned to me and—damn those eyelashes!

"Then I have never met the terrible liars you play poker with," I returned.

That earned me a hint of a smile.

"Come on, give me your worst joke," I said.

He looked at me like I'd just escaped the psych ward.

"Oh, don't give me that look. Your worst joke. Go."

He shook his head. "Fiona, I don't…" he trailed off.

"Okay, fine. I'll go first." I sat up straight and smoothed my hair as if preparing for a presentation. "Why don't crocodiles eat clowns?"

He peeked at me from the corners of his eyes and I swore I saw his lips twitch. "Fine. I don't know. Why?"

I gave him a "duh" look and answered, "They taste funny." I followed that up with jazz hands.

He face-palmed.

"Pretty bad, huh? Your turn."

Mark sat up and looked at me. "What exactly is the point of this again?"

I started to answer before I thought better of it. "My dad and I used to do this all the time when we were waiting—" I stopped myself just in time. "You know, for appointments and stuff. It passes the time."

It was actually one of my sweetest memories of that dark time in my life—my dad smiling at me and telling the worst jokes ever in an effort to distract me from fear or pain, even if it was just for a moment.

Mark let out a short mirthless laugh that startled me.

What was that about? I needed to chill him out.

"Just go with it. Your turn," I prodded.

He looked sideways at me again before giving in. "Fine, let me think for a minute." His eyes went to the ceiling for a moment before he continued. "Okay, prepare yourself. This is horrible."

I wiggled in my seat in anticipation. What can I say? I love a bad joke.

"Did you hear about the fire at the circus?"

I shook my head.

Mark cringed and said, "It was in tents."

I couldn't help it. I giggled.

"You're not supposed to laugh—it was awful!"

"That's why I'm laughing. That might be the worst joke I've ever heard." I still couldn't stop giggling.

Mark just shook his head and I finally got a full-on smile, the same one I remembered from Laney's deck. The same one he's used when he'd acted like a total sleazebag. I'd almost forgotten.

But before I could give it another thought, the double doors to the inner sanctum of the ER opened and a slim woman with dark brown hair, puffy eyes, and a harried expression emerged. "Mark, sweetie," she said, looking bewildered and a bit shell-shocked.

Joke time was most definitely over.

Mark rose abruptly from his chair and went to her, enveloping her in a hug. If the situation hadn't been so sad, the image would have been almost comical—such a slight figure secured in an unbelievably expansive embrace. It almost looked as if he could have wrapped his arms around her twice. Perhaps it would have helped, she seemed so devastated.

I wished I knew what was going on, but I reminded myself that I was a virtual stranger who had no business butting in—even if all I wanted to do was help.

After several moments, Mark released her from his embrace but held onto her upper arms and peered into her face. "Tell me," he said, his jaw tight.

The woman, who I could only assume was his mother, swiped at some fresh tears. "It's bad. He's awake, but he owes some money to some really bad people and they tried to beat him to d-d-death." She started to sob quietly.

I frantically searched for a packet of tissues in my purse.

"Shit," said Mark.

"I don't understand," his mother said. "This kind of thing doesn't happen to people in real life. We need to help him. We need the police but he said no."

Mark cursed again as I finally unearthed the packet and approached cautiously. I handed the tissues to Mark. He spared me a momentary glance and then offered them to his mother.

She turned her eyes to me, a bit surprised to see a stranger with her son. "Thank you," she managed and then wiped her eyes and nose.

Mark led her to a seat across the room and bent down to talk quietly with her. I couldn't make out anything he said, and I just stood awkwardly, not quite sure what I should do. He rose a moment later and approached me. The deep furrows had returned.

"I think I can take it from here."

Oh, okay, that was a bit abrupt. "Sure. Of course," I said and reached out to touch his hand in reassurance. "Take care, Mark."

"Thanks. You too," he said distractedly, but he was already on his way back to his mom.

"Okay, so you know I'm a terrible gossip, but this is *not* gossip. This is just something you need to know but I'm afraid it's going to come out as gossip," I announced as I burst through Laney's front door that evening.

"Um, hi," she said, but she was smiling—she knew me too well to expect any other kind of entry into her house from me.

"Something is wrong with Mark," I said as I stalked into the kitchen and put a bottle of Kim Crawford on her counter—her new *granite* counter, thanks to sweet Nate. He'd been slowly updating the kitchen, and the counters were the latest addition. Before that had come the cooktop, much to my delight. "We've got to figure this out and help him." I brought my mind back to the situation at hand.

I turned around and realized she wasn't there. "Laney?!"

She rounded the corner. "Excuse me, but did you just tell me something about Mark? Mark from Nate's work?"

"Yes! Keep up, woman!"

"I thought you hated Mark." She tilted her head to the side and crossed her arms over her giant rack. I sometimes marveled at her ability to stand up straight with all of *that* going on up front.

"Meh."

"What does that even mean?" she demanded.

"Not important. Get your hot piece of ass in here—we need to talk business."

"My 'hot piece of ass' is still at work so you'll have to settle for me," she said, blowing her hair out of her face. Now that I took a good look at her I noticed that she was dressed in a ratty t-shirt and an old pair of denim overalls, her messy hair partially pulled back. There was dirt smudged on her face—and she was sweaty.

I circled my finger in front of her. "What's all this? Are you a farmer now? I have to say I'm not a big fan of this look."

"Thank you, Joan Rivers," she said, evoking a little sigh of pride from me that she made a fashion reference—one that actually made sense (although technically Joan is no longer with us, but whatever. RIP). "And no. I'm cleaning out Gavin's room." She gestured to the stack of packing boxes in the attached living room.

"Holy shit! Is he finally moving out? Let me guess—one too many awkward midnight encounters in the hallway with the guy who just finished banging his sister?"

Laney choked on the air, I assumed.

"Now all you have to do is get a white noise machine for Rocco and you and Nate can play 'feed the kitty' as loudly as you want. Bow-chicka-wow-wow." I threw in a hip swivel to reinforce my point. Hey, if you can't be real with your best friend then what's the point?

She gave me a look she mostly reserves for Rocco when he sings about genitalia while at the grocery store.

"Hey, speaking of Rocco, where is my little man?" I had an urge to hand out some tickles. I started down the hall to find him and to check out Gavin's empty room.

Laney recovered her voice and called out after me, "I had to send him down the street to play with Aiden. He was unpacking the boxes as fast as I was packing them. I don't think he wants Gavin to go."

I stopped outside Gavin's door. Huh, this was a little sad now that I saw the empty room. All that was left was a stripped-down bed and an old dresser. It was all a bit pathetic. Poor Rocco. Who was he going to learn bad habits from now that Gavin would be gone? Without his uncle around he was never going to learn how to belch the entire alphabet. Nate was a more civilized guy—the most he could probably teach him would be to blame a fart on the dog.

I was actually very fond of Gavin, and not having any siblings of my own, I sort of saw him as my little brother too. When Laney bought her house last year, Gavin had moved in with her to help with Rocco and with renovations on the house. With the arrival of "Tall, Dark, and Holy Hotness," though, Gavin had gotten out of the work on the house. But he was an important part of this little family and, while it was definitely time for him to strike out on his own, it was bittersweet.

Laney joined me and leaned against the doorjamb. "I'm gonna miss his stupid face," she sighed. "But he's promised Rocco lots of sleepover parties, and I have to say it has been getting a little cramped around here. I'm proud of him, though."

"Me too," I said and squeezed her arm. Gavin had basically gone from industrial-strength barnacle to semi-independent adult in the span of the last six months. A derailed baseball career had turned him into a freeloading cloud of grumpiness, and it wasn't until recently that a series of events kicked his butt into growing up and moving on.

He was now working part-time for Nate's family's construction company in addition to coaching advanced level players at the Baseball Academy in town. I may or may not have had a tiny bit to do with the latter, but I'll never tell. *Yeah, right.* I totally abused my parents' contacts to get Gavin an interview for the job, but in my defense, he was completely qualified. He was finally coming to terms with never going to the Big Show and was actually enjoying helping other guys work toward that dream.

"Where is he moving?" I asked.

"He and Brett are renting a townhouse just north of High Point."

"I fear for their neighbors." Gavin and Brett have been best friends since high school and let's just say that they are pretty adept at bringing out the idiot in each other.

"That is no joke," she agreed, swiping her face with the back of her hand and leaving another dirt streak.

I hated to imagine the things Laney had found while cleaning up that room. Perhaps the entire Kim Crawford should go to her.

Or not.

"So tell me this mysterious news you have about Mark Beckett?" Laney nudged my arm.

"Is that his last name? Right. So, I ran into him at the hospital this morning and he was almost as insulting as he was the last time I saw him—well, at first anyway."

"Did he make more short jokes?"

"Yes! What is up with that? Was he traumatized by a politically incorrect circus clown or something?"

Laney snickered. "I have no idea, but that's a solid theory. Now go on."

It's true—I'm easily distracted, but Laney is good at getting me back on track without making me feel like a complete spaz.

"I thought at first that he was hungover because he looked all zoned out and tired, but he had actually been waiting since early morning for his mom. He drove her to the ER to see somebody who'd been hurt. He wouldn't tell me anything about who it was, but he was totally distracted and stressed out. When his mom came out she was super upset and Mark seemed really pissed off. I overheard his mom say that the guy—whoever he is—had been beaten unconscious by somebody he owes money to and that they tried to kill him! It was all very *Sopranos*, but without any of the funny stuff."

"Are you being serious right now?" Laney asked, looking skeptical.

"Dead." Oops. "I mean yes! This actually happened."

Her hands went to her hips. "Holy shit. I'm calling Nate."

"That's what I was saying—we need his help!"

"No—we're gonna need more wine!"

*Chapter Seven*

# TAG – YOU'RE IT

**MARK**

"What the hell, man?!" Nate's voice thundered over the phone so loudly I had to pull it away from my ear. I knew Shortcake wouldn't be able to keep her mouth shut.

"Take it down a notch—I'm not hearing impaired."

"You called in for a personal day and now I'm hearing there is some guy your mom's involved with and he's being stalked by loan sharks. I repeat, what the hell, man?!"

"Oh, it gets worse."

"How is that possible?"

"It's my dad."

Silence. Then, "You've got to be shitting me."

"I shit you not. I couldn't come up with this level of FUBAR if I tried."

"Where is he now? Where are you and your mom?"

"He's still in the hospital and I'm at my mom's with her."

As if the morning hadn't been a treat in itself, this day just kept piling on the shit. After Fiona left us at the hospital I'd been able to talk to a nurse and get some information on the extent of the sperm donor's injuries. He had a broken collarbone, broken ribs, a broken leg (likely from a baseball bat to the knee), and head trauma. Terrific. He would need surgery for the leg and knee and would be in the hospital for several days. I didn't know the status of his medical insurance, and I didn't want to.

Thankfully, I had been able to talk my mom into going home since the nurse informed me that the bastard needed rest and was on serious pain meds. I doubted he even remembered talking to my mom, and I was hoping to keep it that way. Keeping *her* away may prove to be a bit more difficult.

She'd spent the afternoon intermittently pacing and quietly crying, despite my efforts to distract her. She called in to work and got the evening off, although I personally thought it might have been a good way to get her mind off the whole situation. But I got her to eat something in the late afternoon and then finally convinced her to lie down in her bedroom.

I had no idea what to do. And since I couldn't say what I wanted to, which was, "Just leave him there and forget about him," I was at a total loss. So, I'd been sitting on the couch stewing while my mom rested.

On the other end of the phone, I heard Nate sigh. He knew all about our history with my dad. "I can't believe he had the nerve to call her."

"That was my first thought, too, but he was out cold. If you can believe it, he still had her listed as his emergency contact—after thirteen fucking years!"

"What an asshole. And your mom actually wanted to go to him?"

"I will never understand women," I replied.

"I've been told it's an impossibility so don't even try. What are you going to do?"

I swiped my hand over my head for the umpteenth time that day. "I have no fucking clue."

"Did the cops come?"

"Yeah, I guess it's routine in this kind of situation. The old man was out of it a lot, but apparently he told the cops he'd just had an accident so there is nothing they can do if he doesn't want to pursue it or press charges. My guess is he's scared shitless, as well he should be."

"Will your mom listen to you if you ask her to stay away from him? The last thing she needs is some loan shark coming after her once they find out he's got a wife—estranged or not."

"Shit! I didn't even think of that." I stood abruptly from the couch. "This is getting worse by the minute."

"You want us to come over tomorrow and try to help you talk to her?"

"Nah, man. I'll figure it out, but thanks."

"Well, if you change your mind, just give me a call. We're here if you need it."

"Thanks, man. Later."

I hung up and stared at my phone. I did need help figuring this out, but I wasn't about to drag Nate and Laney into this mess. It wasn't their problem—it was a family problem. And I knew just who deserved a call.

I scrolled through my contact list and hit the call button.

"Yo, dickhead! What's up?"

"Jake, you cocksucker, it's time to get your ass home. Dad's back."

It was Sunday night and I sat in my truck outside Piedmont Triad International Airport waiting on my brother. The Zac Brown Band rang from the speakers but did little to distract me. I drummed my fingers on the steering wheel wondering what the hell was taking so long. Jake's flight had landed twenty minutes ago.

Then I caught a glimpse of him in my rearview mirror and the reason became clear. Duffle bag slung over one shoulder, my big brother swaggered out the automatic doors with a tall, stacked blonde by his side. She was laughing at something he said and ducking her head coyly.

Jesus Christ.

Leave it to my brother to use a family crisis to schedule some horizontal refreshment.

I rolled my window down and shouted, "Yo, Jake! Your wife just called and said she's going into labor. If we hurry, maybe you'll make it in time to cut the cord!"

Jake looked at me like he might go all Vito Corleone on my ass, and the blonde practically sprinted in the other direction, shouting some pretty choice expletives behind her. He stomped over to the truck and threw his duffle in the back. "I forgot what a dick you can be," he said as he folded his tall frame into the passenger seat.

He looked the same as always—three days past needing a shave and built like a Mack truck. His hair was buzzed like mine but that's where the resemblance stopped. Jake's looks are more dark, favoring our mother, while mine are more fair, favoring the sack of shit. Jake also has a good four inches on me, a fact he never lets me forget.

"Always here to help." I settled my hands on the steering wheel and pulled away from the curb.

"If cock-blocking is your idea of help, you need me more than I realized."

"Oh please, the only reason a girl would fuck you is if she ran out of batteries."

He turned to me and narrowed his eyes. "I think it's time you shut up, little brother, and give that hole in your face a chance to heal."

I smiled at him. "Good to see you too."

The corner of his mouth lifted a fraction of an inch. "Whatever. Just drive—I can't wait to get this shit show over with."

Jake sighed.

I pulled onto the highway. "You and me both."

"Jake?" Our mom sat on the couch, looking as if she'd just awakened from a dream and wasn't sure if Jake was real or not. She blinked furiously as my brother made his way to her, a giant grin on his face.

"Mom!" Jake exclaimed as he bent to encompass her in a hug and draw her to her feet. She wasn't short, but she was thin and looked frail in his big arms.

She returned his embrace and then pulled back so she could gaze up at him. "What are you doing here?"

"Can't a guy come home now and then?" he teased her.

"Of course you can. It's just such a surprise!" A smile lit her face for the first time since Friday. Thank God.

"Well, I missed you and I happened to have some time off so I thought, what the hell!"

Yeah, not exactly how it had gone down, but good enough.

The fact that she didn't seem the least bit suspicious of the expedient timing of his visit indicated just how addled she was.

Earlier this morning I'd had to drive her to the hospital to check on my dad since she'd threatened to drive herself if I didn't take her. Luckily, he'd been sleeping so she didn't get a chance to talk to him.

Ever since Nate's comment about the thugs possibly coming after my mom, I'd been nervous as hell and I was reluctant to let her out of my sight. But nothing seemed amiss at the hospital—not that I would have known what to look for anyway. It's not as if these guys would be swinging around baseball bats and wearing t-shirts saying "1-800-Loan Shark. Text rates apply." But just to be safe, I accompanied her to the hospital room and got my first look at my old man in eight years.

Time—and the baseball bat—had not been kind to him. His hair was long and scraggly and mostly gray, no longer the neatly combed sandy head of hair from my childhood. The muscular frame I'd never been allowed to forget was also diminished. His face was swollen and colored in various shades of purple, green, and yellow from the beating he'd taken. Had I seen him out of context, there wouldn't have been a single trace of recognition.

There were various tubes and wires attached to his arm and hand while his leg hung suspended above the bed, wrapped in plaster and bandages. I wondered vaguely if the hospital had contacted the correct family. Maybe this was all a big mistake. But then I glimpsed the familiar faded tattoo peeking from the sleeve of his hospital gown and I was swiftly returned to the shitstorm that this week had brought to our lives.

Once the nurse confirmed that his pain meds were keeping him asleep most of the time, I was able to coax my mom to leave.

I took her to lunch at the Village Tavern, hoping to cheer her

THE SPARK • 63

up, but she just picked at her salad and remained distant. Maybe she sensed the fury brewing just beneath my skin and that was the reason for her continued silence on the topic, but I was desperate for her to open up. Thankfully, I'd known reinforcements were on the way.

"I just can't believe you're here." Our mother stared at Jake, dumbfounded. "When you didn't make it home for Christmas I was worried about you." She didn't mean to scold, but I secretly felt a bit smug that her comment piled a little guilt on Jake. He certainly deserved it, in my humble opinion.

He looked appropriately chastened. "I know—I'm sorry. I really couldn't get out of the project we were working on. But there's no need to worry about me, Mom."

I wasn't entirely clear on what my brother did for a living. After his stint in the Marines, he'd seemed to wander the country aimlessly for a while, coming home from time to time. He worked odd jobs and then somehow got involved in landscape design, which took him to Florida. This was unsurprising, as I could perfectly picture Jake sweet-talking rich retirees into installing ridiculously expensive outdoor fountains surrounded by hedge mazes or some such shit. All he'd have to do is turn on the smile, flex his biceps, and throw a little "Aw, shucks" in there and the rich ladies would swoon. My smile hadn't been the only one our mom had worried about.

"I should go get your room ready." Mom brought her hand to her dark hair. "Are you hungry? I should make you some dinner. Where are your bags?" She looked around.

"Don't worry," Jake said calmly and grabbed her hand. "I just have the one bag, and I've already eaten. I'm also perfectly capable of making a bed. Just relax and catch me up on what's been going on lately."

We'd agreed it best that Jake play dumb and pretend he didn't know Dad was back. Hopefully, once he got our mom talking she would finally share some of what she was thinking and we could get a bead on her mindset.

"I have to make a phone call," I said and excused myself from the room. I went into the kitchen where I could still hear their conversation. Part of me felt guilty for putting on a ruse, but the situation was so messed up I could easily let it go.

"Didn't Mark tell you...oh my goodness, Jake. Normally I wouldn't have much to share, but I have some news and I'm not sure how you're going to take it."

"What's that?" Jake asked quietly.

She proceeded to tell him the facts as we knew them, with the addition of a new piece of unwelcome information—it seemed the old man was into these guys for thirty grand.

"Wow," said Jake, the fucking genius.

"I know," our mother replied, but then she went on. "Jake, I just don't know what to do. I've been thinking about it nonstop and I feel like we need to help him."

Shit. Shit. Shit.

I clutched my phone so hard I was surprised it didn't crack.

"Hmm, well, I guess I can see how you'd feel that way." At least Jake was doing a good job of keeping his cool. "There are a lot of things to consider, though, Mom." He sounded like a fucking talk show therapist.

"I know. I don't have that kind of money to give those awful people. But we can figure something out. He's your father."

At this point, I was incredibly fortunate to be standing a room away. There would be no way I could school my expression at that last comment.

Unbelievably, Jake continued with a calm tone, "True, but let's think this out a bit. Do you know if he has insurance? Do you know where he was living when he got mixed up with these guys?"

"Um, well, the hospital said he doesn't have insurance." She seemed to pause.

"Mom, did they have you sign anything at the hospital?"

"No, nothing. Why?"

I could hear Jake's sigh of relief that echoed my own.

"Okay, well that's good at least. Make sure you don't sign anything or you might become liable for his medical bills. You're still technically married."

"Oh my God—I hadn't even thought of that!"

"It's okay. We'll figure this out. Now, was he in North Carolina when he got involved with these guys?"

"I don't know. I just know this is where they found him and attacked him. I really think he was trying to come home to us."

Fuck. Fuck. Fuck.

Again, Jake kept his cool. I was going to have to buy him a beer and stop calling him derogatory names. "Well, that aside, we have to be careful, Mom. It might be best to stay away from the hospital in case these people are watching and they figure out your connection to him. I'm worried they might try to harm you in some way."

"What? Why would they do that? I didn't do anything to them." She sounded breathless at the thought.

"These kinds of people don't think that way. They want their money and will do just about anything to get it. Look what they did to D...dad." He stumbled over the word and I couldn't blame him one bit. "That's probably why he lied to the cops too."

"Oh."

Things were silent for a few moments so I figured it was safe to return. They were both sitting on the couch and Jake's arm rested along the back, behind our mom's head. Unsurprisingly, she looked a bit dazed.

"Anybody need anything to drink?" I asked, trying for distraction so my mom had time to digest the reality of the situation. I was hoping against hope that it sunk in and stuck. We'd have to worry later about her misguided belief that anything but money had brought dear old Dad back to Greensboro.

"Sure," said Jake. "Why don't you bring Mom a glass of wine and I'll take a beer."

"Coming right up," I said, happy to retreat to the kitchen once again.

Jake and I had our fair share of differences and I certainly still held on to some resentment that had built since his abrupt departure years back. But right now?

It was damn good to have my brother home.

## Chapter Eight

# A GOOD BEST FRIEND IS HARD TO FIND

**F**IONA

"I know you told me you and Nate would take care of it but, for reasons I can't examine right now, I can't get the whole thing out of my head. I know he's a big boy—lord knows if he were any bigger he'd need his own small country to fit in. What is up with that, by the way? Isn't there a point where a person looks in the mirror and realizes that there are wimpy people in this world who need the muscle more than he does? Did his mother never tell him about the muscle-impaired children of the Third World?" I rambled, as usual, as I hefted the grocery bags to Laney's kitchen.

A new recipe idea had been niggling at my brain and I'd decided to make use of my guinea pigs again tonight. "Anyway, I hope you like beef tips because I woke up this morning with a hankering for some juicy tips. Yum!"

I heard a sharp intake of breath, a poorly muffled giggle, a deep chuckle, and what sounded like a growl all coming simultaneously from the living room off Laney's kitchen.

Fuckity, fuck, fuck my life!

I really had to stop running my mouth without checking for witnesses first. I turned slowly from the counter and walked to the half wall separating the two rooms.

I thought for one brief moment that I might actually die of humiliation.

*I'm sorry, Mr. and Mrs. Pierce, there was nothing we could do. It was acute systemic embarrassment (which the medical community will henceforth refer to as ASE or perhaps "Fiona's Curse"). She unfortunately brought it on herself—you are aware your daughter was a complete and total wackadoo, aren't you? Again, I'm very sorry.*

On the recliner in the corner of the room sat Laney on Nate's lap, both of them wearing shit-eating grins on their fat stupid faces. Assholes! Rocco played with some monster trucks on the coffee table, and if only I'd been able to stop there, I wouldn't have been forced to see the faces of the two men sitting on the couch, one stern and familiar, the other jocular and completely foreign to me.

Oh yay, I was expanding my audience to include random strangers now. Why did these things always happen to me?

"What's a beef tip?" asked Rocco, lifting his sweet brown eyes to me.

I ignored my flaming face and looked at the child who I decided was going to be my only friend from here on out. "It's a cut of meat that comes from the bottom loin under—"

"Okay!" Laney interrupted, barely stifling another giggle— what was up with her?! "It's steak, Rocco."

"Gross."

Oh well, more for me.

Then, instead of creating a diversion and allowing me to slink back out the front door like a true best friend would, Laney gestured to the couch and forced me to act like a grown-up. "Fiona, you remember Mark, of course. And this is his brother, Jake. Jake, Fiona. Fiona, Jake."

Sending Laney my best "I'll cut a bitch" glare, I tried to regain my composure and step down the two steps to the living room. Of course, my heel caught on the threshold and I bobbled a bit before grasping the wall to regain my balance.

There would be no regaining my pride, however.

I proceeded to the couch and looked up, and up, at Jake, who was now standing politely with his hand out. What did their mother feed these boys? I took his hand as I also took in his slightly naughty smile. Don't ask how I knew it was naughty. It just was.

"It is so nice to meet you, Fiona," he said, appearing quite amused. Oh yeah, this guy was trouble.

"You too," I managed to say. "I'm here all week if you'd like to catch another show."

Jake chuckled and I looked around him—which was not an easy thing to do as it seemed the brothers were both greedy where muscles were concerned—to find Mark, who was scowling for some reason. Okay, so maybe he was mad I ranted about his physique, or maybe it was my inability to stay out of everyone's business.

Whatever.

"Hi, Mark," I mumbled.

"Shortcake," was all he said.

Oh no he didn't!

"So!" exclaimed Nate. "How about those beef tips? Sounds awesome!"

As tempted as I was to claim there was not enough food to go around and then suddenly invent an important meeting that required my presence (because you know, Monday evenings are usually fully booked with work for landscaping receptionists), I sucked it up and cooked dinner for everyone. Who was I kidding? Laney knew I always made too much food, so there would have been no fooling her anyway.

I have to say I was quite pleased with the results of my efforts, and from the little moans and the lack of conversation at the dinner table I'd say my bourbon and honey steak tips were a hit with everyone else as well—Rocco excepted. He did, however, enjoy my roasted garlic mashed potatoes with his hot dog. Future foodie in the making.

At least I assumed it was the food that kept everyone quiet, not the weird tension between Mark and me. Was I the only one who felt it, though? He had me discombobulated. I'd been thinking about him and about the scene at the hospital all weekend, unable to get him out of my head. And while I'd been cooking I'd caught him staring at me several times—it had rattled me to the point where I'd nearly burned the glaze.

*Gah! Out of my head, you brute!*

"Fiona," Jake finally said, wiping his mouth with a napkin. "Will you marry me?"

Ha! I knew it! How could you not like a good beef tip?! I smiled at him.

"That depends, Jake. What can you bring to the proverbial table?" I took my last bite and sipped my wine, determined to focus on brother number two. He was a little yummy himself, but he lacked the eyelashes and general surliness of Mark. Wait. What?

"I can build you a backyard oasis and probably get you a seat at the hottest Bunco night in Florida," Jake said after a moment of thought.

"Tempting," I said, pretending to consider his offer. "But I live in a condo. And I prefer Mahjong. I hope you understand—it's not you, it's me."

"So you're saying I have a chance."

Laney and I laughed and then Nate chimed in, "Seriously, Fiona, that was so good. I'm going to have to up my workouts if you keep feeding me like that."

I smiled at Nate and then I snuck a quick glance at Mark, sure he was going to volunteer to train Nate or something, but he was just sitting back in his chair eyeing me and sipping his beer. Hmm.

"Can I be excused?" Rocco asked, his little lisp making the question quite possibly the most adorable thing I've ever heard.

"Sure, baby," answered Laney, and the little guy ran off to his room.

I got up and started to grab the dishes but Laney and Nate stopped me simultaneously, as was their custom on Fiona nights. I don't know why I still tried.

And then, because I couldn't seem to keep my giant yap shut, I proceeded to butt into everyone's business. "So, how is your mom?" I asked Mark and Jake.

Jake glanced at Mark and they did some silent brother communication thing before Mark finally answered, "She's okay."

To any normal person, this succinct reply would have signaled that it was time to switch topics. But me? I pressed on, for some ridiculous reason. "And her friend who was hurt?"

Mark threw a glance to Nate at the counter, maybe having assumed that Nate had filled me in on some details—which he had *not,* much to my annoyance. I hadn't even been able to crack Laney.

This idea of Rocco as my new best friend was proving to have more and more merit by the second. Sure, he was just a kid, but if I fed him enough ice cream I'm sure he'd go shopping with me. Plus, I'm pretty good at talking about gross stuff and that totally impresses boys.

Jake was the one to finally speak up. "It was actually our father, and he's pretty racked up but he'll pull through." Mark shot him a warning look while my chin hit the table.

Oh my God! It hadn't occurred to me that it could be Mark's dad. That would certainly explain why he and his mom were so worked up at the hospital. "I'm so sorry! I had no idea," I said. "That must be really upsetting. I'm glad he's going to be okay." I continued to ramble.

"That would make you the only person," Mark muttered, effectively shutting me up.

"Mark, everyone here knows what's going on so why not see if anybody else has ideas on how to clean this up quick?" Jake turned to his brother.

I raised my hand like a kindergartner. "Um, I don't think I really understand what's going on."

"And we don't want to bother you with our problems, Short-cake. Right, Jake?" His look was so pointed it was almost comical.

This was all so shocking I forgot to be mad about the "Short-cake" moniker.

Jake looked back and forth between Mark and me as if suddenly realizing something interesting. Huh? Then he smirked like the goddamn troublemaker I'd known he was, and I could practically hear the *bling* bounce off the naughty twinkle in his eye.

*Oh, hell no! Back this truck up before anyone gets any ideas.*

Jake went on, "I'm sure Fiona would be happy to help. So, long story short, Fiona, our dad is a douchebag who our mom is somehow still hung up on—even though he walked out on her years ago—and he has loan sharks after him because he stupidly borrowed a shitload of cash from them. Now he's back in town, we can only assume, to suck us into his shitstorm and all our mom can think about is how to help him and/or win him back."

"Holy hell," was what came out of my mouth.

"You can say that again," Laney said from the sink.

After that, we all migrated back to the living room with our drinks and proceeded to brainstorm a bit. From what I could understand, the goal was to keep their mom as far away as possible from not only their dad, but the hospital's billing department and these guys who had beaten up the douchebag dad.

"Not to be insensitive to the serious topic at hand," I began, "but does anyone else's mind immediately picture Chevy Chase in a shark costume whenever the words 'loan shark' are mentioned?"

"Thank God I wasn't the first one to say it, but I've been dying to!" said Nate, who was then firmly swatted on the arm by Laney.

"Shut up, you two. Am I the only grown up around here?" she scolded. "And besides, that was *land* shark, not *loan* shark," she added quietly. "If you're going to be assholes, at least get it right."

Nate and I just grinned at each other and shrugged before we schooled our expressions. Nate cleared his throat and I looked down at my lap.

"The whole thing is so oddly surreal, though, isn't it?" Mark commented.

Phew—my big mouth hadn't pissed him off again.

"Why can't we call the cops?" asked Laney.

"Because the old man has at least some sense of self-preservation. If he goes to the cops he'll most likely end up with cement shoes, and as long as he's alive there is a better chance they'll keep after him and not go looking for relatives," explained Jake, who then turned his attention to me and said, "I've always wanted to have a legitimate conversation where I could fit in the phrase 'cement shoes.'"

I couldn't help it—I giggled a little. Until I saw the look on Mark's face. If I were Jake, I'd find another ride home lest I be the one to end up in those shoes.

What was up with that? He needed to pull his panties out right quick before his scowl caused premature wrinkles. Did he understand nothing about skincare?

"So what's the end game here?" asked Nate. "Not to be harsh, but do you want to leave him to the mercy of these guys? Or do you want to spirit him off to Mexico or something? Do you want to come up with the money and then threaten him to never come back?"

"I say let them have at him again," said Mark.

Ouch.

"It's not that simple and you know it, little brother," said Jake.

*Aww.*

"I know, but a guy can dream, right?"

"Okay, so option one is out," Nate stated. "How about option two?"

"What's to keep the guys from going after Mom if the asshole suddenly disappears?" asked Jake.

"We don't even know if she's on their radar," replied Mark.

"Best to keep her far away then," concluded Laney.

"Yeah, that's the problem. She wants to be involved," Mark returned.

"Well then, we'll have to figure out a way to remove her from the picture without being obvious while you guys deal with the rest," I said with a little smile, my mind already spinning with plans.

I looked at Laney. "You in?"

"Hell yes."

Nate put his head in his hands and muttered, "Here we go."

I do love a good project.

*Chapter Nine*

# SO MAYBE IT'S A THING

## MARK

"I can't believe I let you guys talk me into this," I muttered to Jake on the way home from Laney's house that night.

The food had been incredible—Shortcake could cook like a fucking champ. I'd spent more than a few minutes watching while she'd chopped, stirred, and sautéed, and I liked witnessing the relaxed pleasure these actions brought to her small features. It had felt oddly intimate, though, so I had tried to force my attention away, to little success.

I'd be lying if I said she hadn't been on my mind since the ER waiting room. How she'd gotten me to smile on a day like that was a complete mystery, one of many where this woman was concerned. The problem was I didn't have time or energy for more complications in my life and she had "complication" written all over her. It's not like I could bang her and then never see her again. Not an option.

After hearing her little tirade about my body earlier tonight, though, I hadn't been able to help myself from calling her "Shortcake." If memory served, that had been part of my opening line the first time we'd met. She hadn't liked it then and she sure as shit didn't like it now. I just couldn't help having a little fun with her.

And I'll admit, after the initial discomfort of discussing what I considered private family business, it was somewhat of a relief to share some of the load, even if it did involve sharing it with Fiona. As always, Nate was great at breaking things down into manageable pieces, and by the end of the evening I felt as if we had some semblance of a game plan.

At one point, Fiona and Laney had excused themselves, ostensibly to put Rocco to bed but it was clear they were scheming.

This made me nervous.

I knew logically that my mom could weather a lot of shit, but in my opinion she was always to be handled with care.

When they returned to the room, the girls attempted subtlety while asking questions about my mom—where she worked, what kind of hours she had off, what her interests were. They eventually abandoned all pretense and just asked for her number. Jake answered most of their questions, although how he knew these things living several states away I had no clue. Maybe he paid more attention than I gave him credit for.

Completely sick of the serious tone the evening had developed, I made a concerted effort to switch topics and soon we were arguing about college basketball—I do so love to torture Nate about his devotion to Notre Dame.

At one point, after a particularly well-placed insult, I dropped the mic and excused myself to the restroom. When I was finished and emerged into the hallway, my attention was grabbed by a low melodic sound coming from one of the rooms. I turned left to investigate instead of taking a right and rejoining the group. Maybe Rocco was listening to music instead of sleeping. I'd been over here a few evenings and I knew the kid liked to stall his bedtime as much as possible.

When I got to his door and peeked in, however, I saw Fiona perched on the side of his bed, singing softly to him. The scene was simultaneously endearing and bizarre. Here was this smart-ass, ball-busting woman—barely bigger than her pajama-clad charge— singing an old Beatles song to the sleepy little boy. She was dressed to the nines in high heels and what I could only assume was a ridiculously expensive designer outfit but strangely looked right at home sitting on a rumpled pile of fire-truck bedsheets.

My skin warmed. I began to feel like an interloper, a voyeur, and tried to back away. In my haste, I inadvertently hit my boot on the doorjamb and immediately drew Fiona's attention.

She stood up suddenly, forgetting her task before quickly checking to make sure Rocco was indeed asleep. That damn hair fluttered around her face and she tried tucking one side behind her ear as she looked at the floor and quietly made her way into the hall. Her cheeks were pink.

"You have a beautiful voice," I whispered, unable to help myself.

"Oh, thanks." Apparently, that hadn't been what she'd expected me to say. "I was just trying to help him get back to sleep. Nightmare," she explained quietly, still clearly uncomfortable at being caught in the act.

"I used to sing to my dog," I blurted out.

*What?! Shut up, you asshole!*

I don't know what possessed me to say that except I didn't want her to feel self-conscious about what I had seen as a genuinely sweet moment—that and, well, it was true. Daisy had loved it when I sang to her—that dog was a huge fan of Notorious B.I.G.

Fiona smiled and looked up at me. Then she started to giggle and I shushed her while closing Rocco's door.

"I'm sorry. That was really rude. It's sweet. Really." She tried to get ahold of herself.

"I have no idea why I said that," I muttered. "If you're done laughing at me, let's go back and torture Nate some more." I tried to scowl at her but it didn't work.

She bit her lip.

Damn, that was hot.

"Deal," she finally said and sashayed her way back to the living room.

Watching her cute little ass as she walked ahead of me, I suspected I was in a bit of trouble.

When Jake and I got up to leave later in the evening, Laney gave us both hugs while Fiona stood to the side somewhat awkwardly. She seemed to finally make up her mind and settled on a smile and wave for Jake and a punch to my arm, after which she let her gaze linger a moment too long on the bicep she'd just assaulted. Was it possible little Miss "Go eat a bag of dicks" didn't find me that distasteful after all?

Interesting.

Jake interrupted my reverie. "What? These people obviously care about you—what's the harm in letting them help?" he asked from the passenger seat of my truck.

"Fiona doesn't give two shits about me. She's just a bored little —emphasis on *little*—rich girl looking for a project." I knew I was laying the denial on a bit too thick.

"Whatever you say, man."

"What is that supposed to mean?" I took my eyes off the road to glare at him.

"It's so obvious. You guys are doing the whole 'I hate you so much I want to fuck you to death' thing."

"That's *not a thing*! And, no, we are not. She thinks I'm a steroid-obsessed idiot and I don't even find her attractive. I've seen small children with bigger tits than hers." Okay, that was a bit overboard. And creepy. So her tits aren't big, but they are definitely there. And I may or may not have noted that they're perky. Kind of like her.

Shit.

"For what it's worth, I think she's hot, if not a bit…what's the word I'm looking for?" Jake closed his eyes in concentration and I hoped he'd just drop it. "Hyper?" he tried and then shook his head. "Dramatic?" He turned to me.

"I think the word you're looking for is 'blond.'"

"That's it!" He pointed his finger at me and I rolled my eyes. "I suppose I could do a whole lot worse than a hot little blonde, though," he mused with a quick glance at me.

I tamped down the rising in my chest. He was so pitifully obvious in his baiting technique I almost felt sorry for him. "Oh gee, Jake," I deadpanned. "Please don't bang her, man." I turned to him and resumed my normal voice, "Is this the part where I'm supposed to growl possessively?"

"Okay, dickhead. Touché. But I know you think she's hot," he said and then smirked and whispered, "Shortcake."

I flipped him off. "It doesn't matter what I think—she hates me and the last thing I need right now is more drama anyway. Speaking of which, what the hell are those two witches going to do to our mother?"

"Who the hell knows, but they seem to have something up their sleeves so I'm all for letting them run with it while we worry about the rest."

And then, apropos of nothing, he said, "Hey, did you know Mom still has middle school trophies on the shelf in our old room?"

I cringed. Part of me was happy that we were dropping the subject of the tiny terror, but the other part wasn't ready to talk about Mom's behavior. "I'm aware." It was no secret that part of her lived in the past—a past that she somehow managed to sentimentalize.

"Who keeps debate team trophies? I mean, sports trophies, maybe..." he goaded me. "I saw those things last night and laughed my ass off. I'll bet Mom has an entire album of pictures stashed somewhere of a pimply little Mark in a crooked tie lecturing like a 90-pound politician at some podium." He snickered.

I wasn't about to tell him he was right. "Laugh it up, asshole."

He seemed to have lost his mind because he proceeded to do just that and practically bust a gut in my passenger seat.

"If you're going to piss yourself, I swear I will pull over and punch you in the throat." He held his index finger up, indicating he needed a minute. "Seriously, out of three hundred million sperm, you're the one who made it? It boggles the mind." And that just sent him off again.

Mom was working an evening shift at her waitressing job, but I decided to come in the house instead of just dropping Jake off, hoping to check in with her. We were relieved that she'd made it to work without comment and especially without trying to stop by the hospital again. I was hoping the information Jake had dropped on her last night was making an impact, but it would be nice to see for myself.

Walking into our childhood home rarely made me think of my father anymore, but that had changed in the last few days. All I could see when I walked into the little duplex now was the stained and time-worn carpet in front of the recliner where my dad used to settle his clay-encrusted work boots and then complain about dirty floors later. And the mirror above the entry table with the crack in the corner from when it had fallen during one of his tirades, only to be picked up and repaired by my mother that night. Then the wobbly oak table in the kitchen where Jake and I had bitten our tongues so hard we'd nearly drawn blood in our attempts to refrain from back-talk as the old man had hurled thinly veiled insults and criticisms.

I could see him plain as day in the farthest chair, his hair combed back, a full plate in front of him and a can of Old Style in his hand. "Joey Walker, now there's a great kid. I'll bet you money his father is damn proud of that one. Did you see that pass he threw last night? And I noticed he doesn't do too poorly with the ladies either, huh? Did you see that cheerleader he was cozying up to after the game? Hooey!"

"Do you know him?" he'd asked me. "What am I saying?" He'd then chuckled. "Of course you wouldn't know a guy like that." His focus had switched to my brother. "Jake, you know him. Maybe if you put in a little more effort at practice you'd get more playing time like Joey, huh? That is some kid. Pass the potatoes, Mary." Mary, of course, being his nickname for me.

My trip down memory lane was interrupted by Jake as he stepped in front of me. My eyes snapped from the table to focus on Jake and the IPA in his outstretched hand.

"Nah, man, I gotta drive home in a bit."

"Suit yourself," he replied and dropped onto the sofa. At least that wasn't the same couch from our childhood. I'd finally gotten our mom to agree to a new one last year when the springs on the old one were literally pushing their way through the threadbare cushions. This new one wasn't fancy, but she'd let me buy it for her and at least I didn't have to risk my nuts being cut off when I sat on it.

She was always touchy when I tried to fix things up at her house, insisting that it was fine as it was and she didn't want me spending my money on her. Since I work in construction, though, I'd been able to make some improvements to the place using spare pieces from other projects. That was how she'd gotten a new foyer floor and kitchen countertops. The kitchen floor I'd had to pay for out-of-pocket, but I didn't tell her that. I just wanted her to have something nice for once in her life.

"Damn, it's weird being back," Jake said as he took a swig and looked around.

"How long has it been anyway?" I let my sudden moodiness spur my comment, knowing full well how long it had been and just wanting to hear him say it. I began to pace the small room.

Oblivious to my mood, Jake replied, "I think it's been over a year—Christmas before last maybe?"

I just grunted in response.

"What crawled up your ass all of a sudden?" my brother asked, trying and failing to pull off a casually amused expression.

"Oh, I don't know—maybe just a bit tired," I said through clenched teeth. The room was starting to feel claustrophobic. I wanted to pick that old recliner up and throw it out on the curb. Fuck, what was wrong with me?

"Oh, just spit it out—I knew this was coming anyway so go ahead." Jake tossed an arm out in invitation.

"Don't try to make it sound like I'm having some kind of teenage hissy fit—if we're going to talk about who the grown-up is in this room, I think we both know it sure as shit isn't you!"

He scratched at the side of his dark scruff. "I'm sorry, okay! I was eighteen. All I could think about was getting the hell out of that man's house before I killed him. Don't you remember what it was like to be eighteen? We're all selfish idiots at that age."

I stopped my pacing and stared at him with incredulity. WTF?!

"Yes, Jake. I *do* remember what eighteen was like—clearly our experiences were worlds apart. You ran off to 'find yourself' and I was stuck here!" He opened his mouth to interrupt but I was on a roll. "*My* eighteen meant taking care of mom and making sure she took her meds every day—making sure she made it to work so she could keep a roof over her head and not lose her insurance. It meant sticking around town working full time and taking classes at community college because God only knew what would happen if somebody didn't stay here to keep an eye on things. That's what it was like to be eighteen, Jake," I spat.

Jesus, it felt good to get that out, but I simultaneously felt like kind of a douchebag—this was practically ancient history and I was indeed starting to resemble a teenager throwing a hissy fit.

Shit.

I slumped next to him on the couch, the fight having left me entirely.

"Exactly how long have you been waiting to say that to me?" He shoved my arm.

"Oh, only about fifteen years. Not long." I sighed.

"I'm sorry, little brother. I know it's no excuse, but I was a young, selfish asshole who couldn't see past the immediate future.

If it's any comfort, I regretted signing up for the Marines about thirty minutes into boot camp."

"Maybe a little. Wait, I thought you liked the Marines?" I turned to him.

"I don't think anybody 'likes' the Marines. I did end up learning a lot and it helped me grow the fuck up, that's for sure. I should have come home after. I should have helped you watch after Mom. I just didn't know how to make it up to you and then I kept putting it off, telling myself you were always better at this shit anyway. I know it was stupid."

"Fuck," I swiped his beer. "You're here now. And you seem to be able to get through to Mom a hell of a lot better than I can."

He grabbed the other beer I'd refused minutes earlier. "That's because I've spent the last several years honing my skills at charming older women."

"Don't. That just sounds disturbing as shit."

"Asshole." He shoved me again.

"Dickhead." I shoved him back harder and managed to push him off the couch.

I *knew* I was stronger than him.

"You're gonna have to get to the gym here in town if you want to keep up with me, big brother."

Just then, the front door opened and our mom walked in, spying me on the couch and Jake sprawled on the floor. She smiled. "Isn't this a nice surprise—my two boys hanging out together. It feels like old times." She seemed to be in a good mood.

"Hey, Mom," we both said simultaneously, making me feel like we were indeed kids again.

"How was work?" Jake asked, picking himself up off the floor, trying not to spill his beer in the process.

"The usual—it was fine." She set her purse down on the entry table and turned back to us. "Oh, and I got the strangest phone call. It was from the girl who was with you at the hospital the other day—Fiona?"

Oh shit.

"What did she say?" I was afraid to ask but did anyway. It was like pulling off a bandage—better to get it over with quickly.

"It was the oddest thing. She invited me out to lunch." She had a small smile on her face, obviously recalling the details of the conversation. She let out a little laugh.

Interesting.

"Anyway, we're going out on Wednesday." She walked toward the kitchen, calling out behind her, "You boys need a snack?"

"Always," replied Jake.

I stayed silent, too preoccupied with what Fiona could possibly have said to not only draw such an unexpected reaction from my mom, but to get her to agree to lunch with a complete stranger.

I *knew* Shortcake was a witch.

*Chapter Ten*

# THE A-TEAM AIN'T GOT NOTHIN' ON ME

**F**IONA

I was like frickin' Hannibal from the A-Team. This plan was coming together like a mo-fo! I wasn't lying when I said I liked a good project—it's one area where my list-making abilities come in super handy.

Even before the Beckett boys had left Laney's house, she and I had schemed out a solid strategy. The plan was to call their mom, whose name we learned was Kelly, and invite her to a welcome-home dinner for Jake that we were planning to host. Who doesn't love an excuse to eat yummy food and drink wine while making new friends in the process? Naturally, the true purpose of the call was to lure Kelly into spending some of her free time with us, therefore keeping her mind off her husband and her ass out of his hospital room.

I called her cell phone and happened to catch her on her way out of work. While the introduction was a bit awkward since I had to mention the hospital, I quickly glossed over it with my typical flightiness and moved right on.

I may have inadvertently implied that her sons and I had known each other for longer than we actually had. Okay, I outright lied, but it was for a good cause! And I did know them through Nate, whom I knew through Laney—and something involving Kevin Bacon makes it okay. Speaking of Kevin Bacon, that dude has gotten scary skinny—eat a sandwich, man.

Anyway, I asked Kelly about Jake's favorite foods when he was growing up and then suggested that a few embarrassing photos would be a good addition, all while drawing her into friendly conversation.

I wasn't too surprised to find that she was a lovely woman with a good sense of humor. And I knew just how to make a mom of two grown men warm up to me. It involved a careful balance of both praising and insulting the shit out of her offspring. Every mom loves to hear good things about her sons while also under-standing that a girl who is blind to their faults or is a pushover is never going to make the grade. Especially with those two beasts she'd raised.

By the end of the call, I had secured a lunch date for Kelly, Laney, and me on Kelly's next day off. She said a cheery goodbye after promising to bring photos with her. I was secretly hoping there would be a few embarrassing shots of Mark as well, but I didn't ask.

"And that's how it's done," I proclaimed to Laney as I pushed the end-call button and set my phone on the counter.

"I have to say I'm pretty damn impressed. You were charming as shit!"

"What a lovely compliment." I glared at her playfully.

"You know what I mean." She scrunched her eyebrows. "You

can talk to anyone, and you're never shy or anything—it's really an extraordinary skill."

"Aww, that's sweet. But you know it's just because I'm so used to making a fool of myself that it doesn't really faze me anymore. I just open my mouth and shit comes out." I paused for a moment. "Wait, that didn't come out right, did it? See? It's true!"

She laughed at me as Nate rounded the corner into the kitchen. I took a moment to admire him, as I often do, and oddly found myself comparing him to Mark. Had Nate's arms gotten a little scrawny since the last time I saw him? No. Not possible—that was only a couple days ago.

My mind wandered back to the moment in the foyer when I'd stupidly decided that an arm punch was a proper farewell to Mark. His arm was like steel and apparently I was starting to develop a steel fetish. I'd practically mentally undressed him right there in the foyer—how pathetic. And from the look he'd given me, I don't think it went unnoticed. Damn. It must have been that story about his dog that got to me. Double damn.

"What's so funny?" Nate asked, pulling my attention.

"Fiona," Laney responded, still smiling at me.

"Naturally," was his comeback so I punched him in the arm. What was it with me tonight? At least Nate had the good grace to pretend it hurt.

"So, I don't really get it," Laney said.

"What? He insulted me so I punched him." Did I sound a bit defensive?

"Not that," she said. "If somebody owed me a bunch of money, why would I try to kill them? Then I'd never get my money back."

Nate leaned against the counter and crossed his arms. "Not that I have any personal experience with this, obviously, but I've seen enough movies that some may consider me an expert." Laney and I both rolled our eyes at him but he continued undiscouraged. "My theory is either they never intended to kill him—just hurt him badly enough to scare the shit out of him—or he'd been screwing them around to the point where they figured they'd just off him and take all his possessions. Then they'd at least have something—and they could go after people in his life for the rest. Obviously, that's what has Mark and Jake the most concerned."

That all made sense, I guess. It also pissed me right the hell off—what had Kelly done to deserve even the threat of something like that? It made me even more determined to help them all out and to befriend her in the process. Us girls have to stick together, after all. Vaginas unite!

There has got to be a potential superhero story with that awesome tagline! It's a shame I'm not into comics.

I managed to make it to Wednesday, the day of our lunch with Kelly, without thinking too much about Mark—or his arms. And by that, I mean I only thought about him a couple times in the shower and maybe a few times at work when I was supposed to be filing. Not bad at all. But even I, the queen of meaningless sex, could admit that this had the potential to become a problem. I mean, casually screwing someone who was part of your friendship network was a terrible idea. Even if that person happened to be hot and used to sing to his dog. I'd just have to try to remember how good he was at annoying me and then I wouldn't want him at all. Yes—good plan.

Technically I only had an hour for lunch but I was good at finagling more time here and there—it was one of life's great mysteries why I got fired so often. Since Laney tended to actually follow her company's policies, we decided to meet up closer to her office for our girls' lunch.

Venturing inside the little Italian bistro in my best skinny jeans and some killer Tory Burch wedge sandals, I spotted Kelly immediately and was suddenly struck by her resemblance to Jake—dark hair, olive complexion, and striking cheekbones. Kelly was also fairly tall, which obviously wasn't saying much coming from me, and was quite beautiful now that her face wasn't streaked with tears as it had been the last time I'd seen her.

It was also clear to me that she was one of those women who didn't know how to play up her beauty and spent very little time on herself. She wore old jeans, a cardigan that was two sizes too big, and not a speck of makeup. I sensed another project looming, and my Inner Fashion Maven cackled gleefully. Unlike Guilt, she was a wonderful house guest.

Kelly hadn't noticed me yet as she stood near the hostess stand gripping her purse while shifting on her feet.

"Kelly!" I approached her with a welcoming smile. Her eyes turned to me and a gorgeous smile lit her face. What in the hell was this woman doing pining over a loser like her dickhead husband? I gripped her hand in both of mine. "It's so good to properly meet you."

"You too, Fiona—thanks for inviting me," she said a bit shyly.

"Of course," I responded and then looked around. "I don't see Laney yet, but let's go ahead and get a table."

She nodded, and by the time we'd been seated at a window table and handed our menus, Laney had arrived.

"You must be Kelly," Laney greeted, shaking Kelly's hand.

"Yes," she smiled, "I've heard a lot about you, Laney. From all accounts, Nate is a very lucky guy."

Laney blushed a bit as she sat in her chair.

"Yes," I agreed. "Nate gets lucky a lot." I opened my menu.

Laney sucked in a breath, but Kelly let out a laugh.

"You'll have to excuse her, Kelly. I would try to explain, but there is really nothing adequate to say." Laney skewered me with her eyes. Anna Wintour was back.

"Please, don't worry about me," Kelly replied with a small smile. "Until I talked to Fiona on Monday I hadn't realized how much I needed a good laugh."

Laney reached out and touched her hand. "I'll bet you do—I know you and your boys have been under a lot of stress this past week."

"Yes, well…" Kelly looked down at her lap, and Laney and I exchanged worried glances. We were supposed to be distracting her, not stressing her out. Shit. "All the more reason to focus on better things—like this dinner you're hosting for Jake. It's very sweet of you," Kelly said, raising her eyes to us again. She fiddled with her water glass, almost knocking it over.

Taking her cue to move on, I said, "Oh—did you remember to bring the pictures? I can't wait to see!"

Her expression immediately brightened and the tension in my gut eased. Kelly pulled an envelope out of her bag and handed it over to me. I leaned toward Laney so we could both have a look.

Sweet mother of Judas Priest! We'd hit the jackpot.

There were, of course, the adorable diaper shots and then the traditional toddler-holding-baby-brother ones. But then we hit the mother-lode of blackmail material. Shot after shot of the brothers together, Jake usually in some pose with his chest puffed out or showing off his adolescent biceps. And then there was Mark—Mark wearing round, wire-rimmed glasses, hair a floppy mess, and weighing about as much as a Chihuahua, and probably with about the same size muscles too.

By the time we got to the last photo—one where Jake had Mark in a headlock with Mark's skinny little ass facing the camera —Laney and I were both in tears.

Kelly reached over and picked up a picture. "They were adorable, weren't they?" This just sent Laney and me off again in another fit of giggles.

"They were...something," Laney managed, swiping a finger under her eye.

"I just never would have guessed that Mark," I extended my arms in the classic giant-fish-story pose, "was ever so scrawny. I mean, he could have given me a run for my money." I laughed. Inwardly, though, I was "mwahaha"-ing as any good villain would do.

"Oh God, I know. He was most definitely a late bloomer. But such a sweet boy—still is." She gazed at the photo with a mother's love.

"We are definitely blowing some of these up—I'm thinking life-sized!" Laney proclaimed, sifting through them again.

I was still stuck on the "sweet boy" comment and the look in Kelly's eyes. No! Mark wasn't supposed to be sweet—he was supposed to be rude and unbearable so I could ignore my attraction to him. Shit.

Thankfully the waitress came to take our order so I could think about something else. Like what kind of dessert I was going to have after lunch.

Conversation flowed easily over lunch and although Kelly certainly wasn't gregarious or particularly outgoing, she did contribute and seemed to feel more comfortable with us by the end of the meal. It was clear though, however much she tried to be engaged and put on a cheerful face, there was a cloak of sadness about her that made me understand Mark's protectiveness when it came to his mother.

The fragility of a parent was an entirely foreign concept to me. I'd spent most of my own life as the fragile one with my elders consistently lending me their strength. What had life been like for a young Mark to assume this opposing role? It was obvious his mother's disposition wasn't merely a result of recent events but one honed over years of struggle.

This thought tempered my good mood, but I maintained my smile as we all parted ways in the parking lot and I headed back to work—all the way thinking about scrawny little Mark being sweet to his mom and then handsome grown-up Mark doing the same. Damn the man. He and his stupid eyelashes and not-so-off-putting muscles were getting under my skin—I could feel it!

I heard my phone signal a new text message on Friday morning as I sat at my desk trying to remember what my boss Jax had asked me to do on his way out the door. My hands had been busy so I hadn't written it down, and I was having no luck recalling it. Oh well. I picked up my phone and saw a number I didn't recognize along with a very strange message.

**Unknown Number:** *I need your help!*

I suddenly imagined myself in one of those movie scenarios where the kidnapping victim discovers a forgotten phone and dials a random number in the hopes that a good Samaritan on the other end of the line will save the day. I could totally do that!

**Fiona:** *I'm here! What is ur name? Do u need me to call the police?*

**Unknown Number:** *Huh?*

It was worse than I thought. This person had obviously been put in a confined space and was running out of air. What else could explain the confusion?!

*Fiona: How much air do u have left? Do u know where u are? I need to give the police something to go on!*

I just hoped I wasn't too late. Guilt would never let me forget it if I let this poor person die!

*Unknown Number: Are you high right now, Shortcake?*

Shortcake?

Shortcake!

This was no desperate kidnapping victim. It was Mark Fucking Beckett.

*Fiona: Mark?*

*Unknown Number: Who the hell did you think it was?*

*Fiona: How did u get my number?*

I quickly put his name into my contacts so he couldn't catch me unawares again.

*Mark: It didn't take Sherlock Holmes.*

Gah!

*Mark: What the hell was all that stuff about the police and air?*

Never being one to actively pursue humiliation—it preferred to find me on its own—I decided to skip that topic.

*Fiona: What do you want?*

*Mark: My mom is planning on going to the hospital tomorrow and we can't talk her out of it.*

Crap! This was about Kelly so I couldn't be mean and tell him to suck it.

*Fiona: When?*

*Mark: Morning sometime. She works in the afternoon.*

*Fiona: On it. Later.*

*Mark: Thanks, Shortcake. I owe you.*

*Fiona:* Stop calling me that.

*Mark:* It's an endearment.

*Fiona:* Endear this!

I followed that up with a lovely middle finger emoji. Thank you, Steve Jobs, for giving me the tools to adequately express my feelings.

## Chapter Eleven

# RULES OF THE PLAYGROUND

**M**ARK

I had to laugh as I set my phone down on the desk. I loved torturing the little spitfire, and now that I didn't have to worry about my mom tomorrow I was feeling much more relaxed.

"What are you laughing at?" asked Bailey as she walked into the office. "And get out of my chair."

Bailey Murphy is Nate's younger sister and the one I never had —or particularly wanted. Like Nate, she works for the family construction company and spends her days dealing mostly with interior design and space planning. The rest of her time is spent insulting Nate and me, as far as I can tell. Well, that and painting. Bailey is actually an artist at heart, but she feels an obligation to the family, and having a real job also keeps her from living in a cardboard box—or her parents' basement. I'm unsure which she would consider to be worse.

"I was here first," I said, pointing out the obvious.

"What are you, eight?" she responded and then reached toward my phone. I snatched it up before she could grab it.

Bailey stands only a few inches shorter than me and, thankfully, she isn't into heels like somebody else I know so she never tops me. Lord knows she'd love it, though, so I make sure to never suggest she dress like an actual girl. Objectively, I suppose she's attractive—long blond hair, bright blue eyes, decent rack—but it's impossible to see her as anything other than just *Bailey.*

"You may as well just tell me. I'll find out eventually anyway."

She wasn't above pick-pocketing or blackmail, so I gave in.

"I was just texting Fiona. I get an inordinate amount of pleasure from torturing her."

"Aw, that's so adorable. I can't imagine why you're single," she deadpanned and then proceeded to try and pull me out of her chair. Silly woman.

I just ignored her as she strained herself for another minute.

"You're not pretty enough to be this much of a bitch, Beckett." She stopped pulling at me and flipped me off instead.

What was it with girls giving me the finger today?

"Oh, I'm sorry," I feigned innocence and rose from the chair. "Did you want to sit here?"

"Asshole," she said and flopped into the chair like the graceful angel she is.

"Who peed in your Cheerios this morning?" I asked her.

"Eww. And nobody peed in my...anything. Just yuck." She gave me a disgusted look—one you might give to, well, somebody who peed in your cereal.

"Come on," I coaxed. "Tell Uncle Mark all about it." I took the seat opposite her and folded my arms on the desk.

Her disgusted look morphed into more of a disturbed frown.

"Are you always this creepy or am I just noticing it now?"

"Shut up and tell me what's wrong."

She waved her hand like she was swatting away an annoying bug. "It's nothing—I'm just frustrated—I'll get over it."

"Frustrated about what? Work stuff or…personal stuff? I would say 'guy stuff' but with the way you dress I'm never sure which way you swing." I gestured to her outfit of khaki pants and a company polo.

She gave me a huge fake smile. "I hope the steroids make them shrink up and a mouse eats them while you sleep."

My hand immediately covered my zipper in an attempt to protect my balls from her insults. "Hey—you know I don't take that shit!"

"Whatever you say, Buffy. Anyway, it's nothing you need to worry about—I'll get over it and be fine by Monday."

"Are you sure you don't want to talk about it? I can try my best to be nice and listen. Scouts' honor." I gave her the salute, or possibly signaled a Vulcan code, I'm not really sure—I was never in the Scouts. But I genuinely cared about her and didn't like to see her upset. If this was girl shit, though, I was going to regret it for sure.

"I'm positive. Now before we deal with the boring-ass bid paperwork, I want to hear about Fiona." She waggled her eyebrows.

"So *you* don't have to share but *I* do?"

"Yup."

"Well, there's nothing to say about Fiona anyway. She's just helping me with the situation with my parents and giving me the added bonus of being easy to pick on. You know how much I love that."

"I'm aware," she responded, leaning forward in her seat and searching for some papers on her desk.

"I'm wondering," I mused, "why is it that you and Fiona both have blond hair but she's the only one who's *blond*?"

Bailey eyed me, started to speak, thought better of it, and then finally said, "You know how I said you were acting like you're eight? I'm thinking that's the same thing you're doing with her."

"Huh?"

"You know, pulling her pigtails on the playground, calling her ugly, spitting in her applesauce at lunch…"

"Spitting in her…what the hell kind of school did you go to?!"

She waved me off again. "Andy Pulaski, first grade—the kid was in love with me but didn't know how to show it."

"Are you sure he didn't actually despise you? It sounds like he hated your guts."

"Eh, I guess we'll never know for sure. The point is, you teasing Fiona is so transparent—you should just ask her out and be done with it."

"I don't want to go out with her!" I insisted. "And besides, I tease you all the time and that doesn't mean I want to bone you."

"Yeah, but I'm the exception to the rule. We've known each other too long. And besides, I find you about as desirable as William Shatner's left nut."

"Ouch."

"The truth hurts, Beckett. Just ask her out. What's the worst that could happen?"

Obviously, she didn't know Fiona very well or she'd never ask that question. I'm relatively certain Shortcake could singlehand-edly bring on the zombie apocalypse and then just shrug her shoulders and suggest a trip to the mall.

"She's going where?" I asked Jake.

I was driving home from work that evening when Jake called to tell me that Mom had changed her plans for tomorrow morning. Thank God.

"I told you—some spa or something."

I had heard him the first time but I just hadn't believed it. Our mother had never been to a spa in her entire life. She isn't a spa kind of person.

But I knew a diminutive mastermind who most definitely was.

"Fiona," I said.

"Fiona," Jake echoed. "I don't know how the hell she did it, but that woman is a genius."

Maybe not the word I would choose, but I was grateful none-theless.

"Anyway," Jake went on, "I called the hospital today and they're planning on transferring the old man to a county rehab facility tomorrow."

"Does Mom know?"

"I don't think so. She hasn't been there since we warned her off on Sunday, but I can't be sure she hasn't been calling on his status. Anyway, I think this might be a good opportunity for us to stake out the place and see if we can spot anybody while he's being transferred—you know, see if anyone is paying close attention or even tailing him."

"I can't believe I'm saying this, but you have a good point. That would be a great time for someone to try to approach him— when he's sort of out in the open with no security to worry about."

"That's what I was thinking too."

"Okay, any idea what time they're transferring him?"

"Sometime in the morning, but they weren't more specific than that," he told me.

"Okay, I'll bring the coffee and doughnuts and pick you up at 7:30."

"Sounds like a plan, little brother."

I couldn't believe we were staking out a hospital for bad guys. My life had suddenly turned into an eighties buddy flick.

I hit the gym earlier than usual the next morning, determined to get in a workout before potentially sitting on my ass all day. Contrary to some people's experience, a workout actually energizes me so I knew I'd be all set for the day. After showering and dressing in old jeans and a long-sleeved thermal, I headed over to my mom's, stopping for refreshments on the way.

"Rise and shine, people!" I shouted as I unlocked my mom's front door and let myself in.

"Hey, sweetie," came her voice from the kitchen. I followed it and found her in an old pink robe at the table with a cup of coffee and a pile of mail. "What are you doing here so early on a Saturday?"

"Jake and I are running some errands," I semi-lied to her as I handed over a fresh latte from the drink tray I was carrying.

"Wow—thanks!" she said, not needing to check what kind of drink I'd gotten her. I knew her vices.

Just then Jake sauntered into the kitchen dressed very similarly to me, only the color of our shirts differentiating us. He went directly for the drink tray and lifted the lid on the only untouched coffee there—we both took our coffee black. After taking a long sip, he finally spoke. "Ready?" he asked me.

"Ready," I replied. "See you later, Mom," I said.

"Not sure when I'll be back but you'll probably be at work so I'll see you tonight, okay?" Jake addressed our mother.

"Sure," she said, distracted by a letter in her stack of mail. "I'll see you later."

We drove toward the hospital mostly in silence as we sipped our coffees and Jake devoured two of the doughnuts from the bag between our seats. I turned up the radio to give us something to distract ourselves, although it didn't do much except eliminate the need for conversation.

When we finally pulled up to the hospital, I parked in the visitor lot and switched off the ignition. "Well, I guess this is it. I feel like we should have brought something with us—like some brass knuckles or a pocket knife. I feel unprepared."

"The goal is not to get arrested, dumbass. We're just waiting and watching—no big deal. Let's go," he said, opening the passenger door and stepping out.

We ventured in the main doors of the hospital and up to the floor where our old man's room was. The nurses' station was bustling and there was a constant stream of people up and down the hallway. How in the hell were we going to spot these guys, assuming they would even show up?

As if sensing my irritation, Jake whispered, "Calm the fuck down. Just pull out your phone and act like a normal person, dickhead."

We leaned against the wall several doors down from the asshole's room for the next hour or so, taking turns strolling around the floor in a (hopefully) casual manner. The only pleasant distraction was a surgically enhanced red-haired nurse who did her own "casual" strolls by our spot in the hall. Her eyes raked over us each time she passed and we returned the favor, but after the first time I just wasn't feeling it. Jake, on the other hand, most definitely was.

"What's your name, darlin'?" he asked on her third lap.

"Lexie," she answered and tilted her head to the side. "What's yours?"

"I'm Jake. This is Mark. Think you can help me out with something, Lexie?"

"Sure." She smiled up at him.

"That patient in room 320 who you guys are moving today— has anybody been around asking questions about him?"

She suddenly looked unsure. "Oh, I can't give out any patient information. Sorry." She attempted another smile, seemingly disappointed she couldn't give him what he wanted.

"No, I don't need any patient info—just wondering if any visitors have been hanging around or asking about him."

She was ready to retreat so I took over. "Listen, Lexie, that guy in there is our dad and we're worried some people who aren't so friendly are looking for him. We're just trying to protect him."

"Oh." She seemed to consider that. "Um, now that you mention it, I did notice a couple guys hanging around yesterday who seemed a bit out of place. They kept walking by the room and then the nurses' station and were clearly eavesdropping. We ended up calling security but they split before security got here. I didn't think much of it until now. We get odd people around pretty often —usually bored from waiting around."

Mark and I exchanged a glance. Shit. "Do you remember what they looked like?" Jake asked her.

She bit her bottom lip in concentration. "They were kind of unremarkable, you know, just everyday guys. They both had on baseball caps—I think one of them had a red logo. The other guy had a leather jacket and they were both in jeans. That's about all I can remember, sorry. Do you need me to call security?"

"No, that's okay," I said. "Do you happen to remember if either of them had facial hair or a noticeable tattoo or something?" Yeah, I've watched some TV. I know some things.

"Oh, yeah, the one guy had a goatee—I do remember that. No tattoos I can remember but they were both wearing long sleeves so ..." she trailed off.

"Thanks, Lexie," Jake said and then winked at her. "Just one more thing—do you think you can find out what time our dad is being transferred without making a big deal out of it—we kind of don't want him to know we're here."

She gave us a curious look and put her hands to her hips. "Show me your ID and I'll see what I can do." Smart girl.

Jake smiled at her and pulled out his wallet, extracting his driver's license and handing it over. Lexie took it to the nurses' station and started typing into the computer. Seemingly satisfied with what she'd found, she returned a few minutes later with the license in her outstretched hand.

"Okay, Jake Beckett. I can tell you the rehab transport is supposed to arrive at 11:00 and he'll be discharged by then."

Jake took the ID and gave her a grin. "Thanks, Lexie. You've been very helpful. Now, maybe you can help me with just one more thing?"

"That's what you said five minutes ago. I do have a job, you know," she scolded but did it smiling. "What else could you possibly need?"

"Your number would be a good start."

"You know, it may be time for you to branch out and try dating a girl with tits she didn't pay for. It opens up a whole new demographic," I suggested to Jake as we walked out to the parking lot. All I got was a pointed look with a raised eyebrow in return.

We were back in the truck, which I'd moved for a better vantage point. That way we could watch, hopefully unnoticed, when our father came out, keeping our eyes peeled for anything suspicious.

After another half hour of waiting with just the radio and our own thoughts, Jake said, "You know, I wanted to be in the FBI when I was younger." He tapped the buttons on the radio looking for actual music instead of commercials or cackling deejays.

"Seriously?"

"Yeah. I thought it would be cool and it sounded interesting too —I could be a real-life bad-ass, you know. Although, now that I'm an actual adult I realize the job doesn't really involve much of that."

"So why didn't you go to college and try going for the FBI instead of enlisting out of high school?"

"Why do you think?" He sat back in his seat, having found a good country station.

Oh, right. "Dad somehow found out," I stated more than asked.

"You know it—laughed his ass off and told me the government would never hire a dumbass like me unless it was to shine their shoes."

God, our dad was an asshole.

"Still, you shouldn't have let him stand in your way," I said, knowing it was unhelpful at best.

He just grunted in return and then pointed to a car backing out of a prime spot. I quickly put the truck in reverse and maneuvered to the new parking space.

"Anyway, you seem to have a good thing going with the landscape design, right?" For some reason, I was set on pulling him from any dark thoughts—ironic given our current circumstances.

"Sure," he replied. "Hey—didn't Fiona say she works for a landscaping company?" He attempted nonchalance. Unsuccessfully.

"Uh, yeah, why?" I asked cautiously, not sure I wanted to know where this was going.

"No reason." Jake shrugged.

Yeah, like I believed that. It was like a dog asking where the shoes were stored and then passing it off as a mere bit of curiosity.

I scoffed. "What—" I began but Jake cut me off, suddenly pointing out the driver's side window.

"Check it out," he said quietly, but with an intensity that made me shut the hell up.

I turned my head to look out the window and saw two guys standing next to a black sedan, smoking. One wore a black cap with a Red Sox logo and the other had on a black leather jacket and sported a dark goatee.

Shit. Fuck. Damn.

I really wished at that moment that Jake had, in fact, followed his childhood dreams and could call in a crapload of reinforcements. But as it had always been and probably always would be, we were on our own to deal with the oncoming shitstorm.

## Chapter Twelve

# THE POWER OF THE PEDI

FIONA

"I don't know about this," Kelly fidgeted in the front seat of my Prius as I parked outside the Youtopia Day Spa in High Point.

"What do you mean? Free mani-pedi! Life rarely gets better than that," I encouraged. I hadn't anticipated her level of discomfort. I mean, I'd figured she rarely had the chance to treat herself, but she looked downright scared. I glanced to the back seat hoping Laney could step in and somehow fix the situation.

Reading my mind as usual, she leaned forward, eying the spa's sign through the windshield. "It's been *forever* since I had a pedicure. You ever had one, Kelly?"

"Not yet." Kelly shook her head and tucked a strand of stray hair behind her ear.

"I was kind of weirded out the first time too, but as soon as the woman started massaging the knots out of my calves I was a goner." Laney sighed.

"They do that?" Kelly asked, incredulous.

"Sheer heaven," I confirmed.

"Girls, you are young twenty-somethings with what I am sure are beautiful young twenty-something feet. Mine look more like something out of a horror movie. I'll be too embarrassed. Maybe I'll just do the manicure."

"No!" we both cried at once.

"The pedicure is the best part—and they always have massage chairs…" Laney cast out the lure and prepared to reel Kelly in.

"And I'm sure they have seen much, much worse than whatever you think you have going on in those shoes. I promise—they won't bat an eyelash."

"Crap. Maybe. I don't know…I guess. Okay. Fine, I'll do it."

"Yay!" Laney and I both did a happy car dance.

"You girls are nuts," Kelly commented, but she was smiling as she opened her door and got out.

I had been due for a mani-pedi anyway, so as soon as my middle finger text to Mark had been sent, I was on the phone with Dr. Brandon asking him for more info on his daughter's new spa. He was happy to put me in touch with Jenny and I escaped the call with only a few short questions about my wellbeing. Overall, a successful chat, I thought.

I went ahead and called Jenny, hoping she'd have three available spots—which was pushing it considering it was Friday afternoon and I was looking for Saturday morning appointments. As luck would have it—for me, not so much for Jenny—the new spa was slow-going and she indeed had more than enough open spots for us. In fact, she offered us all free services in exchange for honest online reviews, hoping to drive in more traffic. I tried to protest but she was having nothing of it, so I just planned on tipping the crap out of our technicians.

Appointments made and Laney on board, I called Kelly and told her about our family friend who'd just opened a spa and needed people to come in and try out the services for free. Based on her hesitancy, I now realized I may have bullied her into it a little—with overenthusiasm and friendliness, I hoped.

But it was the perfect opportunity to kill two birds with one stone. I would keep Kelly away from the hospital and the creepy bad guys (her husband included) and I could begin Inner Fashion Maven's grand plans for a Kelly makeover—insert non-evil cackle. I didn't know anybody who deserved it more than she did, and if she was open to it I was going to be on her like white on rice, or Laney on Nate, or whatever.

We walked through the front door and were immediately surrounded by a lovely spicy-minty scent and relaxing background music that sounded like tiny bells. The entire reception area of the spa was painted an earthy green combined with cream and rust accents, and a beautiful stone fountain sat in the corner bubbling quietly. Comfy chairs lined one wall and tempting products were on display throughout the space. It was, in fact, what I imagined heaven's waiting room to be like. All that was missing were some cherubs and a giant gold gate.

"Fiona!" I heard my name being called and turned to see Jenny emerging from behind the sleek cream reception counter. We exchanged hugs and I congratulated her on the new spa. She and I kind of knew each other from the years our families had been attending the same fundraisers and functions. She was in her thirties and had three kids, though you'd never be able to tell—she was slim and pretty and she rocked an awesome head full of burgundy curls.

"It's so beautiful!" I told her. "You'll be beating customers back in no time."

"Your lips to God's ear," she responded with a smile before introducing herself to Laney and Kelly. "Come on back, gals, I've got you all set up—you just need to pick your colors and then relax." She led us to the back, which was more of the same nirvana but this time with massage chairs.

We all chose our colors—I went with a citrus theme while Laney chose a palette of blues and Kelly chose clear.

*Clear.*

I did not think so. I grabbed the bottle and put it right back. "You can't pick clear! At least if you're going to do the clear look you need a French manicure."

"What's that?" she asked and I refrained from crossing myself —just barely. I looked up and down the colors and pulled out a pretty pale pink and a slightly darker one. "How about these? The lighter one is for your hands and the other is for your feet. You're probably the only one who's going to see your toes, so why not have a little fun?"

She agreed and we all sat down in our cushy chairs at the manicure tables. Jenny declared she was doing mine, and she introduced us to Laney's technician, Evelyn, and Kelly's technician, Nari.

"This is Kelly's first mani-pedi so go easy on her, Nari," Laney teased.

"You're kidding," replied Nari. "You just relax and I'll take care of you. We won't be able to keep you out of the spa by the time we're done with you today." She smiled at Kelly and got another in return.

Phew.

Thirty minutes later, we were sitting side by side in our massage chairs while Jenny and the gals worked on our feet.

Kelly let out a giant sigh. "I can't believe I've never done this.

What was I thinking?" She had her eyes closed and her head leaned back.

Nari laughed as she applied the scrubby stuff to Kelly's legs. "I told you."

"And I don't know what you were talking about with your feet being old people feet or something," I said.

"They are," she insisted. "I've been working on my feet for thirty-five years. It does things to a woman's feet."

"Nari, be honest, how bad are her feet?"

Without hesitation, Nari replied, "Not even top 100 in nasty feet. You wouldn't believe the things I've seen."

"Amen!" said Jenny and Evelyn at once.

We all laughed, even Kelly.

I decided here was my opening. "Jenny, do you do other services too? Besides nails and massages?" I asked.

"We're starting out with just this for now, but we have more space and we'll have hair styling, facials, and waxing if we can get things going soon. I'm actually a stylist, but I'm a certified nail technician too so right now this is what I'm doing."

Excellent.

"Don't you think Kelly would look great with a cute layered bob?"

"Ooooh," said Laney. "I like it."

Jenny considered Kelly with her professional eye. "That could totally work with some caramel highlights. That would rock."

"Stop right there, girls," said Kelly who was leaning back with her eyes closed again. "I'm still getting used to the idea of having painted nails so don't rush me. And, besides, stuff like that needs upkeep and I'd rather eat than have pretty hair."

I knew not to push too hard, so I let it go. Sort of. "We'll skip the highlights then," I said quietly and Kelly gave my arm a shove.

An actual shove! This was awesome. I looked over at her and her eyes were still closed but she had a grin on her face.

I had promised to have Kelly home in time for her to run a few errands and get ready for work—and I kept my promise, pulling up to her house with time to spare. She'd gone quiet again on the drive home, but I was hoping it was just because she was super relaxed. Turned out, not so much.

She turned in her seat so she could see both Laney and me. "Can you girls come in for a minute? I have something I need an opinion on." She looked nervous as all get-out again.

Shit.

We didn't even answer. We just opened our doors and followed her into the house. It was one side of an older duplex and it was a bit dated, which I had sort of anticipated, to be honest. I could see where little updates had been made here and there, but nothing disguised the age and wear of the place. The tile in the entryway appeared almost new, but the carpet had definitely seen better days. A nice couch sat along one wall of the living room, but the rest of the furniture looked old and beaten up. The kitchen counters and floor were not original to the house and I could see Mark's hand in all of it. Despite the mix of old and new, the entire place was tidy and free of clutter. Kelly definitely liked her living space neat.

She led us to the table in the small kitchen and invited us to take a seat. Once we were all sitting, she withdrew an envelope from the stack of mail sitting on the table in front of us. She handed it to Laney.

"Does this mean what I think it means?" Kelly asked.

Laney opened the envelope, took out the letter, and read it over.

"Crap," she swore and handed it to me.

It was a plain sheet of white paper with just a few words printed on it.

*You have one week. $32,000 cash.*

"Shit," I said and put down the paper.

We all just stared at each other.

"I kept telling myself it must be a bad joke or something, but it's not, is it?"

"We have to call Mark," I said.

"No!" Kelly exclaimed. "I don't want to worry him or Jake. I'll figure something out."

"But you can't!" insisted Laney. "You need their help! And we should call the cops too—this is a threat!" She pointed to the paper. "It's one thing if your husband doesn't want to call the cops but now they've threatened you, so you can call!"

Kelly just shook her head. "But it's not an actual threat. There's nothing the police could do about it," she said.

Laney and I both read the paper again. She was right. It was deliberately vague.

"I'm going to the hospital to see Jim tomorrow and find out where the money is. Then I'm going to get it to these people." She pointed to the paper.

"What makes you think he still has any of it? Wouldn't he have handed it over the first time instead of being beaten half to death?" I asked, wondering if Kelly was thinking straight.

Kelly shook her head again. "I don't know—you'd have to know Jim. He's so...stubborn and always sure he's in the right. He *could* still have at least some of it. Anyway, I'm going to find out tomorrow. If he doesn't have it, I'll figure something else out from there. These guys obviously know about me but they don't know about the boys—and I intend to keep it that way."

"I understand you wanting to protect them, Kelly, but they'd want to do the same for you. They're worried about you."

"I know, but they don't need to be. As soon as we get this money thing worked out, things can go back to normal."

Laney and I exchanged a glance.

"Normal like 'last-week-normal' or normal like 'with Jim'?" I asked, afraid of the answer.

"What do you mean?" She seemed genuinely puzzled.

"Well, from what Mark and Jake said, not that it's any of my business you know, but from what they said it sounded kind of like you maybe, you know, still kind of had—"

"Oh for God's sake," Laney cut me off. "What she's trying to ask is if you still have feelings for your husband and want him back."

Kelly's head jerked back. "What would make you think that?"

I mumbled, "Mark and Jake may have mentioned something or other…"

"Oh," she said and looked down at the table. She remained silent for a few moments before speaking again. "The whole middle-of-the-night hospital thing was just so crazy—I'm not even sure what I said to them. It was all so shocking, you know?" She lifted her head. "Seeing Jim again and especially in those circumstances—it took me a few days to get my head on straight."

"So…you don't want him back?" Laney asked.

Kelly gave a slight laugh that held zero humor. She tilted her head back and blinked like one does when trying to stave off tears.

We waited silently, hoping she'd elaborate. After getting a handle on her emotions and bringing her eyes back to us, she did.

"My boys, they remember all the bad stuff, you know?"

Laney and I both nodded, waiting for her to continue but afraid of what we'd hear.

"But I remember the beginning. I was so in love, and I have to believe Jim was too. There is nothing as magical as young love, and God we were young. I was seventeen. He was nineteen and was going to be my knight in shining armor, taking me away to a life that would be so, so beautiful. It felt like no one else in the world could possibly have a love as pure and strong as ours—it would last forever. We were kids." She shrugged.

"The thing is, change happens gradually, not overnight. Things…happen. Real life happens. Lord knows I should have been a better mother and stepped in when Jim got out of line. But it's so easy to see that in hindsight. Looking back, I just remember being tired and I remember making excuses—at least he didn't hit us, at least he didn't do drugs. I understand it's no real excuse and never will be. He was just so clever in the way he put us down and made us feel like we should be grateful he even put up with us."

She gave another humorless laugh. "I'm not stupid. I don't actually want him back." She ran a hand through her long hair and looked up at the ceiling again. "I guess part of me just wants to feel worthy of *someone* wanting to come back for me, even if it is my loser husband. I know that sounds ridiculous. It *is* ridiculous."

My heart broke into a billion pieces and my throat was so tight with tears that I didn't dare try to speak. One glance at Laney showed her similarly affected, her cheeks streaked with tears she hadn't been able to hold back.

I reached out my hand and gripped Kelly's. Laney did the same on the other side. We held on for dear life.

There were two things I was certain of at that moment. One, this was something even an entire day at the spa couldn't make a dent in. And two, I was going to kick the ever-loving shit out of Jim Beckett. They might be tiny, but these fists were gonna fly.

## Chapter Thirteen

# LOU AND TERRY AND THE SUCKER PUNCH

## M ARK

*Fiona: Where r u?!*

There was no way I was about to tell Fiona I was sitting in my truck outside the hospital looking at two thugs who may be planning on kidnapping or killing my father as soon as he emerged.

I ignored her text.

It was 12:30 and we still hadn't seen any signs of our old man or the transfer vehicle. Jake had just returned from a little recon mission where he'd gone through the back of the hospital and confirmed that our father was still there. As is typical in healthcare, things weren't running on time.

The goons—I was trying out different terms to refer to them and I may have found a winner—were back in the black sedan and Jake and I were doing our damn best not to be noticed.

My phone chimed again.

*Fiona: Where the hell r u?!*

"You gonna answer that?" Jake asked me, leaning forward in his seat and looking as restless as I was.

"No."

Before I could move a muscle, he'd snatched my phone and put a hand over my face to push me away from him.

"Fiona," he said with a smirk as I grabbed my phone back and punched him in the arm.

"Next time it will be your pretty little face," I warned him.

My phone chimed yet again and Jake smothered a laugh.

*Fiona: Mark, if you don't tell me where you are I will publish this picture on Instagram, Twitter, and my Facebook page.*

What followed this was something I had difficulty wrapping my brain around. It was a photo from when I was about 12 and Jake was maybe 16. He was standing shirtless, flexing his bicep on one arm while choking the crap out of me with his other arm. I was maybe 80 pounds soaking wet and was wearing my damn glasses and a bow tie. How in the hell did she get this picture?

And then I remembered who I was dealing with.

*Mark: Let's not do anything rash, Shortcake. I'm at the hospital.*

*Fiona: Perfect. On my way.*

Fuck!

*Mark: DO NOT COME HERE!*

*Fiona: Don't you shouty caps me! I can go where I want!*

If the goons didn't get to me first, this girl was going to be the death of me.

*Mark: Seriously, Fiona. The bad dudes are here. Stay away and keep my mom away!*

*Fiona: Shit. Okay.*

I could breathe again.

*Fiona: R u okay?*

*Mark: We're fine. Just watching right now. Nothing has happened.*

*Fiona: Should I call the police?*

*Mark: No! What is it with you and the police? Is this a fetish thing?*

*Fiona: What? Please speak English.*

*Mark: No cops. Dad is being transferred to rehab. Do NOT tell my mom.*

*Fiona: She's at work anyway. Had a lovely time at the spa.*

Jesus H. Christ.

*Mark: We're gonna follow the rehab transfer to make sure he gets there safe. Will text you later.*

*Fiona: Stay safe. Later.*

I read her last text and then noticed that Jake was staring at me with a shit-eating grin. "Do you realize your face went through about thirty emotions in the last five minutes and at one point you actually growled?"

"No I didn't."

He nodded with that stupid-ass grin still glued to his face. "You've got it bad, little brother."

"Whatever. She just drives me crazy," I lied.

He put on a mock frustrated face and balled his fists. "Oooh, that little minx, she just drives me so crazy I'm gonna fuck the hell out of her."

What an asshole. "You know, Jake, all I can think of right now is how jealous I am of all the people who've never met you."

He laughed, completely unoffended. Douchebag.

"Oh shit," he said, his expression sobering. "Here comes the transfer." He pointed out the windshield to a vehicle that resembled a combination of an ambulance and a van. On its side were the words "Guilford County." This vehicle was either taking someone to rehab or to prison. Either would be fitting.

I looked to the sedan and saw that the driver had opened his door.

Jake and I both opened ours, but we hadn't yet determined exactly what we were going to do.

"I'm thinking you may have been right about those brass knuckles, little brother," he said quietly.

My heart was beating a mile a minute as the vehicle came to a stop and the transfer driver got out. He was not a big guy—by any means.

Just then, the double automatic doors of the hospital parted and there was our old man on a stretcher, looking not a whole lot better than the last time I'd seen him. A lone woman in scrubs was pushing the stretcher. Shit. We needed more people around, prefer-ably ones with muscles and weapons.

"Is that him?" asked Jake, his voice surprised. I forgot he hadn't seen our father in fifteen years.

"Yup."

"He looks so…" Jake started.

"Old, I know," I said.

"I was gonna say small, but yeah. Holy shit."

"Speaking of holy shit, here we go," I said as I gestured to the sedan where both men had now emerged and were heading slowly toward the transfer vehicle.

We let them get a head start and then fell in behind them, careful to keep a good distance.

They were about twenty feet from the vehicle when the one with the goatee shouted, "Yo, Jim! Fancy seeing you here. Haven't seen you since Vegas."

We picked up our pace and closed the distance a bit. I could see my father turn his head to them and then mouth the word "Fuck."

The orderly and the driver seemed to hesitate, not quite sure if this was a friendly meeting or not.

That would be a firm "not."

"Lou, Terry, hey," said the old man, feigning cheerfulness. "Uh, you can see I'm not really up for visitors right now."

"Yeah, what happened, man?" said Lou or Terry, whichever one had the Sox hat on. At this point, they were about five feet from the stretcher. The driver and orderly, seemingly having decided this was an exchange of friendly pleasantries, went about their business and began loading our father into the back of the vehicle.

"Oh, you know…" said the old man, nervous as shit.

"Oh yeah," said the thug with the goatee. "I think I heard something about that. You should be more careful who you hang out with, Jim. Maybe you should spend more time at home—with your pretty wife."

"Oh shit," said Jake at my side.

"Yeah, maybe," was all the old douchebag said. Son of a bitch!

"We'll stop by your house next week and check on her for you —see how she's doing while you're healing up. Sound good?"

"Uh…" said my piece-of-shit father.

"It's all set then, next Saturday. Later, Jim."

And they walked away, right past us and back to the sedan. Jake and I pretended to be in conversation as they passed and the doors of the transfer vehicle slammed shut with a bang.

It was official. Our old man was the shittiest husband and father in the world and we were all up shit's creek without a paddle.

It turned out I didn't get a chance to text Fiona to update her—she wasn't patient enough to wait. By the middle of the afternoon, she'd found Jake's number and we both had three new texts along with a renewed threat to post more incriminating photos if I didn't "call her ass immediately."

I also had an apology text from Laney.

And another from Nate.

Exactly when had Shortcake become an integral player in this debacle? How had she wormed her way into this so deeply that she now required regular "briefing"?

Still, not wanting to subject myself to widespread ridicule over social media, I dialed the little harpy's number while my brother made himself at home in my kitchen and grabbed a soda from the fridge.

"The bad guys know about your mom," she said as soon as she picked up the call. "She didn't want me to tell you and I've been going back and forth about this for hours, but I'm so worried for her, I just had to tell you. And now I'm probably going to hell, or at least Karma is going to have it out for me. I'll probably break my leg or lose my job—of course, that's probably going to happen anyway, but whatever. Anyway, I'm prepared to suffer the consequences if it means we can protect your mom. I was thinking I could hire a bodyguard for her or, you know, buy an attack dog. Although what we'd do with the dog when this is over, I don't really know. My building doesn't allow dogs over thirty pounds and I doubt we could find a good attack dog that small. And now that I think about it, I'm not sure I'd want an aggressive dog as a pet anyway. You think we should go with the bodyguard instead? Maybe I could find a hot guy close to her age and it could be like that movie, *The Bodyguard*, except he and your mom would stay together in the end. Oh, and nobody would die," she finished on a breathless gasp.

"Shortcake!" I finally shouted when she stopped for a beat.

"Yeah?"

"Shut it!" I said, trying to get a moment to take it all in. She was like a forest fire—once she got going it was fucking hell to stop her.

"Rude!" she responded but did, in fact, shut it.

"I know they know about my mom. The question is, how do you know?" I mentally braced for an answer I knew I wouldn't like.

"They sent her a threatening letter. Can we please call the cops now?"

Shit.

"Hold tight. Where are you?"

"My place."

"Where's that?"

She gave me the address and I told her I was heading right over.

"Just call up and I'll buzz you in when you get here. In the meantime, I'll call my parents' driver and ask him if he knows any hot older bodyguards. Drivers usually know these things, don't they?"

I couldn't take it—I hung up on her.

I put my phone on mute in case she called back and then relayed all the details to Jake.

Let me rephrase—I relayed all the *pertinent* details to Jake. I left the crazy where it was—in a high-rise building downtown.

"I'm heading over to Fiona's to find out as much as I can. I'll drop you off at Mom's and you see if you can find this letter."

"Shit. Okay," he said and we both headed back out. "You know, Florida is much less dramatic than North Carolina."

"I'm thinking after this shit blows over I might need a vacation —you'd best prepare for a houseguest."

I parked on the street a block down from the high-rise. Damn, this girl was money incarnate. I work in the business and I know how much condos go for in a building like this.

Way out of my league, just like her.

Wait, no. I didn't want to be "in her league" anyway. That's the kind of thing relationship people think. I don't date—I fuck and run. So who cares how much money a chick has? It's never been an issue when she's under me. Not that Fiona was going to be under me, or over me, or against the wall, or on the kitchen table— hey, with all those fuck-me heels she wears, who can blame my male brain for wandering there from time to time? Or all the time. Dammit.

I buzzed her.

No response.

I buzzed her again.

Still no response.

I called her on my phone.

After five rings, she finally picked up.

"Yes?"

"Buzz me up, Shortcake. I'm getting strange looks out here."

Indeed, there was a guy who watched me buzzing repeatedly and felt it necessary to comment, "Damn, man, you must have pissed her right the fuck off."

"Oh, I'm sorry. Did you want to talk to me? Because it sure didn't seem like it when you *hung up on me!*" she shouted.

"It was just a bad connection," I blatantly lied.

She muttered something unintelligible and then I heard the buzzer go off. I was no moron—I grabbed that door as fast as humanly possible since I was certain there would be no second chances, regardless of loan sharks and goons and my little spitfire's need to be a do-gooder.

The entire lobby area was decorated and designed in a very clean, modern style. A bit minimalist for my taste, but then again, it seemed that rich people often paid more for less. I found the elevator and, I must admit, I was a tiny bit disappointed to see she did not live in the penthouse, but on the floor below. If she'd had an entire penthouse to herself, it would have made it that much easier to dismiss her completely as a spoiled little rich girl who was just dabbling in my family's drama for entertainment. Not that a condo on the fourteenth floor of this building would be anything to sneeze at.

I imagined Fiona in my mother's dilapidated house and felt a twinge of both humiliation and anger that I couldn't quite reconcile. Fiona was simultaneously too good for the abysmal place and not good enough for it—or my mother, or me, or Jake for that matter. It made no sense, but the familiar feeling of never being good enough produced an amazing amount of resentment that built over time like an unnoticed thorny weed and often stung innocent passersby. It was yet to be determined if Fiona fell into that category or not. She'd never struck me as innocent at any rate.

The elevator took me up to her floor and I found her door, which was propped open a few inches. I took this as an invitation and entered her condo, ready for her verbal attack and the possibility of physical assault as well.

I took in the place. Yup, money.

The apartment and its furnishings weren't particularly stuffy or ostentatious, it was just that everything in there was expensive. Expensive in the way where it doesn't scream it cost a mint but it would probably automatically repel dusty cargo pants or beer in a can. The owner of said items would find himself mysteriously thrust into the hallway with no clear understanding of how he'd gotten there while the couch pillows inside would wipe their imaginary hands and say, "Well, now that that's done let's get back to being splendidly rich."

I was so distracted in my perusal of the condo that I didn't see Fiona at first. Then I wondered how I couldn't have spotted her right off. She was, for once, not wearing heels. In fact, she was barefoot. She was also dressed in form-fitting jeans and a simple wide-neck white t-shirt—which, let's face it, probably cost as much as the couch I'd bought my mom. Her hair floated about her face as usual and I realized she wasn't wearing any make-up.

My Shortcake stood in the threshold of the kitchen with a wounded look on her face and red puffy eyes. She'd been crying. The mere thought that either I or my situation was the cause of the tears had me wanting to take back every negative, sarcastic, insulting thing I'd ever thought about her or said to her. My gut roiled at the same time it was hit with the biggest sucker punch I'd ever felt or imagined. Because despite all my big talk, my history, and common sense in general, she was *my* Shortcake.

She was mine.

What on God's green earth was I going to do with this revelation? It turns out that standing there like a big fucking jackass was the only move I had.

Brilliant.

## Chapter Fourteen

# WE DO LIVE IN A DEMOCRACY, AFTER ALL

$\mathcal{F}$IONA

In my defense, I didn't really think he'd show up after he hung up on me like an asshole. But by the time I realized he was indeed downstairs and wasn't going away, I refused to primp or even apply so much as a swipe of lip balm, and I just buzzed him up. So what if I looked like a twelve-year-old homeless person? Oh, wait, that thought was too depressing—I'd totally want to embrace a twelve-year-old homeless girl and adopt her. So what if I looked like a very short crack whore? That was better. Mark would just have to take me as I was. No, I didn't mean *take me*, I meant *put up with me*. That's what I meant. Wait, did I just compare myself to a crack whore? *Get it together, Fiona!*

When the door swung open and Mark stepped inside, my breath hitched a bit. He was dressed in a *very* form-fitting olive green long-sleeved thermal, an old pair of jeans that were worn in *all* the right places, and work boots. He had that creased brow and a day or two of scruff on his face, and my lady bits decided they liked this look very much. A fire started down below from just the kindling of his scruff and the spark from his sheer hotness. How had I thought all of...*that*...was excessive? He was fucking sexy as hell!

He looked like he'd just walked off a runway and I looked like I'd just walked out of a crack den. This was completely counter to the familiar order of things in my little world. *I* was runway! *He* was gym rat material—rude and conceited. Right?

Oh, of course not. I'd known for at least a week that he was more than that. Much more.

His eyes finally found me and Uterus spoke up. "*Fallopian Tubes, Vagina, and I have all voted and the results are in —JUMP HIM!*"

Well, crap. I could usually reason with Fallopian Tubes and Uterus, but Vagina? There was no swaying her. In fact, she and Inner Fashion Maven were often in cahoots as they shared a mutual hatred of Guilt and a mutual affection for hot sex. Thank God Clit hadn't weighed in or I'd already be across the room and climbing Mark like the human mountain he was. Everest be damned! It was Beckett I would conquer!

Shut. The Fuck. Up.

I had to gather my wits. This was not about crack whores, female anatomy, or mountains that needed scaling. This was about a very real threat to good people and I needed to clear my freaking head.

"Shortcake," was all he said as his shoulders dropped and he lost any sense of defensiveness he'd entered my condo with. "What's all this?"

I was confused. "Um, my condo?" I asked more than said.

"No, that's not what I mean. The tears, Shortcake?" He approached slowly, his thigh muscles straining his jeans.

*Panty Dropper, party of one!*

"Don't call me that," I said with only half the indignation I'd meant to use.

He was standing directly in front of me by that point. I looked down, suddenly self-conscious at my appearance when I had been steadfastly resolute just minutes before.

I felt his finger on my chin, lifting my face so he could look directly at me without having to bend down. I realized this was the first time he had ever touched me and I felt goosebumps rise on my arms. It really was quite ridiculous how big he was in comparison to me. I wondered for a moment what those muscles were called that rose above a person's collarbone to create that slope Mark had. Then I dismissed that thought altogether as I caught his scent and nearly swooned. What was that? Whatever it was, it had the effect of a hot fudge sundae on all my various lady parts because they all swooned simultaneously, leaving me responsible for keeping our entire body upright. Bitches!

"I like calling you that," he responded quietly. "Please don't spoil it for me."

I was evidently under some kind of spell he'd cast because I inexplicably said, "Okay."

*Okay?!* What? I hated when people pointed out my height—it was so patronizing. Like I wasn't aware of my size already and just needed a freakishly large person to point out something my tiny scale-appropriate brain couldn't possibly configure on its own! *Wow, thank you for pointing that out—I was wondering why I had so much more oxygen down here. Feel free to go on with your business, you freakishly tall human being, you.* Gah!

But apparently, Mark was now using some sort of wizardry on me because I capitulated like a puppy with a peanut-butter-filled Kong.

*"What the hell, Fiona?"* cried a new part of my subconscious. I wasn't familiar with this one. *"Pride,"* she introduced herself.

*Oooooh. Wow, it's great to meet you—I think we need you right about now.*

*"Yeah, no shit,"* she said. But before she could say more, Mark cut in.

"I don't like seeing you cry. Are these tears about my mom? Please say you just watched something sad on TV or missed a giant sale instead," he said as his thumb swept over my right cheek.

My knees wobbled and I could only hear Pride as a very faint echo in the back of my brain yelling, *"Hold on!"*

"I just…don't want any of you getting hurt," was what I managed without breaking down again.

This afternoon, I had waited until I'd dropped Laney off and was safely ensconced in my own space before I'd broken down. I cried my eyes out at the unfairness of it all. Why were some people so cruel? Why did Kelly have a shit husband who, even after disappearing for years, could still rain hurt down on her and her kids? Why did my family have money when *she* was the one who needed it to protect her family? And why did people like me, who had those financial resources, have to fight a different battle—one that money couldn't win? It was all so misaligned.

Of course, I knew without asking that if I were to offer the money it would ruin any kind of friendship I may ever hold with any member of their family. I would forever be the little rich girl who offered her "spare change," oblivious to the true struggle it was to live a normal life. If it were only that, I probably would have risked it regardless, but I knew they would never accept my money in a million years. I wasn't the only client Pride had, of that I was certain.

So, I did what any normal girl would do—I sat in my apartment, broke down in tears, and downed a pint of Ben and Jerry's. All right, I may have also had a couple glasses of wine, only remembering after the first sip that wine and ice cream don't really go together very well. Somebody needs to invent alcohol-infused ice cream. Oh yeah, I guess that's kind of what frozen margaritas are. Oh well. Moving on.

Anyway, it was at that point the phone had rung and it had been Mark, *finally* calling me back, so I'd gotten my act together and told him about his mom and the note, even though Guilt gave me hell about it. Oh, what did she know anyway?!

I did make the decision, though, to keep some of Kelly's business private—certainly the emotional and very personal struggle she'd shared with us, but also the fact that she was going to see Jim tomorrow. I was hoping the bad guys would stick with their plan and leave her alone until next weekend, but it was still a bit risky. And I knew if I told Mark, he and Jake would try to stop her—to protect her, as usual.

Their care and concern for her was indeed very sweet and endeared them to me, but I knew only too well what it felt like to constantly be on the receiving end of such care. It was always well-intended and came from a place of love, but to be reminded how fragile, how breakable, you are on a constant basis can have the unintended effect of making you feel even more broken. It can make you forget that you *can* be strong if given the chance. So, I wanted to give Kelly that chance, and hopefully it wouldn't turn out to be a mistake. That's why I was planning a little stake-out of my own in the morning. I've watched *Enter the Dragon*—I've picked up some things. Nobody was touching a hair on Kelly's head.

"Shortcake," Mark said again and then wrapped me up in the

same hug I'd witnessed him giving his mother last week—the one where it seemed his arms could wrap around me twice.

And I needed it.

I reveled in it.

I let out a huge involuntary sigh and burrowed right into his chest where I was again consumed by his scent—something woodsy and earthy—and the goosebumps turned into a whole-body shiver.

"Are you cold?" he asked.

"Yes," I lied.

At which point he bent down, picked me up as if I were a child, and carried me over to the sofa where he plopped down with me sprawled sideways across his lap—kind of like he was Santa and I was a big baby, only in a sexy way. Okay, drop the whole Santa thing—that analogy is totally inappropriate. Just focus on the big hot guy.

He grabbed the cashmere throw I keep over the arm of the sofa and bundled it around me, tucking it almost up to my chin. It made me smile stupidly at him.

"Better?" He smiled back and looked at me with his amazing brown eyes bordered all around by those obscene eyelashes.

"*What's taking so long?*" asked Uterus.

"*Yeah, enough with all the boo-hooing—just sit on his face already!*" Vagina chimed in.

"*Shut up, you filthy little whores!*" scolded Pride.

I had to work very hard to block these bitches out or I was definitely going to throw common sense out the window and start feeling Mark up.

"So," Mark interrupted the turbulent musings in my mind, "tell me more about this letter and everything that happened."

Oh, right, back to regularly scheduled programming—except that I was sitting on his lap and his thumb was stroking my arm.

"Um, well, we went to the spa and it was really fun—your mom is great, by the way—and we got mani-pedis. See?" I lifted my feet from under the throw to show him my toes.

He grinned. "Very nice, Shortcake."

"And I had to talk your mom into getting her nails painted an actual color instead of clear—can you believe that's what she picked out?" I looked up into his face again and I could practically see his internal struggle to maintain patience.

Oh, right, back on track, then.

"Anyway, when we were done and were dropping your mom off she asked us to come in to have a look at something. It was the letter from those loan sharks."

"What exactly did it say?" he asked, tension lining his mouth. His thumb had stopped moving.

I concentrated and tried to remember the note. "It said something like, 'You have a week. $32,000.' I'm pretty sure that's what it said because Laney and I insisted it was a threat and your mom should call the cops, but Kelly pointed out that the way they'd written it wouldn't necessarily be seen that way."

"Shit. The price went up by two grand. I guess I shouldn't be surprised," Mark said, shaking his head. "And it goes along with the timeline we overheard at the hospital."

"So what exactly happened over there? You had me worried."

He looked at me intently and then, I kid you not, bent and kissed the top of my head!

What was going on here? Had I blacked out for a week and we were now people who hugged and kissed? Or, in the midst of a coma I don't remember being in, had his mother decided to adopt me, making me his little sister who he affectionately kissed on the head? Help! I don't know what's going on!

*"Calm down and pay attention,"* Guilt said. *"This is a lot for him to take in so give him some leeway without freaking out like a thirteen-year-old with her first crush."*

Right.

His thumb started making circles on the back of my hand this time. Oooh, that looked really good with my new manicure.

Mark's voice pulled me from my consideration of our hands. "Not much, really. The thugs approached my old man and issued a very thinly veiled threat to my mom if they don't get their money by next Saturday. The asshole just laid there like the useless pile of bones he is."

I brought my hand to my throat. "Oh my God—poor Kelly. This is so unfair! What are we going to do?"

"Well, first, *Jake and I,*" he said while giving me a pointed look, "are going to convince our mom we've got it covered. Then we're going to use a contact at the hospital to get the old man's address. From what those guys said, he's probably not living here in North Carolina—just came back to try and hide and be the parasite he is. We're going to go snooping and see if we can find anything to sell or—if he's dumb enough, a safe assumption at this point—see if he has any hidden cash. That is, if the thugs haven't already tossed the place."

I nodded my head. That sounded like a pretty decent plan to start with.

"What did my mom say about the note?"

Hmm, here's where things got tricky. I'm relatively certain it's wrong to lie to someone while they're cuddling you and just kissed you on the head.

"She was upset, obviously. I don't know. We just did some girl talk?"

"Is that a question?"

"Um, no?" Dammit all.

"Again, is that a question, Shortcake? What aren't you telling me?"

I huffed. "Some things are just private, Mark—between girls."

"There's not anything important you're not telling me, though?"

I tried to evade. "Well, if you consider stories about your childhood important…" I trailed off, hoping I'd distracted him enough.

"Yeah, about that—I can't believe my mother gave you those pictures!"

"Aww," I teased. "Are you embarrassed that you used to be as tiny as me?"

He just narrowed his eyes and squeezed me.

"Careful, He-Man, you may just crush me with your big bod if you don't watch out. I will say, though, that seeing those pictures gives me a little insight into why you and your gym have such a bromance going on."

He scoffed. "Whatever. I just like being in shape, Shortcake."

"Uh-huh," I said, eying him up and down quite leisurely.

And at that moment I became acutely aware of some very specific movement under my bum. Let's say a *rising* of sorts.

Oh my.

*Oh my!*

I abruptly sat up and practically jumped off his lap—this was so confusing! I threw myself across to the other end of the sofa and tossed the cashmere blanket on top of his lap to cover any evidence. My sharp movements caused some groaning and grunting from Mark. Perhaps I hadn't been very graceful in my panic to escape the confusion-inducing penis salute. Ugh. Kill me now.

What was wrong with me? I was completely attracted to him, and I now had hard evidence (*oh, come on, I couldn't resist*) he was attracted to me too. *He* only did casual sex—*I* only did casual sex. On paper, we should be boning right now. Well not actually *on* paper because that might involve paper cuts in some extremely inconvenient—*oh, you know what I mean!*

Only it wasn't that simple and we both knew it.

Time for distraction!

I snuck a peek at Mark. He seemed to still be recovering from my unintentional assault to his man parts.

"So, there's one thing I think you haven't considered in this grand plan of yours to ransack your dad's place."

"Oh yeah?" he muttered with his eyes closed, head resting on the back of the sofa like he'd just run a marathon. Seriously? How badly could it really have hurt?

"Yeah. Assuming he lives far away, if you and Jake both go then there won't be anybody here to protect your mom in case the thugs decide to come calling early."

His eyes opened and shifted to me. "Crap. You're right." He sat up, seemingly back to normal. "Maybe I can ask Nate…no, I don't want to put him in harm's way, especially with a family to worry about."

Damn straight. "That's why I'm going to go with you, and Jake will stay with your mom."

*What? Did I just say that?*

"What? No," said Mark.

Phew.

Then he tilted his head, looked me over slowly from head to toe (turnabout being fair play and all, I suppose), and announced with complete certainty, "Actually, that's a great idea. Can you get off work if need be?"

*Shit. I'd really done it now.*

*"Yay!"* cried all the lady bits, even Guilt and Pride because being helpful is a good quality in a human being.

"Sure," was all I could say. It seemed I was out-voted.

I believe I'm the only person I know who lives in a democracy consisting of a slew of imaginary crazy people and only one actual human.

Oh well…road trip!! I just hoped it didn't interfere with my stake-out. I was one busy bad-ass woman.

*Chapter Fifteen*

# THE CHRISTOPHER COLUMBUS OF LIKE

MARK

I had absolutely no fucking idea what I was doing. This was akin to braving a new world—I'd never had *feelings* for a girl before. And I'd certainly never wanted to hold one on my lap, unless of course she was straddling me.

After Fiona had kicked my hard-on and practically crushed my nuts in her attempt to scramble off my lap, I'd thought all was lost and she was repulsed. Then I remembered how she had thoroughly checked me out—the very perusal that had caused said hard-on— and I recognized the deer-in-headlights look on her face.

She was just as perplexed as I was, and more importantly, as turned on as I was. I already knew she was mine, as foreign as that thought was, but I was guessing she didn't yet realize I was hers. All of which would be remedied by the concentrated alone time we'd have while traveling to, and subsequently searching, my dad's place, wherever that may be.

So, back to the plan. A call to Jake was in order so I pulled my phone out of my back pocket and hit connect on his contact, keeping Shortcake in my sights all the while. She fidgeted like mad in the corner of the sofa. It was fucking cute. And now that my dick had recovered, it was clamoring its approval. However, as soon as my brother picked up the phone, it did the appropriate thing and calmed the hell down.

"Yo," Jake greeted.

"Hey, you find anything?"

"Not a thing. She must have taken it with her. You at Fiona's?"

"Yeah. Don't worry about finding the note. Bottom line is we already know the deadline is Saturday, but the amount has been upped—thirty-two grand."

"Shit."

"Yeah. So, the plan to search his place is still on, but Fiona brought up a good point. If we're both gone, who's going to watch out for Mom in case the goons get restless?"

"Right—crap."

"So I think you should still get the address from Lexie, but then Fiona and I will go to his place." I kept my eyes on her and she smiled nervously. Then she stood and headed for the kitchen, mimicking a drinking motion on the way. I'd let her go for now.

"What the hell, man?!"

I maintained a calm demeanor. "We've got it covered."

"I hope you know what you're doing," he said.

"Not a fucking clue," I responded once Fiona was out of earshot.

To which Jake laughed his fucking ass off.

"Okay, it's all set," I told Fiona when she finally came back to the couch carrying a glass of red wine in one hand and a beer in the other. "Jake is going to get the address tomorrow and then, depending on where we're headed, we can either leave tomorrow afternoon or Monday morning. How does that work with your schedule?"

I noticed she sat about as far away from me as possible as she set her glass on the end table and picked up her phone from its spot on the coffee table. She tapped at it for a moment and then put the phone to her ear.

"Hey, Ollie, it's Fiona," she greeted the person on the other end of the line, then paused and laughed before saying, "Oh, you know me too well." And then she giggled.

I decided I hated this Ollie person.

"Yeah, I was hoping to switch things around and get Monday and probably Tuesday off…uh-huh…uh-huh…oh, really? Uh-huh. Okay, thanks hun. Later." And she hung up the phone.

Hun?

"So?" I asked with my teeth clenched, hoping she didn't notice how hard I was gripping my beer bottle. That was new. Apparently, I was the possessive, jealous type.

"Ollie is going to smooth it over with Jax so I can get both Monday and Tuesday off in case it takes that long."

"Ollie, huh?" I asked, failing colossally in my attempt at nonchalance.

Fiona turned to me and cocked her head to one side. Then a little smirk hit her face and I wanted to drag her back to my lap and kiss it right off her.

"Yes. Ollie. He's great," she said oh-so-causally as she picked her wine glass up and took a sip.

I growled. Huh—seemed like Jake was right for once—I did in fact growl around Fiona.

Okay, so this was how we were going to play this game? She was going to run away like a frightened rabbit and then turn around and try to make me jealous? This rabbit obviously didn't know who she was dealing with.

I rose from the sofa, taking one last pull on my mostly full beer. "Well, Shortcake, I should probably get going—got some shit to take care of."

Her head snapped up and she almost spilled her wine. "Already?"

Ha! Don't mess with the bull if you don't want the horns, little rabbit. I play to win and I hate losing, especially now that I knew what I wanted.

"Yup. I'll call you tomorrow with the details once Jake gets the info." I fake stretched and knew my shirt lifted to reveal a portion of my abdomen and happy trail. I heard a little whimper from her side of the couch but pretended not to notice. "Thanks for the beer," I said as I headed for the door.

I heard her scramble off the couch and her glass nearly crash into the table in her haste to set it down. "Oh, okay. I'll walk you out." I felt her come up behind me at the same time I grabbed the door handle.

I turned momentarily and saw her tongue poke out to swipe over her bottom lip. Damn, this was not as easy as I'd hoped, but I stood my ground. "Later, Shortcake." I stepped into the hall, pulling the door closed behind me just before I collapsed against it as quietly as possible. I looked down at my tented jeans and silently promised my dick that I would make it up to him.

"Atlantic City? Seriously?" I asked Jake.

"I shit you not."

This just kept getting better and better.

It was Sunday mid-afternoon and I was in the trailer at my current work site when Jake's call came in. I'd decided to come in on a Sunday to get things organized in anticipation of my unexpected time off. The guys had assured me they would cover for me, but I didn't want to be a bigger pain in their asses than necessary. Getting as much organized as possible should ease the way and make things go smoothly in my absence. But I forgot all about the blueprints and work orders littered in front of me when I heard the words "Atlantic City."

There was nothing intrinsically wrong with Atlantic City other than our father living there being the biggest cliché ever. But it was not lost on Jake or me that this was the place our old man had always talked about as being some kind of mecca we'd all visit one day when we had money and could make a big deal of it. I think he'd figured he could spend the vacation gambling while our mom took us to kid-friendly activities and venues. He would spend as little time with us as possible and call it the best family vacation ever.

So, I suppose we shouldn't have been too surprised when Jake's flirting with Lexie had brought this information to light. Jake had looked it up on the map and it was only an eight-hour drive—no problem for an overnight trip, but not really feasible for a round trip in one day.

Fiona and I would have to get a hotel.

"All right, man," I said. "Text me the address and I'll let Fiona know we're leaving in the morning."

"No problem. I sure as shit hope you guys find something. All my money is tied up and I can't get it fast enough. In the meantime, I'll keep wracking my brain and see if I can figure out a way to borrow a shitload of cash on short notice."

"Hopefully it won't come to that, but if it does, I've got some saved and available. Not enough, but some."

"Well, I guess we'll see," Jake said. "By the way, I'm at Mom's and she's not around—hasn't been all afternoon. Think we should be worried?"

"Nah, probably just got called in to cover for someone at work."

"Okay. I'll text the address. Later, little brother."

I hung up and was about to hit connect to call Fiona but decided to text her instead. I still didn't want to expose my hand too much.

*Mark: Destination New Jersey—tomorrow morning.*

*Fiona: OK, what time?*

*Mark: 7:00 and pack a bag—I'll pick you up.*

*Fiona: OK—I'll bring the music.*

*Mark: No way, Shortcake. My ride, my tunes.*

*Fiona: Whatever.*

She followed that up with a devil-face emoji. Hey, it was better than a middle finger. I set my phone down and got back to work, but I did it with a grin this time.

*Chapter Sixteen*

# YOU CAN'T TEACH AN OLD DOUCHEBAG NEW TRICKS

**F**IONA

I set my phone back down and looked across the table at Kelly, thankful that Mark had texted me instead of calling. I didn't know if I'd be able to maintain a casual vibe if I had to actually speak with him, given what I'd just found out from his mom. It was all I could do to remember to throw a little sass in the text exchange so he wouldn't be suspicious.

So, it turns out I'm not as sneaky as I thought. When I'd ventured out in the morning for my super-secret stake-out, I'd been all kinds of confident. But apparently, parking your bright blue Prius right by the building's entrance goes against the very first rule of a super-secret stake-out. I also suspect turning the radio up and jamming out to Twenty One Pilots may conflict with rule number two.

I was just getting to the good part of "Stressed Out" when I heard someone yell my name and knock on the passenger side window.

Kelly.

Oops.

I turned the music down and put on my best sheepish smile as I lowered the window.

She folded both her arms on the door frame and peered at me. "I'm not even going to ask," she said, shaking her head.

I thought about making up a story about why I was there, but even I'm not talented enough for that level of bullshit. Instead, I pointed at her and said, "I've got your six. You go do your thing and I'll keep my eye out for bad dudes!" Turns out reading military-themed romance novels had taught me important lingo for this kind of operation.

She just shook her head again, in resignation I assumed, and said, "In that case, you may want to move your car and keep the music down if you don't want to attract attention." It seemed somebody had watched better movies than I had.

"Roger that!" I gave her a thumbs-up and put the car in reverse. She watched me park, and I waved before she turned and entered the building. I checked my phone for reminders, then for texts, and then I played a game of solitaire. This stake-out stuff was boring as shit. I couldn't believe I'd forgotten coffee!

After what seemed like forever, but was probably only about twenty minutes, I spotted Kelly practically sprinting out the front door of the building. She made a bee-line for my car and I quickly lowered the window again.

Her cheeks were pink and her eyes were a bit wild as she looked in at me. "Holy crap!" was all she said before standing back up and looking around the parking lot. "Let's get out of here. Just pick a place and I'll follow you," she said before racing off to her car.

She didn't have to tell me twice. I put the car in gear and

headed straight for Starbucks, making it in record time. It was all I could do not to explode from anticipation while we got our drinks and finally sat down at a secluded corner table.

"Spill it, woman!" I demanded, and Kelly finally got down to business.

As it turned out, Jim being moved to rehab was no big secret and all she'd had to do was ask at the hospital to get the info. Then she'd headed on over to confront him and had immediately spotted me in my super-secret stake-out position by the fucking front door. Sheesh. I hurried her past that part and on to the dirt.

"So, once I'd signed in and finally found his room I was so nervous," she said.

"Of course." I nodded in understanding and sipped my iced coffee.

"But I gave myself a pep talk and then I just barged right in. He has a roommate and I think I may have scared him with the look on my face," Kelly said with a little smile. "Anyway, I walked right up to the bed and just said, 'Jim' in a really snarky tone of voice." Her face scrunched up in a perfectly appropriate snooty countenance. Awesome.

"What did he do? What did he say?" It seemed all my patience had been used up in the parking lot.

"I have no idea what I ever saw in that man—you wouldn't believe it. He smiled at me. *Smiled* at me! And then he went on with 'Kell, honey, you look great—I'm so glad you came—blah, blah, blah.'"

"He did not?!" My jaw dropped. What a douchebag. "I have got to call Laney and get her on speakerphone for this—do you mind?"

Kelly just waved me on, confident as can be, and I dialed Laney. She picked up immediately and we filled her in before

Kelly continued. Laney must have been just as anxious as I was to hear the story because she didn't even give me shit for not including her in the super-secret stake-out.

"So I told him to cut the crap," Kelly said with a little smile. "Luckily, he didn't remember a thing about seeing me in the hospital, he'd been so drugged up, so I was able to fudge a bit about the details. I told him I already knew why he was back in town and there was no way on earth I would help him out of the mess he'd made. I might have threatened more bodily harm as well." She covered her mouth, obviously a bit surprised at her own boldness.

"Good for you," Laney chimed in.

"Oh, it gets better," Kelly continued and sat up straight in her chair. I loved seeing her on fire like this—it was such a change from the meek woman I'd met last week. "He totally tried to back-track once he knew I wasn't going to fall for his 'oh honey, just help a guy out' crap. He's such an idiot. He told me he has a line on a 'sure thing' and that's why he needed the cash he'd borrowed. The problem is the money for this sure thing needs to be in the investor's hands by next week and he's still a little short." She grinned and raised her eyebrows.

I gasped and brought my hand to my mouth. "You didn't?!"

I may have created a monster.

"I sure did!" Kelly said, leaning back in her chair.

"Did what?" Laney screeched over the phone's speaker. "What?!"

Kelly spun her coffee cup on the table. "I told him I may have a little cash squirreled away and I might be interested in making an investment myself. But I made it clear I wasn't going to just hand it over to him. I wanted to be fully involved and make sure he didn't just run away with my cash. He tried to act all offended, but then I pointed out that he was the one who'd come to *my* town in the first place so I knew he didn't have any other way to get more cash."

"So wait, he still has the cash from the loan sharks?" Laney asked.

"Yup," said Kelly.

"Oh my God," Laney and I both said.

"Now to the best part," Kelly continued, totally on a roll. "Being not just a giant idiot but also the world's biggest jerk, he's managed to alienate just about everybody he's ever known. And now that he's laid up and can't get himself back home—which happens to be Atlantic City—to get the bulk of the cash, who do you think he's sending?"

At that point, I couldn't hold in my hilarity any longer. Laney and I proceeded to laugh our asses off.

"What a moron!" I heard Laney cry over the phone.

"Oh, that's not all." Kelly's expression suddenly turned dark. "Since he's safely tucked away in rehab for a while, his plan is to wait it out until he gets the payout from the sure thing. Then he'll pay the loan shark back with more interest and be done with it. He said by then we'll both be rich."

She took a breath and continued, "It was very important to him, though, that I go get his money right away and have it in his hands before Saturday." She looked at me meaningfully. "He has no idea I got a direct threat from these guys and I know that Saturday is the deadline."

I sobered up completely then. "So he was just going to let your ass swing out there while he sat in a secure facility with the cash?"

"Yup," Kelly replied quietly.

"I am going to kill that asshole!" Laney shouted from the phone.

"You'll have to get in line after Mark and Jake find out about this," I said.

"No!" Kelly cried. "Like I said, I don't want them involved. I'm going to talk to my boss and hopefully get a few days off so I can drive up there and get the money. Jim told me where he stashed it so it won't take long. And if I can't get the time off, I'll just have to deal with it and find another job—it won't be the first time I've been unemployed. Better unemployed than dead, though, right?" She said.

It had been at this point in the conversation that Mark's text had come in saying we were leaving for New Jersey in the morning. After our quick text exchange, I looked at Kelly.

"Um, I have something to tell you."

She looked suspiciously at me as I continued.

"Mark and I are already planning a trip to Atlantic City in the morning." I closed one eye and turned my head a bit, steeling myself for her reaction.

"What?!" she and Laney said in unison.

"Well," I tried to defend myself, "Jake and Mark were planning on going up there and searching Jim's place and I pointed out that it may be a good idea if one of them stayed in case the thugs came after you in the meantime. So, I volunteered to go with Mark."

"Wait, wait, wait," Kelly interrupted. "How do they know the thugs are after me? And how do they know where Jim lives?"

At this point, I had to decide whether to rat myself out or to rat Mark and Jake out for keeping their exploits from their mom. Guilt hung her head at the mess I'd made, and I decided full disclosure was probably best. So, I told Kelly the whole thing about me confessing to Mark about the note—but not about her visit to Jim in rehab—and how he already knew she was in danger because he and Jake had overheard the guys at the hospital.

"Look, Kelly, we all just care about you and don't want you to get hurt. Don't be mad at us." I put on my best innocent face.

She sighed. "I know, sweetie. I should have suspected something like this when you showed up at the rehab place earlier. And had I not just pulled off a little con of my own, I might be more upset." She reached over and squeezed my hand. "Besides, I know Mark is impossible to stop once he gets an idea in his head. As long as everyone is careful and we can pull this off without anyone getting hurt, I guess I can deal with it."

"Fiona…" I heard Laney say.

"Yeah?"

"Are you sure you know what you're doing?"

"Don't worry about me. We'll lay low, pick up the money and come right back. I promise." Then I turned back to Kelly. "One more thing—can you avoid Mark until we're gone and not go all 'mama bear' on him? I'll have to fess up about everything before we get to Atlantic City anyway, and that way he'll have a day or so to calm himself and won't come down on you so hard for going to see Jim on your own. Win-win." I explained.

She seemed to consider that. "Actually, that sounds like a pretty good plan now that you mention it." She gave me a little smile.

"Let's do this thing!" I said and toasted her with my coffee.

The next morning, I was up bright and early, determined to make the most of the time with Mark before I had to go piss him right the hell off with my news. Hopefully he'd get over it quickly, though. In the long run, it did basically solve the problem so he had to be happy with that, right?

I checked my purse one more time before stepping into the elevator to go down and meet Mark. Despite his rejection of my mad deejay skills yesterday, I had three new playlists on my phone and I was determined to win him over with my superb taste in music. Also on my phone was the detailed description of the hiding place of the money, so I had to make sure I didn't forget to bring it. Not that I could survive even an hour without my phone, much less an entire road trip.

I stepped out into the spring sunshine and drew my Prada sunglasses down over my eyes. I was dressed comfortably for the long car ride, but that didn't mean I had to forego designer apparel. Instead of stilettos, I had opted for platform espadrilles and a three-quarter-sleeve silk romper with a gorgeous paisley print. I also carried a light sweater since I knew we were headed to colder weather. My overnight bag—okay, my suitcase—was stocked with a mix of spring and winter wear since I wasn't sure what to expect.

As soon as I stepped on the sidewalk I spotted Mark exiting his truck. I sucked in a breath. He was in comfortable attire as well, not that it made me comfortable at all—in fact, it made my heart rate pick up and my palms sweat. He hadn't seen me yet so I took my time looking him over. He wore gray cargo pants, those same work boots, and a tight as hell t-shirt with a weathered denim button-down over it. The denim shirt was completely unbuttoned and the sleeves were rolled up to expose his corded forearms. I remembered those arms around me on Saturday and I tried to swallow but my throat was suddenly dry.

Just as my eyes reached his face he noticed me standing there. I thought he would look me over too, but his eyes just did a cursory sweep of me before homing in on my suitcase.

What? Where was flirty, affectionate Mark from Saturday? I wanted my head kiss at the very least. Thank God I was so used to being confused or this turn of events would have had me in a tailspin.

"Seriously?" he asked, hands on his hips.

"What?" My hands perched defensively on mine in response.

He tossed a hand out, gesturing to my suitcase. I considered for a moment that maybe he was as impressed as I was that Diane von Furstenberg had a designer luggage line, but then I remembered who I was dealing with.

"We're going for *one night*, Shortcake."

I huffed and lifted my chin. "Well, it'll be cold up there and I wanted to be prepared." So maybe I wouldn't necessarily need *two* pairs of boots, but one pair had a sturdier heel on the off chance that we'd have to do some running from mobsters. It was New Jersey, after all.

And maybe, just maybe, I had packed some additional articles to make sure I looked extra cute. My head was still telling me that hooking up was a bad idea but I didn't have much confidence in my grip on my control. Did I mention it had been a long time since I'd gotten laid? Based on the recent tirade from my lady parts I assumed people in Australia knew the status of my sex life. We were all getting desperate for some attention of the non-battery-operated variety.

"And besides," I said to Mark, "you have this giant truck. What do you care?"

He finally gave me the up and down appraisal I had been waiting for and seemed to make the mental connection that a full suitcase ensured a variety of visual distractions for his man brain. At that point, I got a shrug and a small smirk. "Suit yourself."

Aha! I had him now.

He approached and got right up into my space. I refused to back up, assuming this was a test of some kind. Based on his casual departure from my condo yesterday, he was obviously up to something. He just raised an eyebrow, along with one side of his mouth, and then reached down for my suitcase, never breaking eye contact. He lifted the case as if it weighed no more than a handbag and placed it in the bed of his truck. I started to object, worried what would happen if we ran into rain, but then I stopped myself. I'd have several battles to fight on this journey and this one was definitely not worth it.

I took his hand when it was offered to help me into the cab of the truck. I'm pretty sure my head only came up to the door handle, but there was the running board thingy for me to step on so he didn't have to completely lift me up into the seat. I settled in while he rounded the front and I pulled out my phone before securing my seatbelt. Mark hopped effortlessly into the driver's seat and started the engine.

"So," I said, "I've got three playlists all lined up. Are you by any chance a Justin Bieber fan?"

His hand froze on the key and I could practically hear his jaw crack.

Oh goodie—this was going to be fun.

*Chapter Seventeen*

# SHAKEN AND STIRRED

## M ARK

This was going to be a nightmare.

Fiona sat in her cute-as-fuck little outfit and fiddled with her phone, no doubt trying to figure out how to connect wirelessly to my truck's sound system. That should take her awhile, considering my truck had nothing but a good old-fashioned radio and a CD player. In the meantime, I pulled from the curb and started toward the interstate.

She was apparently ready to move on to a new topic. "Can we stop for coffee?"

I was beginning to comprehend just how long this trip was going to take. "Sure, once we get out of town we can get coffee from a drive-thru, but if it's going to make you have to take a leak every ten minutes, then you have to get the smallest one they have."

"Whatever you say, big man."

I was surprised she didn't fight back.

"Speaking of big," she said and I choked on my own saliva.

"Are you okay?" she asked, smacking me on the back.

I did my best to recover. "I'm fine. What were you saying?"

"Well, ever since I saw those cute pictures of you as a kid I've been meaning to ask you about the whole working-out thing. What exactly do you do to get all of *that*?" She gestured vaguely up and down in my direction.

"Why?" What was she up to?

"Just making conversation. Geez, you don't have to be so sensitive." She went back to her phone, huffing a bit in frustration.

"I go to the gym," I responded.

"Well, duh," she said and I could just hear the eye-roll in her voice. "What I mean is, what do you do at the gym?"

"Lots of stuff—cardio, some machines, and mostly free weights. You planning on starting a training regimen, Shortcake?"

"Um, no. I don't exercise," she said as though I'd suggested she join a BDSM club or buy the generic brand of...anything.

"How can you not exercise? That's so unhealthy!"

"I don't like it." She brushed some invisible lint from her thighs. "I find the whole thing sort of ridiculous."

"Excuse me?" I was taken aback and a little offended, to be honest.

She proceeded to enlighten me. "Take weight lifting, for instance—it's just a lot of picking stuff up only to set it right back down. What's the point?"

I literally had no response to that. Talk about ridiculous—I was beginning to wonder if this girl was actually of this Earth or was, in fact, some strange alien sent to test my patience and sanity.

She continued, "And besides, it makes me all sweaty and stuff." She did a full-body shiver.

"That's how you know you're doing it right."

"No thanks. I'm generally a pretty healthy eater so I think I'm all set."

"Suit yourself," I said as I checked my blind spot and pulled onto I-40, "but don't come crying to me when you hit thirty and your metabolism shuts down. You're cute now, but you short chicks need to watch out when the pounds start piling on." I couldn't help myself—I loved getting a rise out of her. And she kind of deserved it after completely dismissing what I considered to be an essential part of my lifestyle.

She gasped in indignation as I'd known she would. "I cannot believe you just said that!" She slapped my arm.

"Hey! No assaulting the driver." I turned the radio up just to annoy her some more. An old Rascal Flatts tune filled the cab.

She reached over and snapped the power button off. "Did you just call me short *and* fat?"

"No, Shortcake. You need to listen better. I said you're *going* to be fat." I tried and failed to keep the smirk off my face. This was fun.

"I cannot believe you *ever* get laid with the way you speak to women."

"There's not much speaking involved, sweetheart." I raised an eyebrow and tilted my head toward her. She looked at me as if I'd just asked her to smell my finger. God, I was doing an awesome job at being an asshole.

Why was I doing this again?

Oh right, we had a long trip ahead of us and I couldn't afford to have her being all sweet and adorable like she'd been in her apartment this weekend or I'd do something stupid like tell her about my *feelings*. She already thought she had the upper hand on me anyway and that couldn't stand.

Although, she's incredibly hot when she's mad so it was

entirely possible we wouldn't make it to Jersey without me having to pull over and feel her up in my truck anyway.

*Don't act surprised—you should understand me by now.*

"Did you have to train hard to become such an asshole or is it in your genetic code?" she asked and then gave a little gasp as she realized what she'd just said.

I guess fun time was over. I couldn't blame her—I had done a good job of riling her up. That didn't mean it felt great being compared to my dad, maliciously or not.

"Mark, I'm sorry," Fiona said quietly. "I didn't mean it like that. I…"

"It's okay, Shortcake. I deserved it. I was acting like an ass—it's just so easy to piss you off I couldn't help it."

"No—" she began but I cut her off.

"Really, it's fine. And I mean that in the way a guy says it's fine, not a girl." I gave her a grin so she'd know everything was okay.

"Fine," she said and crossed her arms, sinking down in her seat. I didn't miss the little smile she tried to keep to herself.

We stopped to get gas about halfway into the trip and Fiona practically sprinted to the restroom. I knew she'd been bluffing when she promised the large coffee she'd ordered wouldn't slow us down.

After I filled up, I decided to go inside and pick up a drink and a snack. I found Fiona perusing the snack selections as well, with a bag of Cheetos in one hand and a bright red slushy in the other.

I came up behind her and whispered in her ear, "I see you're making those super healthy choices you were telling me about."

She jumped in surprise and nearly dumped her slushy. "Don't scare me like that!"

I just chuckled and grabbed a bag of peanuts for myself.

"I don't know what it is about road trips, but my body somehow sends a signal to my brain telling it to do very bad things," she said as she reached for a Snickers bar.

I almost choked. "Do tell," I managed to say.

"Huh?" She just shook her head and sashayed her way to the check-out counter. I took my time selecting a drink before following her.

This trip was going to be even longer than I thought.

When we stepped back out into the sunshine, she pulled her sunglasses on and said, "You know, I was only teasing about Justin Bieber. I actually have excellent taste in music. I even have some country on my playlists just so you know." She gave me a smug smile.

"Well, it doesn't matter what you have because unless you're planning on listening to it on headphones there isn't any way to play it in my truck."

"What do you mean? You just plug it in or you do the whole Bluetooth thing."

"Shortcake, what year do you think my truck was made?"

She looked from me to the truck and back again. "Oh," was all she said before sauntering over to the passenger door.

I followed to help her in, kicking myself for forgetting that we come from totally different worlds. She was all upper crust and I was all "Eat your crust cuz there ain't no more food in this house." What in the hell had made me think any kind of relationship—my first relationship—would work between us?

I helped her up into the cab and stalked back to the driver's side, my mood suddenly cloudy. It wasn't until a few minutes down the road that I noticed Fiona had unearthed a bunch of shit from her bag and was setting it up on the bench seat between us.

"What are you doing over there?" I asked.

"I'm exercising one of my many skills—resourcefulness."

And then, from a tiny black box on the seat, came the crystal-clear sounds of Parachute's "Kiss Me Slowly."

I looked at the box and then at Fiona. She gave me a killer smile that made me want to pull over, and then she just closed her eyes and leaned her head back in her seat with a sigh.

Well, color me impressed. My little Shortcake was full of surprises.

This was what I got for letting Fiona handle the directions. And, for once, I was not being a dick about gender roles. She and her GPS had gotten us perfectly to our destination—or rather, *her* destination.

"Yes we are," she said for the third time as she wrapped her sweater around herself and grabbed the door handle. The temperature here was a definite drop from North Carolina.

I held her arm to stop her.

"We are not staying at a fucking five-star hotel, Fiona! The valet parking charge is probably more than a night at the Days Inn, which is where I *told* you to direct us!"

"First of all, this is a *four*-star hotel, and second of all, I'm using points so it won't cost anything anyway. Just cancel your reservation."

"You knew I was going to be pissed off so you purposely didn't tell me," I hissed at her.

"Precisely." She gave me a breezy smile and hopped out of the truck. "I'll go check us in while you take care of parking. Oh, and don't forget to tip the valet." She winked and sauntered off to the entrance, her cute little ass swaying.

Shit.

Well, there was no way I was letting the valet park my truck. Once we checked in, we'd have to pull it right back out of parking again so we could go to my old man's place. That meant two tips— not gonna happen. I reluctantly let the bellhop take Fiona's suitcase and tipped him a couple bucks. I then waved off the valet and went in search of street parking. This would never have been an issue at the Days Inn.

A half-hour later I made my way through the entrance of the ridiculously over-the-top hotel and pulled out my phone. Turns out the valet parking is a racket—there is exactly zero street parking within a mile of this place. Good thing I was in shape— another thing I could add to the list of reasons Fiona should work out.

Or not.

Honestly, I'd hate to see her any other way than she already is.

I thought about going up to the desk and asking about my room, but I figured a call to Fiona was needed since it was surely in her name. She picked up and spoke before I could say a word.

"Where in the hell have you been? Never mind, don't answer that—just come up. We're in room 1244." She hung up before I could utter a syllable.

One room? This just got more interesting.

Unfortunately, this hotel was huge and it was like navigating through some rich person's idea of a corn maze. It was almost as if they didn't want you to find the elevators so you would just spend all your time on the main level blowing your money. Oh wait, I'm sure that was exactly the point. By the time I finally found the elevators and made my way to the twelfth floor, my patience was waning.

I knocked on the door to room 1244 and it was immediately opened by Fiona who had, in the time it had taken me to park the car and find the room, transformed into an exact replica of a ski bunny from a James Bond movie. She was wearing fur-lined boots, skin-tight pants, and a fluffy cream sweater with a big drapey neckline. The lights in the room were dimmed and a fire roared in the fireplace behind her—yes, this room had a fireplace. I felt as if I'd been transported to an alternate universe. I half expected a butler to appear out of thin air and ask me how I liked my martini.

"Exactly how long have you been here without me?" I asked, still in shock.

She stepped back to let me in and then closed the door behind her. "Yeah, about that, what the hell took you so long? Did you get into a wrestling match with the valet over your truck keys?"

I continued to look around and noticed that, in addition to the sitting room with the previously noted fireplace, there was a full kitchen, a dining area, and several doors leading to other rooms. I answered absently, "No, I didn't let him park my truck."

"What?" She had her hands on her hips and her hair was floating around her face as always. God, she was stunning. I felt that punch to the gut again.

I shook my head to recover my wits. "We're leaving in like five minutes to go to the old man's place. Why would I pay to have my car parked for five minutes?"

She took a deep breath and then bit her bottom lip and closed one eye.

Shit. This could not mean good things.

"Mark, there's something I need to tell you."

Yeah, those are perhaps the most dreaded words in the English language for a guy—and for good reason. They are usually followed by phrases such as "I'm pregnant" or maybe "I have crabs" or "Sorry, man, I didn't know she was your mom." I was suddenly having flashbacks to the hospital when I'd welcomed the idea of a prostate exam to escape my reality. What the fuck was wrong with my life that all these horrible alternatives were beating out my actual circumstances? I braced myself and forced my eyes to meet hers.

She took another deep breath and then said quickly, "I know where the money is."

*Chapter Eighteen*

# THE PROS AND CONS OF WHITE KNIGHTS AND BAKED POTATOES

$\mathcal{F}$IONA

I still had one eye closed, hoping it might shield me from some of the blowback I knew was coming.

Part of me—okay, it was mostly Inner Fashion Maven and Vagina—had thought that if I dressed cute and set the right mood he'd take the news a little better. I'd been fooling myself that it would have any effect. Nevertheless, I'd had the bellhop light a fire and I'd changed into my best sexy/cozy New England outfit, even if it was just New Jersey. I'd also booked us a lovely little two-bedroom suite on an upper floor with a balcony and some great views, even though it was freaking freezing out. Hey, they were my points—I may as well use them.

"Excuse me?" His jaw was tight and his eyes narrowed. Yup, no appreciation for ambiance.

"I know where the loan shark's money is." At this point, I switched things up and decided confidence was the right tone to strike, so I raised my chin and looked him right in the eye with both of mine this time.

"Are you shitting me right now?" He advanced on me.

"No. I am not shitting you. Your dad never spent it. He hid it to use on a bigger deal and we need to go get it—that is, if the bad dudes haven't figured out where it is already. But, honestly, if they had I doubt they'd still be after your parents."

He looked around as if searching for an explanation some-where in the room before bringing his eyes and tense-as-hell face back to me. "Do you mind telling me what the hell is going on here?" He tried to keep his tone measured, but it was like attempting to contain a raccoon in a paper bag—or his chest in one of his ridiculously form-fitting t-shirts. Didn't these shirts come in a bigger size? I swear it seemed as if most of his shirts would be snug on a baby for God's sake. Did he do this on purpose to distract me?

Oh right, back to the topic at hand. I gave him the short version of his mom's exploits and tried my best to put a positive spin on the whole thing by reassuring him that I'd had her six with my stake-out—I thought the macho phrasing might make me sound more credible. Yeah, that didn't work so well. I knew he was upset about his mom possibly being in danger, but then he turned the whole thing on me.

I did not think so!

"Since when are you heading this operation?" he snapped at me.

"I'm not! If anyone is, it's your mom. She finally grabbed her lady balls and took charge!" I threw right back at him.

"Her what? Don't talk about my mom like that. This was all your idea, wasn't it? Before you came along my mom never would have done a thing like this."

I huffed and stomped my cute booted foot. "And why is that, Mark? Is she too weak and vulnerable to take care of business like a man would?" I let the sarcasm drip from my tongue.

"You don't know anything about her—or my family!" He turned around and stomped toward the kitchen. Then, realizing he had nowhere to go from there, he turned around and stomped toward the door.

Like I was letting him walk out!

I lowered my voice and tried to let the anger and tension ease. "I know more about it than you think I do, and I know your mom doesn't need to be coddled nearly as much as you assume she does. You need to open your eyes and see that even though she's had struggles, she is *not* weak. She's a strong person who hasn't had the chance to show it. You're too busy taking care of her to notice that she needs to find her own way on her own terms, Mark." I was suddenly pleading with him and I was so afraid he'd walk out.

"So you know everything about everything, is that it?" he asked, but I noticed that, like mine, his tone had calmed a little and he wasn't reaching for the doorknob anymore. However, his back was to me so I couldn't be sure of his emotions without seeing his eyes.

"No, Mark. I don't know much at all in the grand scheme of things. But I know you are a wonderful and caring son. I know you love her more than anything, but you can't protect her from every-thing. Nor should you."

He finally turned around and faced me again. "And it's just that easy? Just let go?"

"No, of course not. It's not all or nothing. But let's just take things one step at a time. We've got a great lead here and there's something we can finally do to fix this mess." I took a hesitant step toward him.

He ran a hand over his head in clear frustration and then flung it out toward me in a last-ditch effort to prolong his waning tirade. "Fiona, you can't just go sticking your nose into everybody's business and think you know what's best for everyone."

Gah! I was so sick of being accused when all I was doing was trying to help! "Mark, I'll stick whatever I want wherever I want. You can't tell me where to stick my…my…stuff! I'll stick it where I want!"

Take that!

He smirked and gave his head a little shake. "You'll stick it where you want, huh?"

Huh? How was this suddenly funny?

"Yeah!" I responded with deadly seriousness as I crossed my arms over my chest.

He took me in from top to toe and then inexplicably threw his head back and roared with laughter.

"What?!"

He just kept laughing and eventually bent at the waist with the power of it.

"Have you lost your ever-loving mind?"

Maybe he was in shock. Is maniacal laughter a symptom? No, pretty sure it's not.

"Well," I said, "I guess this is what you get from hanging out with Gavin and Brett so much. Do you need me to call a doctor?"

He started toward me again, having laughed so hard there were actual tears gathered on his ridiculous eyelashes. Uncertain of his motives, I backed up a step—I mean, who knew what he intended in his current mental state? Undaunted, he advanced further and abruptly bent down, gathered me by my thighs and lifted me up off the ground.

"Aarrgh!" I shrieked, unable to extricate myself and completely confused as to what was happening here.

He gave one last chuckle and just said, "Shortcake," as he lowered me to slide down his body until we were nose to nose.

Ooh, tingly.

His eyes hit mine before they traveled down to my mouth and I realized what was happening. Mark Beckett was going to kiss me!

I watched as his head tilted slightly to one side and I considered for one millisecond that maybe I should stop him, but before I knew it his lips covered mine and I told all my inner voices to take a hike. Mama was gettin' some.

The kiss was slow and exploratory—no intense assault or plundering as I might have anticipated from this giant man—just a beautiful, sensual teasing of his soft lips against mine. After a moment, he pulled his head back a fraction, presumably to assess my reaction to the surprising turn of events, but I was having nothing of it. My hand slipped up to the back of his head and pressed him back into me as my mouth sought his again. He emitted a low growl and the next thing I knew, one of his hands pulled my thigh up alongside his hip and I could feel his hardness press against my pelvis. I may have moaned a bit at that point, and I nipped his bottom lip so he would get the message that I needed to taste more of him.

Our tongues explored each other and my head was filled with that wonderful scent I now just associated with Mark's pure maleness. All my senses were buzzing as the kiss progressed into a frenzied clashing of lips, teeth, and tongues—our hands wandering in the need to feel as much of each other as possible. My hands decided to prioritize and tried to find his ass, but the damn things couldn't reach with him holding me above the ground like this. So, I decided to improvise and went for his arms and shoulders.

Holy. Shit.

This was undoubtedly the nicest body I'd ever come in contact with, and my fingers were ecstatic to have free reign to explore all the various dips and curves available to them. Mark was just so hard—everywhere—but surprisingly warm as well. I could only imagine how much more fun this would be without his shirt.

I was so caught up in my own voyage of discovery, I hadn't noticed that one of his hands had made its way to my ass, because of course *his* arms could reach—totally unfair. I swear his palm encompassed the entirety of one of my ass cheeks, but I couldn't dwell on any feelings of booty-inadequacy because it was clear that whatever he was feeling he was liking a whole lot, if you know what I mean.

His lips left mine and trailed a path down to my neck, and I couldn't help but tilt my head back to give him better access as he kissed and nipped his way down to my collar bone, brushing aside the neck of my sweater as he descended.

Oh wow. This was good. Really good.

And then came three swift knocks on the door.

Shit! No!

"Ignore it," Mark mumbled into the crook of my neck where his tongue had started doing wonderful things.

"Yes," I responded on a moan, not quite sure what I was saying yes to.

The knocks came again.

Mark growled for real this time.

Then I remembered. "Shit. I ordered room service. I totally forgot," I groaned.

"We don't need food." He still hadn't moved his head. "Just sex. Lots of sex."

Aaaand then I realized what we'd just been about to do and

remembered why it was not such a great idea. Not to mention, we should be focusing on the money and getting the scary-as-shit situation ironed out—not sex! Damn hormones!

"Mark, you're going to have to release me so I can get the door. I may be feisty, but even I can acknowledge that me trying to best you physically would be an exercise in humiliation."

He finally raised his head and scowled at me, but the effect was lost because his eyes were all sexed up and soft. Damn, I could get used to that look.

But now was not the time. He reluctantly set me down, and I was surprised to find that my knees didn't hold me up quite as well as they usually did. I steadied myself with a hand to Mark's chest and then walked as nonchalantly as possible toward the suite door, thankful I'd donned my sturdier boots—see, packing for every eventuality was a smart move after all.

It also turned out my instinct to save myself with room service worked out, just not in the way I had intended. I'd originally placed the order for a steak dinner when I'd been anticipating needing something to distract Mark when I confessed. In the end, the dinner had saved me from unintentional sex instead, though I wasn't entirely sure how to feel about that. Sometimes a girl doesn't want to be saved, even if it comes with a side of loaded baked potato.

I let the server in and stood awkwardly to the side as he set our dinner out on the dining table. I wanted to look at Mark to gauge his mood, but couldn't bring myself to do it, so I finally went after my purse to retrieve a tip. The server asked if I'd like him to open the wine but I declined and walked him to the door.

"So," I finally said as I forced a smile and met Mark's eyes, "I hope you like filet."

## Chapter Nineteen

# DEAD HOOKERS CAN'T DO THE RUNNING MAN (TOO FAR? MY BAD.)

## MARK

I scrubbed my face with my hands and let the cool water hit my back as I lathered up. At my age, I should be used to the occasional cold shower, but Fiona was a whole different story. She had damn near lit me on fire and my cock was still screaming at me to just go out into the main room and take her against the wall.

After the best kiss of my life and the mood-crushing interruption from room service, I hadn't been up for steak, even if it was filet mignon and probably cost as much as my grocery budget for a month. There had also been Fiona's swift change in mood, which didn't sit well.

Did she regret our kiss? Well, I suppose calling it just a kiss was a bit of an understatement, but still. I hoped like hell she didn't regret it because it was happening again when the time was right. We may be playing this little game right now but I hadn't forgotten the end goal was to win her over, as strange as that still sounded in my head.

So, I'd asked her where the bathroom was and took my bag in for the obligatory cold shower. I'd promised to return for dinner in a few minutes and told her to start without me. Good thing, too, because this was not working. Cooler temperatures alone were not going to calm my raging hard-on so I had to take the situation in hand.

Ten minutes later, I had changed into fresh clothes and felt a bit more relaxed thanks to the shower activities. I ventured out into the main living space again and spotted Fiona leaning against the kitchen counter biting her lip and staring out the window. When I passed through her line of sight she seemed startled and her cheeks immediately pinked. Oh yeah, she wasn't unaffected by our kiss in the least.

I was hoping we could pick up where we'd left off after we ate and grabbed the money, even though I still thought her story was too good to be true. But I was willing to go check out the location if there was even a remote possibility we could be over and done with this crazy-ass situation. Half of me could believe my old man had acted so selfishly and idiotically, but the other half knew it couldn't be that easy. I guess we'd see.

"Hey," Fiona said with an awkward little wave. "I thought I'd wait for you." She gestured toward the table where the plates still had those silver dome covers.

"You didn't have to," I replied, but she didn't meet my eyes. I sighed. "Look, I can tell you feel uncomfortable about what happened between us, but you don't need to. We can just set that aside for now and focus on food and then the money if that will make you feel better."

I hated to see her discomfort and I reminded myself not to act like a Neanderthal and attack her over the table. I could be patient.

*No, really.*

She sighed in return and the tension seemed to drain right out of her. "Thanks." She graced me with one of her beautiful smiles. "I think the craziness of this whole situation is finally catching up with me."

"You know, Shortcake, I realize I haven't thanked you for your help and I really should be showing you better appreciation instead of constantly yelling at you like I seem to do. So, thank you, Fiona," I said, chagrinned.

She kept smiling as she sat down gracefully in her seat at the table and gestured for me to join her. "You're welcome."

"Are you sure this is right?" I asked for the tenth time since we'd gotten in my truck.

"I'm absolutely sure—stop being such a wimp," Fiona responded.

I couldn't even let her comment get me riled up, I was so confused. "I just can't picture my father ever walking into a place like this."

"What's that supposed to mean? 'A place like this.'"

"Well, you know."

"No, please enlighten me. Exactly what is wrong with this place?"

"There's nothing *wrong* with it, I mean if you like that kind of thing, but you don't know my father—he'd never be caught dead here."

She swung the passenger door open and said, "Maybe that's the whole point. Ever think of that?"

And then she jumped out of the truck and strode toward the entrance of the most garish nightclub I'd ever laid eyes on. The outside looked like a neon flamingo factory had vomited all over it and I was relatively certain the inside wouldn't be any subtler.

I reluctantly opened my door, knowing I had to stay with Fiona, even if it may be more for my sake than hers.

"You'd better hurry and catch up to me, Champ, or they're gonna be all over you," she said as she strutted in her hard-on inducing boots and laughed.

That was all I needed to hear to get my ass in gear and race to catch up. She could call me a wimp and laugh all she wanted as long as she didn't ditch me in the middle of a gay nightclub in New Jersey on Go-Go-Boy night.

When Fiona had said she knew where the money was, I'd assumed it was hidden somewhere in the old man's apartment, but I should have known it wouldn't be that simple.

After our dinner, I had gone to get the truck and told Fiona I'd meet her at the hotel entrance in twenty minutes. There was no way I was going to do the valet thing and go retrieve her from the room like a gentleman. I was all for wooing her in the long run, but I had my principles and the gentleman stuff could wait. That valet wasn't getting a dime from me.

Sure enough, when I pulled up the expansive drive, there she was. Gone was the ski bunny ensemble. Instead she now wore a low-cut slinky green top with skin-tight jeans, spike-heeled black fuck-me boots that went clear up to her thigh, and a shit-hot leather jacket.

Holy. Fuck.

She was a wet dream come to life.

She sauntered over to the truck before I could get my wits about me and open the door. I felt like a douchebag when the valet helped her up into the truck and she gave him a huge smile and a tip. Dammit.

"Um, you look, you look…amazing," I mumbled like a complete moron.

She smiled, pulling on her seatbelt and settling a black leather satchel on the seat between us. "Thanks."

I just sat there until she actually had to prompt me to move.

"Um, Mark, there are people behind us waiting to pull up."

"Oh shit. Right. Sorry." Still behaving like a fucking moron, I hit the gas a little too hard and the tires squealed. Could this get any more embarrassing?

Fiona tried and failed to cover a laugh in the passenger seat.

"So, where to?" I asked, attempting to gain some control over my behavior. My plan to play it cool was going all to hell.

She pulled out her phone and tapped a few times. "Looks like his apartment is about fifteen minutes from here. Take a left at the next light." She proceeded to direct me to what turned out to be a run-down converted motel in a shitty part of town. This did not surprise me in the least. There were several late model cars in the parking lot and a few lights were on in various windows. We parked in front of unit 122 and got out.

My eyes swept the parking lot, and the hairs on the back of my neck stood up. I didn't see anything out of place, though, so I chalked it up to adrenaline. When I turned back to the unit, Fiona was turning a key in the lock and opening the door. Shit!

"Wait!" I said and jumped toward her, startling the crap out of her.

"What?!" she screeched and jumped back.

"Nothing. I just didn't want you to go in first in case there was anybody in there or, I don't know, anything I wouldn't want you to see."

"What, like a dead hooker or something? This situation may be strange, but I highly doubt we're going to find a dead body in there." She shook her head at me. "You watch too much TV."

"All the same," I said as I pushed in front of her and entered the apartment, switching a light on as I did.

The place was a complete disaster. It was obvious that Lou and Terry had already tossed it, and my hopes of finding the money were immediately dashed.

Fiona, on the other hand, walked right in completely unfazed.

"Shortcake, I think we're too late."

She just continued to walk through the filthy place, stepping effortlessly around overturned chairs and dresser drawers until she got to the sink outside the bathroom. There, she crouched down and pulled a small flashlight out of her satchel.

WTF?

She reached behind an exposed pipe and tried to move her head as far under the unit as she could in an effort to get a better look.

"Aha!" she declared and popped out from under the sink, holding up a small key. "Victory!"

And then she proceeded to do a very adorable version of the running man while singing some made-up rap about not messing with the A-Team. It was a little unreal and a lot crazy.

I finally had to put a stop to it. "I hate to interrupt your little touchdown celebration, but do you mind telling me what the hell is going on?"

She stopped dancing. "Oh, right. Well, this little old key goes to a padlock where the money is."

"Seriously? And where is that?"

"At some club. Your dad knows the owner and the lady lets

him keep a locker in the staff room. I didn't get the whole story, but I have the address. Let's roll, Chief!"

I shook my head. "You are something else, Ms. Pierce."

"I know." She winked at me and I felt that sucker punch again.

Ten minutes later, as I followed her into my first gay club, I was feeling a whole other kind of sucker punch. *Oh, don't judge— you weren't there. And, by the way, is it really that surprising that a guy whose dad called him Mary might be a little sensitive in this area? I'll wait for your apology.*

*Um, still waiting.*

## Chapter Twenty

# PICK A PENIS! ANY PENIS!

**FIONA**

I felt kind of bad that I'd been evasive about the club. I'd known what we were in for the moment Kelly had given me the name of the place—there aren't too many ways to misinterpret "The Manaconda Club." I'd figured Mark would do better if given less time to contemplate potential upcoming scenarios.

I was not surprised to have him right on my heels as I opened the door to the club and found my eyes and ears assaulted by what I could best describe in two words—flash and fierce.

It. Was. Awesome.

If not a bit loud for the night's purposes.

Club music pounded from the speakers while colored lights skittered across the crowd that packed the central dance floor. Bodies jumped, shimmied, and swayed to the pounding beat. Every few yards was a circular platform standing high above the main floor and each had a very fit half-naked—okay, more like four-fifths-naked—young guy dancing on a pole. In addition to the scorching entertainment was a long black bar against the side wall where several bartenders stood under more neon lights, serving up cocktails and joining in the vibrant mood set by the crowd.

This was Monday night in Atlantic City? I was suddenly pissed we'd missed the weekend goings-on.

With my eyes darting around so quickly to take everything in, I didn't immediately notice the very large mustachioed man standing to my right. He wore black pants and a tight black t-shirt that could have given one of Mark's a run for its money.

"ID and fifteen-dollar cover," he said to me. Then he looked Mark over quite thoroughly and said, "No charge for you."

I had to stifle a laugh as I reached into my bag for my money and license, but when I went to hand it to the bouncer I saw that Mark had already paid my cover and was trying to pay for himself as well. The bouncer wouldn't take the extra money so Mark scowled and put it back in his pocket.

"Hey, is it always this busy on Mondays?" I asked loudly as he checked over my ID

The large man bent down to be heard over the noise of the club. "Nah, just once a month on Manaconda Monday." He gestured toward the platforms. "Go-Go Boys."

"Gotcha," I responded when he handed back my license. Then I remembered we'd better get down to business. "Is Angie around tonight?" I asked.

That got me a sharp look. "Whaddya want with Angie?"

I gave him my best smile, the one that got me out of trouble at work all the time. "I'm a friend of a friend—just need to ask her about something."

He looked at me with suspicion. Apparently, gay mustachioed

men from New Jersey were immune to my charms. Huh. Well that sucked.

"Angie doesn't have friends, and we don't need any trouble here."

Shit, this was going to be harder than I thought. And now this guy was going to be watching us like a hawk.

Out of nowhere Mark grabbed my hand and said, "No worries, Toots! Let's get our fine asses on the dance floor." And then he dragged my stunned-as-hell ass into the crowd.

"Holy shit! Did you really just say that?" I laughed and shouted up at him once we were safely away from the bouncer.

"I had to do *something*—you were painting giant bullseyes on our backs!"

"Oh my God, wait until I tell Nate and Laney—oh, and Jake too—I have his number now. Could you maybe say it again so I can take a video? It would just be easier if I could send out a mass text," I pleaded with him but just got a snarl in return.

"Look, we're gonna have to figure out a way to get into the staff room without being caught. Any ideas? I would say we could go with distraction but this whole fucking place is one big distraction." He scowled as he looked around.

Okay, this was clearly not his scene. Fair enough.

"Well, there's always at least one straight bartender at gay clubs so I could try to find one and flirt my way into the staff room with him," I suggested.

"No fucking way."

So, that was a firm no. I guess he had a strong opinion on that idea. "Well, why don't we just look around? Maybe we'll get lucky."

It turned out my choice of words could not have been more

perfect. As we made our way around the club, I couldn't count the number of times Mark got hit on and/or had his arms groped. His face was beet red by the time we got to the back of the club where the bathrooms were, but it was unclear if the color was from embarrassment or fury. I didn't ask.

We ventured into a darker hallway that had four closed doors. Two were restrooms, although it was impossible to tell if they were designated for any specific gender since they were both just marked with abstract paintings of penises.

Hmm, the painting style was actually quite nice—I wondered if the artist took on any other subjects besides dicks. I'd have to file that thought away for later.

The other two doors in the hallway were unmarked. One of them had to be the staff room.

I casually wandered by the first door and tried the knob. Locked. Mark saw what I was up to and blocked me from view as I tried the second. Unlocked. I slipped in and closed the door behind me before Mark could object or utter a syllable.

"Staff only, sweetheart," came a voice from behind me. "You don't like dicks in the bathroom with you then this ain't the club for you."

I turned around and saw one of the bartenders from earlier leaning against a locker and eying me. I flipped my hair, hoping I had managed to single out a straight one, but it had no effect.

"No offense, sweetcheeks, you're all kinds of adorable and those boots are hot as shit, but you need to turn around and scoot."

Damn.

"Oh, sorry," I giggled and worked the hell out of all the dumb blonde I had in me. "I thought this was the girls' room."

It got me nowhere. He stayed put. "Like I said, across the hall —just pick a penis."

Had I not been desperate to get to the very lockers he was leaning against I would have found this situation hilarious. Unfortunately, this wasn't the right time.

"Right," I said, giving up the ruse. "Later." I turned the knob and walked out, slamming right into a very firm chest belonging to a very annoyed Mark.

"Stop doing that!" he demanded.

"Okay, fine. But that was definitely the staff room. There's a bartender in there and he does not mess around."

Mark scowled at me again. Somebody sure was grumpy.

"Give me the key and make yourself scarce. I'll take care of it."

I put my hands up in the air in surrender. "Fine, if you think you can do a better job then be my guest." I handed him the key. "The lockers are along the far wall and from what I could see there were only a few with locks."

"Got it. Now go hide in one of the bathrooms in case the guy comes out."

"Wait, don't you need a bag or something? That's why I brought this." I held up the satchel.

"Shit," he grumbled. I could totally understand him not wanting to carry a woman's bag, but it wasn't very girly—in fact, it was pretty utilitarian. And given where we were…

Mark snatched the bag from my grip and I snuck into one of the penis rooms, entirely unsure what to expect.

Huh. Well, it turns out it was just like any other bathroom. I was sort of disappointed—I kind of felt the door treatments promised something a bit more exciting. Oh well, may as well pee while I was there.

I did my business, washed my hands, ran my fingers through my hair to smooth it and did as much primping as possible without my bag, all while chatting with the guys and girls who came in and out. But there was still no sign of Mark. At this point it had been ten minutes, so I chanced a peek into the hallway. No Mark—just a group of drunken guys making their way to the back exit for a smoke.

Where in the hell was he?! I closed the door again and leaned against the sink, tapping my fingers on the surface.

Just then, the door burst open and in came Mark, looking flushed. He grasped my hand and pulled me so hard I almost lost my balance. He practically sprinted out of the bathroom and made a beeline for the back exit, with me stumbling along behind him. Crossing the threshold, I begged for him to slow down and only then did he seem to realize I wasn't capable of moving like a cheetah, heels or no heels.

"Sorry," he said as he slowed his pace a touch and rounded the side of the building toward the front parking lot and his truck.

"Well?" I was dying to know what happened.

"I got it," was all he said.

"Seriously?!" I jumped up and down and squealed. "Oh my God. This is so awesome! I can't believe you did it. How did you get past that guy?"

"I don't want to talk about it," he said as he opened the passenger door and lifted me up into the seat, not waiting for me to assist at all. He slammed the door and stalked over to the driver's side.

Uh oh.

As soon as he got in, he cranked the ignition and we sped out of the parking lot. I don't think either one of us had any idea where we were going, but I was just as happy to escape as he was. I had to sit on my hands and bite my tongue really hard to keep from quizzing him, but I was *dying* to know what had happened.

Five minutes later, he pulled into the empty parking lot of a grocery store and cut the engine. "Now don't get too excited until we count it—I don't know how much is there." He handed me my satchel and I opened it, peering inside.

In addition to my own things, there was a plastic grocery bag filled with stacks of cash. Now, I may come from money, but to me that meant credit cards and vacations and awesome clothes. I had never actually laid eyes on this much cash in my life. It was so strange. I pulled out the grocery bag and handed several stacks to Mark. We both began counting.

Forty-seven thousand dollars. *Forty-seven thousand dollars!*

We looked at each other once it had been tallied and I finally got a grin out of him. I returned it and then his morphed into a full-on killer smile. "We did it, Shortcake."

I couldn't help it. I jumped across the bench seat and kissed the shit out of him.

After he got over his initial surprise, Mark joined right in with gusto. Even though the position was awkward with the bag and money between us, we managed to engage all the right parts. His tongue swept across mine and had me moaning as I grasped the back of his head, wishing for the first time that he had longer hair so I had something to hold onto.

One of his hands traveled down to my waist and he effortlessly lifted me over the contents of the seat and onto his lap. I squeaked a little in surprise but he quickly silenced me with his mouth over mine again. I breathed him in and let out an inner sigh as my hands started to wander. They didn't make it very far, however, because just as things were getting good there was a tap on the driver's side window.

My first thought was that we'd been caught by cops making out like teenagers in a steamed-up truck. But then it occurred to me that cops probably wouldn't knock on a car window with the muzzle of a gun.

Shitballs.

## Chapter Twenty-One

# TRIP TO JERSEY: $200, ROAD SNACKS: $30, CONNING AN ASSHOLE: PRICELESS

M ARK

"Sorry to interrupt your little make-out session, but we need a word," came the voice of the man holding the gun. A man whose name I knew to be either Lou or Terry.

Dammit.

I'd been so thrown by the events at the club I hadn't given thought to anything other than getting the hell away with the money. I had to try to smooth this over and protect Fiona. I suppose the good news was we had the cash so I hoped like hell that would be enough.

Fiona's mouth was agape and she was staring at the gun, speechless. I lifted her gently off my lap and placed her as far from the weapon as possible.

"Shortcake, look at me," I coaxed.

She finally tore her eyes from the window and held mine. Her gorgeous green eyes were wide with terror.

"It's gonna be okay. I'm just going to give them the money. You stay in the truck, do you hear me?"

She must have been in a bit of shock because for the first time in her life she didn't utter a word. She just sat there and gave one jerky nod.

I opened the door and looked back at her one more time before stepping out to face Lou and Terry. "Stay here."

I closed the door behind me, bag of cash in hand, and stepped as far away from the truck as I could without alarming them.

They were both dressed in leather jackets and jeans, just like any other guy. Just like me, in fact. The only glaring difference was that the goateed guy held a gun.

"You amateurs can't spot a tail for shit," he said, and then thankfully tucked the gun in the back of his waistband.

Somehow I didn't feel so bad that I lacked that particular skill. I was hopeful that this was the one and only occasion in my life where I might give someone cause to tail me.

I put my hands up in a defensive pose. "We don't want any trouble. We have the money."

"Yeah, no shit. Why do you think we were tailing you? Now put your hands down before somebody sees us and thinks this is a car-jacking."

I did so immediately. While this might have been my first time working a "deal," it was obviously something Lou and Terry were way more practiced at. I deemed it prudent to go with the voice of experience here.

"We figured your old man would spill the beans to someone sooner or later. It was just a waiting game. Now, you mind handing it over so we can get outta here?"

"No problem," I said and reached into the bag.

"At least step behind the truck, kid. Jesus, it's like you're begging for the cops to show up," the second guy said. "Fucking amateurs, Lou," he mumbled.

Again, I did not feel the least bit inadequate for not knowing the appropriate etiquette for this situation.

And, bonus—now I knew which one was Lou and which one was Terry.

I moved behind the truck and they followed. I mentally counted the stacks as I walked so I would pull the correct number out on the off chance they'd let us keep the rest.

I unexpectedly heard Lou say, "Sorry about scaring your girl with the gun. Just had to make sure you weren't going to try to skip town with the money and disappear."

I turned to him. "Do we look that stupid?"

"Well, no, but given who your old man is, the odds weren't in your favor if you get my meaning."

"Point taken," I responded since that did indeed make sense. "So, if we hand over the thirty-two grand you'll just let us go?" I was afraid there was too much hope in my voice.

Terry scoffed as if offended and Lou said, "Yeah, kid. Despite how it might seem, we're really not all that bad. We run a business just like anyone else."

I wasn't about to argue the point. I just wanted to get the hell out of here. I started to hand over the bundle I'd gathered when Terry cut in.

"The price actually went up to thirty-three. Gas money, you know." He scratched his chin.

"Of course," I said as if I were an idiot for not thinking of it myself. I reached into the bag for another thousand and handed it over.

Terry counted all the money and nodded to Lou before putting it in a Health Foods grocery sack, of all things. Apparently bad guys liked to eat organic.

Lou held out his hand and I had no choice but to shake it. "Nice doing business with you, kid. If you ever need a loan…"

"Yeah, thanks. I'll keep you in mind." I began backing up toward the driver's side, unwilling to turn my back to them until they were gone.

"But you best tell your old man if we ever see his face again he won't be as lucky as he was this time."

"If I ever have the displeasure of speaking to him again I'll be sure to pass that right along," I responded.

Lou grinned and they turned and walked to their car. I waited until they'd pulled out before getting in the truck and closing the door.

"Did that just happen?" came Fiona's incredulous voice from the other side of the truck. I looked over and noticed she had her window open—she'd heard the whole damn thing. Her green eyes were wide and wild.

"Yup, pretty sure it did." I held up the bag with the remaining cash. "And we just became fourteen thousand dollars richer." I couldn't help the smile that spread across my face.

She lost the shocked expression and returned my smile. "Well, big man, I'd say you damn well earned it!"

The first thing we did once we were safely back in the hotel suite was call everybody and tell them that the situation had been taken care of and we could all breathe easy. It felt fucking great to share that news. We did not share the bit about the gun and the extra money, however, since we didn't want anyone to worry about the first and we had no idea what to think about the second.

The next thing we did was order a bottle of champagne from room service. I didn't even particularly like the stuff but it seemed obligatory given how much we had to celebrate.

After the server popped the cork and was appropriately tipped and ushered out, Fiona turned to me for a toast.

"To conning a con-artist," she said, and I had to laugh as I clinked my glass with hers and we each took a sip.

"Now," she continued with a grin, "are you going to tell me what happened in that club?"

I cringed. I so did not want to talk about this, but since she was the most tenacious person I'd ever met, I knew she'd get it out of me sooner or later. I had an inkling she was even worse than Bailey.

"Fine," I gave in.

"Wait, wait, wait!" Fiona said. "I need to get comfortable for story time." She proceeded to set down her champagne flute and practically undress. First to go was the leather jacket and then came the boots. She had absolutely no clue what a turn-on this whole scene was—with the descent of each boot's zipper my dick responded in the opposite direction.

This girl was going to kill me.

By the time she finally settled on the sofa in just her slinky top and skin-tight jeans, I was a fucking mess. I sidled my way to the other end of the sofa where I plopped myself down and immediately snatched up a throw pillow to hide the bulge behind my zipper. I was wishing I'd at least thought to keep my jacket or button-down on. My t-shirt and pants didn't hide much.

"Okay, I'm ready," she said, taking a sip from her drink.

"Right." Thinking back to the club helped my awkward situation resolve itself. "It really wasn't a big deal—I was just way out of my comfort zone, that's all."

She glowered at me. "That's not how you tell a story. A story involves details and must contain any dialogue that was exchanged." She gestured as if addressing a small child. "Adjectives and adverbs are also much appreciated. Try again." She nodded encouragingly.

What was this? The story-time version of "Mr. Mark Visits the Go-Go-Boys"?

I scowled back at her and continued, "Okay, okay. So, I went in the staff room and that bartender was still in there. He wasn't rude or anything, but he was obviously going to kick me out. Before he could, I asked him if Tony was around tonight."

"Who's Tony?"

"No idea. I just figured we were in New Jersey so it was a safe bet that somebody named Tony worked there."

"You're smarter than you look," Fiona cupped her chin and said with a teasing smile.

"Gee, thanks. Anyway, turns out my hunch was right and he said Tony would be in later. Now this is where the awkward part comes. I don't think this guy and Tony like each other too much because the bartender guy suddenly became much more friendly." I was hoping to leave it at that.

No such luck.

"Oh? Do tell," she said. She didn't even have the decency to try and cover her excitement at my night's torment.

"God, you're nosy! And you're getting way too much enjoyment out of this."

"Oh, I definitely am. Now go on." She was a puppy waiting impatiently for a walk.

I huffed out a sigh of frustration but continued. The sooner this was over, the better. "Fine. He introduced himself and then started to hit on me and ask me all sorts of personal questions."

Fiona covered her mouth in a failed attempt to stifle her laughter.

"I'm glad I can amuse you, Shortcake."

"I'm sorry, I'm just getting the most spectacular visual." She then proceeded to snort and it all just descended from there as she lost her mind.

I scrubbed at my hair. "Let me know when you're done and I'll finish the story." I took a large gulp of my champagne and got up to fill my glass again.

"Is it safe to continue, or did you pee your pants?" I asked once I was resettled on the couch and her hilarity had subsided somewhat.

She just nodded, apparently afraid to speak yet.

I rolled my eyes at her and prepared for further humiliation. "I was so close to the money, I just had to play the part. So, I told him Tony was driving me crazy and I was trying to shake him loose but he had some of my shit stored in one of the lockers. Since I had the key, it must not have seemed too suspicious to him. I took a look and all the locks were combination locks except one, so I opened it and got the money. You want some more champagne?" I asked, standing up again.

"Oh no you don't." She pointed at me. "There's something you're not telling me. Spill it!" she demanded.

I knew I'd been too quick with my ending. Dammit.

"God, you're good at nagging. Did you earn a Girl Scout badge for that?"

She rolled her eyes.

"If you must know, while I was blocking the locker from his view, he may have grabbed my ass and said some really inappropriate things in my ear. There. That's everything. You happy?" God that was embarrassing.

She beamed. "Oh, more than you know. I'm adding this to the part of the story where you called me Toots. Ha! Now where is my phone?" She began searching around for it.

"Not a chance in hell." I snatched her phone from its place on the coffee table and put it in my back pocket before sitting back down, essentially blocking her access.

"Oh, come on. Let me have my fun. What was his name?"

"Whose name?"

"Duh, the bartender! You said he introduced himself. Did you give him your number?"

"Are you insane?"

"I won't stop until you give me my phone."

"No way in hell."

"He was awfully good looking now that I think about it. You two would make a cute couple," she continued to tease. "Now hand it over!" She put her hand out and stomped her bare foot on the floor.

"No." I crossed my arms.

"Isn't it so great that gay marriage is finally legal?" she goaded.

"Actually, I do think it's great. And I'm sure what's-his-face will find true love in due time."

At that, she growled and then let out some kind of maniacal battle cry while launching her entire body at me. I didn't move a muscle as she exhausted herself trying to pry my body forward with a variety of moves. After a few minutes, she admitted defeat and slumped over my shoulder with her head resting on the back of the sofa. This put her ass at a particularly delightful level, and I uncrossed my arms so I could give it a few encouraging pats. "There, there," I said and circled her thighs with my arms.

She lifted her head and leaned back so I could see her face. She was flushed from exertion and her blond hair was a wild mess. "Did you just pat my butt like a baby and say 'there, there'?"

"Well, I wouldn't say you were like a *baby*."

She blew some wayward strands of hair from her face. It was all kinds of cute.

"It's okay, Shortcake. Maybe you'll do better next time," I told her and then flipped her down so her back was flat on the couch and I was hovering over her.

"You're going to kiss me again, aren't you?" she asked, a bit breathlessly.

"I was giving it serious consideration." I lowered my face so our noses almost touched.

"I don't know if this is a good idea," she said.

"Kissing? I think it's a great idea." I smiled at her.

"You know what I mean—getting involved."

"It's just a kiss. And, besides, we're celebrating."

"Very funny. We have mutual friends. What happens when one of us is done with the other?"

This was where I had to tread lightly. I couldn't see a time when I'd be done with her, as foreign as that idea was to me, and as talented as she was at annoying me. But she was skittish as hell and I suspected she was more like me—or like the old me—than I'd realized. She didn't do relationships. At least not yet.

"Let's just play it by ear." I was hoping that response would work.

"But I kinda like hanging out with you. You're not nearly as irritating as I thought you were." She smiled.

"Again, gee, thanks."

"What I mean is, if we have sex a few times and then move on, won't it be awkward? I don't think I've ever been friends with someone after sleeping with them."

I hadn't either, but I wasn't going to share that bit of info.

"You worry too much. And besides, you never know what will happen."

"Yes I do," she responded, all lightness gone. Shit. This was the look of a girl who had baggage. Normally that would have sent me running for the hills, but I found myself getting worked up on her behalf.

Had she been hurt? Had some guy treated her like shit and thrown her away? I had to save those thoughts for later and focus on the moment.

"Shortcake, let's take it one step at a time. You know I'm attracted to you. Are you attracted to me?"

"You know I am. That's not the problem."

"As far as I can tell right now the only problem is that we're not kissing," I tried to joke but it did nothing to break through her solemn mood. So, I felt compelled to say, "I promise I won't hurt you. You can trust me." I kissed her nose. First I was kissing her head and now her nose? This was uncharted territory for me.

For some reason, the small kiss brought tears to her eyes. "That's not what I'm worried about either."

"Tell me what I can do to make this better." I kissed her forehead. "Do you want me to let you go? If that's what you want, I will. Just say the word."

She bit her lower lip and blinked the tears away, then looked me dead in the eyes for what felt like minutes but was probably just seconds. With that, she seemed to come to a decision.

"No, don't let me go. Just kiss me."

So, I did just that.

## Chapter Twenty-Two

# OH DEAR GOD THAT IS HOT

**F**IONA

*What was I doing?* I mean, I knew what I was doing—I was kissing this incredibly hot man. This man whom I'd discovered was so much more than some simple-minded, conceited meat-head. He was funny and caring and generous, and he took care of his own. He was also very interested in what I thought and did—even when I let my mouth wander from the topic at hand, he seemed to find me somehow entertaining. And he wanted good things for me. It was all so unexpected, but here I was in a hotel room in Atlantic City making out with a guy who felt so utterly right I didn't know what to think about it all.

But it didn't matter if it felt right. I wasn't the one for *anybody*. Not that Mark had exactly declared his undying love or anything, but I could feel it in my bones that he wanted to pursue something —as counter as that was to all my initial impressions of him. But any relationship that went beyond sex was asking for trouble.

Sex was easy—it was physical connection with a few laughs

thrown in. A relationship meant transparency. It meant vulnerability. It meant he would find out who I really am and all the things about me that are broken. It meant he would have the power to break me and I would most certainly break him eventually. It would end in him being disappointed at best—heartbroken at worst—and me cuddling up with Guilt for an ice-cream marathon and listening to her say, "*I told you so.*"

And now that I knew him and what he was all about, I could just picture his reaction when I finally confessed about the cancer and its side effects and about the distinct possibility it could come back. Anytime. He would want to take care of me—I'd seen it with his devotion to his mother—and I would suddenly be fragile, just like I am with my parents. I was so sick to death of being weak—to see that reflected in Mark's eyes might just kill me.

*"How many times do I have to tell you to stop your boo-hooing?"* said Vagina. *"If you miss out on this chance to get some, I will cut you!"*

*Take it down a notch, bitch, and give me a minute. Geez Louise!*

But, dammit, she was right—what was I doing wasting my time with all these negative what-ifs? I was smack dab in the middle of Sexy Muscle Magic Land and I was having a pity party instead of enjoying the rides! And besides, I didn't know for sure that he wanted anything other than casual sex so this could work out great. Yes, let's go with that.

*"Now you're talking!"* said Uterus and all the other girls, except Guilt and Pride, but they're a bit prudish anyway.

I yanked my brain back to the moment just as Mark's mouth left mine to trail down my neck and give me a whole-body shiver—how did he do that? While he focused on my neck, I maneuvered myself to finally cop a feel of that ass.

Wow. Consider me a convert—exercise is awesome! Let's hear it for all those reps!

My hands caressed and stroked wherever they could go—his hips, his back, his shoulders. I had no idea the human body could have that many ridges and contours. It was time to get his shirt off and get a better look.

I pulled his head up from my neck and couldn't resist another kiss before I said, "Mark, if you don't take your shirt off I'm going to tear it in two." His eyes were a little glazed over, as I'm sure were mine, but he grinned and then rose to his knees.

Holy shit—that was a sight!

He then reached behind his head with one hand and pulled his shirt off in a single fluid motion, revealing a chest, abs, shoulders and...everything a man like him had going on. In other words, I think I stopped breathing and was technically dead for a moment.

Laney and I have often discussed this ultra-sexy and impressive male talent of removing a shirt in this manner. We both firmly believe they know exactly how it affects a woman—not that we're complaining. We decided to try it ourselves one time but had very little success. Laney's enormous rack got in the way during her attempt and I had to help her extract her arms from the straight jacket she'd created. My attempt wasn't much better—I was able to get the shirt off but it completely messed up my hair and stretched out the neckline of my Stella and Jamie shirt. Also, Laney declared that it really wasn't as sexy when a girl did it.

Oh right, back to Mark and his incredible bod—*you should know by now I'm scatterbrained, so just deal with it!* His shirt was quickly discarded and I got to take in the full view.

Unfortunately, my little viewing party was cut short because Mark was on top of me again seconds later. But I had been right in guessing that my sensory journey of his body would be so much better without a shirt. His skin was smooth and hot, with the contrasting hardness of his muscles beneath—and there was that heady scent that filled my brain with all sorts of naughty thoughts. I was going to have to find out what cologne he wore and keep a bottle with me when our little affair was over.

*Gah—stay in the moment, Fiona!*

By this point, Mark's hand had slipped under my blouse and was pushing it up above my bra. I helped by lifting my arms and head so he could pull it off. Now it was his turn to check me out, but in truth, there wasn't a whole lot there. I hoped he wouldn't be disappointed. If his growl was anything to go by, I guess I had nothing to worry about. His head dipped down and his lips blazed a trail from my waist up to the center of my mostly non-existent cleavage. He lifted his eyes to mine and I noticed his pupils had almost overtaken his brown irises. And I swear his damn eyelashes batted themselves at me!

"Your skin is amazing," he said, and then leaned back down and took a little bite of my neck—just hard enough to make me groan. I was so turned on at this point I couldn't unhook the front closure of my lacey bra fast enough. I needed his mouth on my breasts ASAP. Luckily, Mark could read my mind and immediately covered one firm peak with his lips while his calloused hand caressed the other. A wave of relief coursed through my body at his touch. It felt like my whole being had been waiting for this—for his touch and possibly for this particular man. It was such a startling and unfamiliar feeling.

I didn't have time to dwell on the thought, though, because everything moved at lightning speed after that. We couldn't get our clothes off quickly enough and before I knew it, my legs were wrapped around his waist and he was lifting me up and striding toward the master bedroom. Yes, please!

"*Yippy!*" I heard the girl parts shout.

He put a knee to the bed and lowered us both down, his mouth crashing down on mine in a frantic kiss. I kept my legs locked around him and caressed his arms, reveling in their warmth and strength. It was like running my hands over a relief map, but in a super sexy way.

"Oh my God," I panted into his mouth as my center clenched. "More."

He didn't need to be told twice. His hand smoothed over my booty and thigh until it found its way between our bodies and his thumb found my clit, stroking and circling until I thought I'd go mad. And then I believe I did go mad as my orgasm suddenly crashed over me and I continued to pant and moan into Mark's mouth, feeling like I was losing my grip on reality.

He bit my lower lip gently. "You are so fucking sexy when you come," he groaned.

Just as my heartbeat was beginning to slow, he suddenly got up off the bed and I started to panic. That is, until I realized I was finally getting my first full-body view of naked Mark and– holy mother of male perfection! This guy was like a living breathing statue, the title of which would be "Oh Dear God, That Is Hot!"

The moonlight coming through the window cast a gazillion shadows across his sculpted body, and the breath left my lungs again. I had never seen such a thing in real life. His hip "v" was so cut it was a capital "V" with an exclamation point!

"Where are you going?" I managed to croak through my breathless state.

"Condom," he responded and then turned around presumably to find his pants in the other room. Oh, this view was just as delicious as the first. Exactly how many muscles comprise the human ass? I pondered that for an extra couple seconds before stopping him.

"Here," I said, rolling over to open the nightstand drawer. "I'll bet the Days Inn doesn't supply condoms." I looked over my shoulder at him and noticed his eyes planted firmly on my bare ass. Huh, he seemed to think my booty was nice the way it was too. This guy was great for my ego.

I held up the condom and he quickly climbed back onto the bed to lie next to me.

"I may have been hasty in my judgment of this hotel." He took the condom and ripped the packet open with his teeth, while I moved my hands down to encircle his rigid cock and begin to stroke him. He groaned and allowed me to explore him for a few moments before he nudged my hands aside and rolled the condom on. Somebody was impatient.

Having been deprived of the pleasure of stroking his cock, my hands moved to his chest and flattened against his pecs. I could both hear and feel his chest rumble at my touch, and my heart sped up again.

This was really happening. God, I hoped I wasn't making a mistake, but at this point everything felt so good and so right there was no way Guilt or Pride or any army of inner girl voices could stop me.

As Mark finally pressed into me, he actually sighed my name. I moaned in response like a wanton hussy, a role I was just fine with. We began to set a perfect rhythm and his mouth sought mine out again.

"You feel so fucking good," he groaned between wet kisses.

In response, I wrapped my legs around him and held on for dear life as our tongues and lips explored one another and our bodies joined over and over. I flicked his ear with my tongue and felt him shiver over me as he continued to thrust and I met his every movement.

I may have lost consciousness at one point when he lifted my leg up to rest on his shoulder and his thrusts became almost frantic. In this new position, I had a clear view of his gorgeous face and chest and he kept hitting the exact right spot. It was so good I was essentially just a lazy ball of goo, not really contributing anything and just letting his muscles do what they do best.

It. Was. Fucking. Hot.

Mark began to grunt with effort and intensity and I could tell he was as close as I was. I grabbed onto his hips and bit my lower lip hard—that was all it took to send us both over the edge. It was quite possibly the best orgasm of my life, and if Mark's gasping breaths were anything to go by I was thinking his had been damn good as well.

He collapsed next to me, thank God, as I was guessing the full weight of him would smash me like a bug. "Shortcake," he said on an exhale, "I'm pretty sure you're going to be the death of me." His labored breathing continued and I could do nothing but laugh and plant a kiss on his chest. He lowered his chin to look at me. "Not that I'm complaining, you understand." And then we both pretty much passed out.

It had been quite a long day, after all.

## Chapter Twenty-Three

# IN FOR A PENNY...IN FOR AN UPHILL CLIMB

**M**ARK

I watched Fiona sleep, feeling only slightly like a creeper. It was going on two in the morning and I knew I should get some shut-eye for the drive home, but I couldn't seem to make myself settle in. Fiona had passed right the hell out after our earlier activities. I'd taken care of the condom and come back to the bed, where I pulled back the covers and shifted her so her head rested on a pillow. Then I couldn't help myself so I rearranged her as she had been earlier, with her head resting on my chest and her arm across my stomach. That was better.

If I hadn't been sure about how right she was for me before tonight, I was damn certain now. Somehow this tiny, feisty, beautiful spitfire had been made just for me, and I thought back to all the times I'd given guys like Nate shit for being pussy whipped. I actually got it now, and it didn't even make me feel like a girl as I'd assumed it would. That right there is what I call personal growth.

Now the hard part would be keeping things low-key until Fiona came around to the same conclusion. But I could do it—I would do it. There was no other choice. She was mine and I wasn't letting her go. With that thought, I finally felt the weight of my eyelids and I drifted off, looking forward to another day with my girl.

"Sour cream and onion or salt and vinegar?" she asked. Apparently, now that we'd had sex she was willing to share her snacks with me.

I had awoken this morning to Fiona trailing kisses down my sternum and I'd be lying if I said I couldn't see myself waking up to that every morning. We'd rolled around in a tangle of limbs and lips and tongues for a while before taking the action to the shower where we managed to spend a good half hour going down on each other. Then I had no choice but to demand she brace her hands against the shower wall so I could take her from behind. I had to say I was gaining a whole new appreciation for this fancy hotel and its endless supply of both hot water and condoms.

When we were both sated and clean, we realized how late it was and quickly packed up our things so we could get on the road. This time I didn't object when Fiona ordered the large coffee. I knew we'd be stopping for snacks every couple hours anyway so what difference did it make? Fiona was not only a chatty traveler but a hungry one as well, not that she hadn't earned that appetite after the last twelve or so hours.

We were just pulling out of rest stop number two when she asked my chip preference. "Neither. I'll just stick with my peanuts, thanks," I told her.

"You just love your nuts, don't you?" she asked.

I was preparing a nice little comeback along the lines of, *"You seem to like them too,"* when I looked over and noticed she was just smiling and humming to herself, oblivious to the blatant double entendre she'd just dropped. I couldn't bring myself to respond so I kept my laugh to myself but couldn't contain my smile.

That caused her to lean over in the seat and kiss my cheek. Damn, this girl was going to be a handful and I didn't think I'd want it any other way.

How had I gotten here? A few weeks ago, I was swearing off relationships or even just simple repeats. Suddenly I was putty in this girl's hands. Damned if I could do anything about it now, though. I'd just have to steel myself for the verbal beat-down I'd get from all the guys.

Oh well, in for a penny…

"How about one of your playlists, Shortcake?"

We arrived back at her condo after dark and we were both exhausted. I didn't know how to play the sleeping-over card, so I took her lead when she yawned and said she was going to take a quick shower and crash. I pulled her suitcase from the bed of my truck and offered to carry it up for her, but she insisted she'd get it on her own since it had "those wheelie things."

I could take a hint so I didn't press the point. Shortcake was getting skittish again. I did, however, make sure to give her a searing kiss before sending her through the doors of her building. Let her stew on that for a while.

I knew Jake and my mom would be waiting for me to stop by

so they could grill me about the trip. I'd been thinking about that extra money, too, and had concluded that my mom should just take it. If anybody had earned it, she had, and the old man could just assume the loan sharks had taken it in return for their trouble.

As predicted, the lights were on inside the little house as I pulled into the drive and parked. I barely had a chance to get up the front steps before the door flew open and I was tackled in a giant bear hug by Jake.

"I can't believe you fucking did it!" He smacked me on the back hard enough to dislodge something vital before pulling back and patting me on the shoulder. "You did good, little brother." He was all smiles.

I fake scowled at him. "Maybe you could show your appreciation by getting me a beer instead of manhandling me."

He laughed. "Coming right up." He moved back to the doorway and was replaced by our mom who hugged me as well, only hers was the normal type, not the kind that caused internal bleeding.

"I can't tell you how relieved I am to see you in one piece. I was worried sick." She took my face in her hands and inspected me for any damage.

"It all went fine, Mom, but I do have a bone to pick with you," I started to scold.

"I know, I know, you're mad I went to see your father without telling you. And you did some scheming of your own without telling me. What's done is done. Let's focus on the good stuff." She held my eyes firmly.

"I can do that," I finally said.

After we'd settled in and Jake had gotten me my well-deserved beer, I told them about the extra money and my thoughts on it.

"I can't just take it! It's not mine. And who even knows where he got it," my mother objected.

"Mom, you can definitely take it, and you should." Jake backed me up. "He probably got it gambling or playing poker anyway. Just think of it as back child-support."

I pointed to my brother. "Exactly."

"I don't know," she said and bit her lip. "And what about my taxes—won't it look strange if I suddenly have fourteen thousand dollars?!"

I waved her off. "There are ways around that—we'll figure it out."

"At least give me a little time to think about it, okay."

"Sure," I said and Jake nodded his agreement even though we both knew, in the end, she would get the money whether she agreed or not. She always resisted when I tried to pitch in financially, but this time I was standing firm, especially since the money was coming from the sperm donor's pocket.

"Hey, I'm meeting up with Nate and Gavin for a game of pool. You should come," Jake said.

I was torn. The drive had wiped me out, but I was afraid if I went home to my empty bed I'd just think about Fiona. "Maybe just for a bit," I said.

We kissed our mom good night and then took separate vehicles, Jake borrowing our mom's tiny car. The visual of him cramming his six-foot-four-inch frame into the compact vehicle had me chuckling as I pulled out of the drive and headed for the bar, ironically named "Jake's." What could I say? It was our favorite place even if it did have the same name as my dickhead brother.

It turned out the whole crew had decided to hit Jake's tonight. Brett, Gavin, Trey, and Court—another guy from work—were shooting pool, and I spotted Nate at the bar picking up another round.

"Hey! It's the man of the hour!" he called out when he caught sight of me.

I just grinned and stole one of the beers the bartender had just set in front of him. I took a sip of the draft—a nice hoppy IPA. Nate always had great taste in beer.

Jake walked up to the bar and I noticed he was rubbing the base of his spine. "Goddamn car—that thing is designed for the vertically challenged."

Which of course made me think of Fiona, again. I groaned.

"What's up with you?" asked Nate, giving me a sideways glance.

"Nothing. Let's play some pool."

Gavin and Brett cleaned up the floor with all of us, although Trey and Court were still insistent that they could turn things around. Seeing the writing on the wall, Nate, Jake, and I bowed out and took a seat at a nearby table. We all switched to water, knowing we'd be driving soon.

Once we were settled, I gave the recap on the Atlantic City adventure, this time including the parts about the gun and the extra money. I pointed at Nate. "You cannot tell Laney about the gun or she will flip the fuck out about Fiona."

He put his hands up. "I hear you. If she found out she'd have your balls and I don't think I could live with the guilt."

I knew he was right. Laney was protective of Fiona and would definitely, and rightly, blame me if any harm had come to her best friend. Thankfully it hadn't. In fact, Fiona had been amazing.

"Why in the hell are you smiling at the thought of having your balls cut off?" my brother asked.

"I wasn't smiling."

"Yes, you were," they both said at the same time.

"If I was, it wasn't about my nuts, I can promise you. I was just thinking about Fiona. You should have seen her up there." I shook my head. "That girl isn't afraid of anything."

"There it is again," said Jake, gesturing to my face.

"What?" I asked.

"Holy. Shit," said Nate, sitting up straighter.

"What?!" I demanded this time.

Jake looked at Nate and then back at me, seemingly as confused as I was. Until his lips slowly turned up and he threw his head back with a barking laugh.

I was starting to get pissed. I took a quick drink of my water and then slammed it back on the table.

Nate looked dumbfounded but Jake slapped his palm on the table. "I knew it! You totally boned her!"

Oh shit.

It wasn't as if I was going to keep this a secret forever, but I was at least hoping to secure things up with Shortcake a little more tightly before the entire world weighed in.

"You did, didn't you?" Nate asked, finally having recovered his ability to speak.

"Something might have happened. That's all I'm going to say. And that does not go beyond this table!"

"Man, have you met Laney? There is no way she will let me live if she finds out I knew this before she did," said Nate.

"Maybe Fiona already told her?" I offered up. "As far as I can tell, she has absolutely no filter so it's apt to come up soon. Just work with me."

"Yeah, okay."

Meanwhile, Jake was still having a good time at my expense. "Hate-fucking is supposedly really hot, not that I've ever experienced it personally, but I can see the potential. All that energy refocused on fucking each other's brains out." He hooted.

"Hate-fucking?" Nate looked at me. "Seriously?"

"Yeah," Jake responded before I could. "Those two are always bickering and driving each other crazy. It's classic—annoyance channeled into a good screwing."

I put my head in my hands. Shit.

Nate was pissed. "I actually care about that girl and you'd better not use her or treat her like shit. I mean, I know she doesn't do relationships either, but that doesn't mean you're allowed to be an asshole."

Double shit. I now had confirmation of my suspicions that Fiona wasn't into relationships. This was going to be a difficult road ahead.

"It was *not* hate-fucking and I was not an asshole." I lifted my head again and shot daggers at Jake. "It's complicated. Besides, is it really anyone's business besides mine and Fiona's?"

Nate took in my expression and seemed to come to a satisfactory conclusion. "Okay, okay. I get it." He put his hands up. "I've just got to look out for Fiona—she's kind of the crazy, foulmouthed little sister I never had. Oh, wait, I *do* already have one of those." He smiled.

"It's cool, man," I told him and then turned to my asshole of a brother. "It's almost as if you're *asking* to be punched in the throat. Why is that?"

"Damn, little brother, I'd forgotten how fun it is to get under your skin." He grinned at me.

I vowed at that moment to never torture a child of my own by providing him with a sibling. Then I sat with my water, contemplating my next move.

There were two things at the top of the list—say goodbye to dear old dad, and get Fiona to fall for me.

Piece of cake.

Fuck.

*Chapter Twenty-Four*

# LIAR, LIAR, PANTIES ON FIRE

**F**IONA

It was the following afternoon and I yawned as I sat at my desk and checked my phone for the tenth time in the last five minutes. Nothing.

Which was fine since I didn't want to pursue anything with Mark anyway, right? It was an adventure and we had some hot sex. Best to leave it at that.

Oooor, maybe doing the friends-with-bennies thing would be the better choice. We could make it work even if we had mutual friends to deal with. It wasn't like either one of us was going to want to take it up a notch and have an actual relationship or anything.

Ugh. This was hurting my brain.

The phone rang and I jumped in my seat, only to realize it was the office phone. Oh right, my job. Oops.

"Good afternoon. Precision Lawns and Landscaping. This is Fiona. How can I help you today?"

"Hey, Fiona! Just the girl I wanted to talk to," said the voice on the other end. It was familiar but I couldn't place it.

"I get that a lot, but I'm afraid you have me at a disadvantage. Exactly who is this?" I asked with a light-hearted tone.

"You wound me, Fiona. It's your future husband—that is, if I can convince you to develop an interest in Bunco."

I smiled. "Hi, Jake. Why are you calling on this line? Don't you have my cell?"

He laughed. "Mark deleted your contact. He said I only manage to screw things up when I open my mouth so I'm not allowed to talk to you out of his presence."

I couldn't help but giggle. Hmm. Interesting.

"What can I do for you today? I'm assuming you're not calling about lawn service since you don't live here."

He didn't respond right away. "Actually, that kind of *is* why I'm calling."

"What do you mean?" I was genuinely confused at this point.

"I did some checking around and your boss Jax has a really impressive reputation around town."

For some ridiculous reason, his comment gave me a little kick of pride—which was so misguided since I'd only worked here a couple months and the only thing I contributed to the business was answering phones and forgetting to fill the coffee maker.

"Well, that's nice to know," I responded, still not understanding where this was going.

"All right, I'm just gonna lay it out for you. I'm considering moving back to the area and I want to work with the best. That happens to be your boss. Any chance I could get an introduction? If I'm overstepping or that makes you uncomfortable I totally understand, but I thought it wouldn't hurt to ask."

I was totally shocked. "You're moving back? When did this

happen? Does Mark know? Does Kelly know? Oh my God, she will be so thrilled. This is so exciting! Now our welcome home party can be for real. Oh wait, you're not supposed to know about that—forget I said anything. Oh my God, this is so exciting! Oh, and of course I'll introduce you to Jax, although it might actually work against you. I'm not exactly the best reference, but we'll figure it out. Wow. Just, wow!"

"Take a breath, Fiona. I said I'm considering it. It's by no means a sure thing. I have lots of things to think about."

I scowled into the phone. "Party pooper. So, in other words, keep my mouth shut? You so picked the wrong person, Jake, you know that, right?"

He laughed. "Just do your best."

"You mind me asking what caused this sudden turn-around? From what Mark has told me, you have a pretty sweet gig down in Florida." I leaned back in my chair and twirled a pen in my hand. I immediately dropped it. Why do people always make that look so easy?

"Yeah, well, things aren't always exactly how they appear," he said. And boy did I know a thing or two about that. "And besides, this whole debacle with my mom and dad has got me rethinking some things."

"That's understandable. Well, I'll do my best to keep my mouth shut but I can't make any promises. I can, however, promise to introduce you to Jax."

I grabbed another pen and jotted down some notes about the meeting arrangements before we said our goodbyes.

"I still don't understand what we're doing here," Laney said as I prowled the fragrance counters at Macy's. She trailed behind me with her Caribou hot chocolate in hand. I would never understand how she couldn't recognize coffee as humankind's greatest invention—well, that and Diane von Furstenberg's wrap dress. It really does look good on everyone, you know. And now that I think of it, penicillin wasn't such a shabby invention either...oh well, I digress...

It was Thursday and I still hadn't heard a peep from Mark. *It had been two days, people—two days!* So, I had concluded that our hot night of sex was a one-and-done kind of thing. This was not entirely surprising, even though I found it remarkably disappointing for reasons I did not want to contemplate. Sometimes you don't realize what you want until you don't get it. There has to be a song in there somewhere.

Anyway, I thought I'd get confirmation that our one-nighter was in line with Mark's general MO and he hadn't, say, fallen off a cliff in the last two days. That info was definitely worth a trip to Caribou Coffee where I could casually quiz Laney. Then I could put the whole thing to rest and move on with normal life—life without *Sopranos* dudes and guns and Manaconda Mondays and road trips and sexy muscled arms and searing kisses and toe-curling orgasms and sweet hugs and—oh for Christ's sake!

I hadn't seen Laney since the weekend so we'd agreed to meet up for a coffee/hot chocolate date after work. I had been so busy obsessing about Mark I hadn't even spilled the beans about Jake's potential move back to Greensboro. Yay me!

She and I still had the dinner to plan and I was dying to know if anyone had been to see Mark's dad to share the news that his money was gone—boo hoo. But I could not bring myself to text or call Mark. A silent brushoff was enough—I didn't need verbal or text confirmation from the source himself.

I waited for Laney at a table by the window, having already ordered both our drinks, and I was trying to come up with the best way to casually ask about Mark's sex life. Ugh, this was going to be hard. I'd finally resolved to just wing it in my normal spazzy way when Laney walked through the door.

"I know, I know, Skechers are not appropriate work attire. Ward off the fashion demons and move on," she said as she approached the table and dropped into the seat opposite me.

I took in her outfit which did, in fact, include Skechers, but I had to give her points for her cute asymmetrical top. However, since I knew it amused her, I crossed myself and whispered a request for forgiveness on Laney's behalf to Inner Fashion Maven and Christian Louboutin while I was at it. "Done," I said.

She rolled her eyes at me, took a sip of her drink and sighed. "Nate picked Rocco up and they're going out for guys' dinner so I've got the whole evening free."

"Yay—that's awesome. Maybe we can grab dinner after this or something. You know we still have to plan a party for Jake," I began.

"I was just thinking about that today. I know it started as an excuse to hang out with Kelly, but I'm still excited to do it," she said. "But first, I haven't even seen you since you got back from Atlantic City. I need the full recap!"

I leaned forward in my seat, eager to finally share the good stuff. "I already told you just about everything, but I did leave out one juicy bit. You have to swear not to tell Nate, though, or Mark will lose his shit." I proceeded to tell her all about the club and the guys who had a thing for Mark's hot bod.

We were both laughing like idiots by the time I finished. Laney snorted and then said, "Too bad for all those guys Mark doesn't swing the other way. I get the impression he's a total manwhore—

he could have lined up a record number of dates." She continued to giggle, but my mood fell flat on its face.

Shit. This was the information I'd come here for, so why did I feel like someone had just sucked all the air out of the room.

Unfortunately, I wasn't able to mask my emotions quickly enough to avoid Laney's notice. She smiled and crinkled her eyebrows at me in silent question. I attempted a grin that I'm sure came off as more of a grimace and then tried to hide behind my coffee. Her smile died right there on her face and her left hand came up to rub her cheek. Shit! That was her tell.

"Oh, Fiona," she said.

"What?" I responded, setting my coffee back down and shooing her with my hand. "It was no big deal. I've had one-night stands before. So what?"

She rested her elbow on the table, still cradling her face. "I guess so. But you don't really seem okay. What happened? I mean, I don't need the details of the deed itself, but did you guys talk about it? Did you know what you were getting into?"

"No…I don't know. We didn't talk about it—before or after—but we'd been kind of dancing around each other so I suppose it was bound to happen." I picked at the seam of my coffee sleeve.

She grabbed my hand. "About what I said before, I don't know for a fact that he just does hook-ups. It was just a guess. I mean, maybe you guys can do the casual thing like you usually do. Unless that is, you want…do you want…do you want a relation-ship?" There was way too much hope in her voice.

I huffed. "Oh, God no. You've known me for how long and you ask such a question? I'm a little worried about the state of our friendship." I attempted to joke but even I knew it rang false.

"Oh." She pulled her hand back and picked up her hot choco-late again.

"What?"

"It's just that I guess part of me was hoping you'd finally be open to a relationship. That's all."

Yeah, no shit. She was about as opaque as cling wrap.

But she looked so darn sad I was kind of mad at myself for disappointing her.

"Look," I said. "I may not be 'relationship girl' but I can admit that maybe I was hoping for a friends-with-benefits deal."

"You said 'was.' Why can't you still do that? And then maybe see where it goes…"

Gah!

"Because he hasn't called or texted since he dropped me off on Tuesday, and I can't stop thinking about him and I am going out of my mind mentally reliving the best sex of my entire life!" I blurted —maybe a touch too loudly judging by the pinch-faced glares I was receiving from the two older women across the way.

Oops.

Well, clearly neither one of them had ever screwed a man who was built like a fucking mountain and was sweet to his mother. Dammit.

"Oh my God," Laney said.

I knew that look—and that tone of voice.

Retreat!

"You like him."

I rolled my eyes at her. "Well, of course I like him. Do you think I have sex with people I hate? Who does that?"

"No, I mean you *like* him."

I scoffed at her, "Yeah, right. You know what I like?" I slammed down my almost empty coffee cup. "I like how he smells. It drives me out of my ever-loving mind and makes me think things I never think. And it lights my panties on fire!" I looked over to the disapproving, awesome-sex-deprived women. "That's right, ladies. Panties. On. Fire. And I'm not even a liar!" I pointed at them and taunted like some mentally unstable version of a coffee-house poet.

At this point, Laney took over since I had evidently lost my mind. "Let's go," she said as she stood and gathered my purse along with all her things. I stood up and beelined for the door ahead of her. I was done with this. I wasn't going to let some man turn me into a nut-job!

Laney attempted an apology to the women who had tragically never been to Sexy Muscle Magic Land and then raced to catch up to me as I stomped down the sidewalks of Friendly Center in my four-inch heels.

"Where in the hell are we going?" Laney asked. When I didn't answer, I heard her mutter, "Well at least I wore comfortable shoes."

So now we were at Macy's, trolling the men's fragrance department on the hunt for whatever that damn intoxicating cologne was that Mark used to lure me in and catch me unawares.

I turned to Laney to explain my strategy again. "I'm going to buy a big-ass bottle of whatever it is he wears so I can do some good old-fashioned immersion therapy and rid myself of my damn Pavlovian response to that scent!" I was white knuckling the theory that it was his scent, not the man himself, that had tricked me into possibly having—*gag*—feelings.

"I guess," said Laney, in a pathetic attempt at encouragement.

"There are too damn many of these." I looked around helplessly, which was a little sad because I don't think I've ever in my entire life felt anything less than blissful at a department store.

"Maybe I can help. Describe the scent," Laney pitched in with much-needed enthusiasm. This is why I love this girl.

I thought about Mark's scent and my lady parts immediately sighed. *Shut it, bitches! Mama has demons to exorcise!* I blocked them out and tried to concentrate. "I don't know—a little spicy and kind of herby and woodsy, but in a way that's like a favorite blanket you bring out from an old cedar chest." I was staring off into space and almost missed her stifled snort. "What?!"

"I hate to break it to you, but you've got it bad."

Did I just say I loved her? Well, forget that. She was dead to me.

I groused, "Oh shut up and help me find this shit."

Laney snickered and then dutifully approached the first counter.

## Chapter Twenty-Five

# LADY GAGA WOULD MAKE A TERRIBLE NINJA

FIONA

"I've got some news," Laney sing-songed over the phone later that night.

"You found the cologne?" I asked excitedly. Maybe Nate had known what it was all along! Or not, because that would be weird.

We had completely struck out at Macy's, and by the time we'd smelled the fortieth scent our olfactory senses were numb and everything had started smelling like old feet dipped in sporty deodorant. We'd finally given up and decided to grab dinner, where we vowed not to discuss Mark and/or the events that led up to me shtupping him.

Instead, Laney told me about Nate's increasingly peculiar behavior, but this time she wasn't finding it worrying. Instead, she was getting a kick out of it. This was a surprising, but welcome, turn of events.

Apparently, Nate was up to something because twice in the past week Laney had come up behind him, unintentionally startling him, and each time he had jumped sky high and then stuttered and stammered like Woody Allen. The man was undoubtedly guilty of something.

"He wouldn't..." I began. I could never see Nate cheating on Laney, but I had to make sure her mind wasn't going there.

"No, no—definitely not," she reassured. "Both times I surprised him he had been typing into his phone and tried to hide it from me really quickly."

"Umm..." I uttered and then stopped because wasn't this exactly the type of behavior a cheater would exhibit? *Sorry, Nate, I have total faith in you, but whatever you're up to you need to be a bit subtler, dude.*

"No, you don't understand. He doesn't have a password on his phone and he's always asking me to answer it for him or check his texts when his hands are busy. That means he's been planning something online." She raised her eyebrows and smiled.

The lightbulb finally turned on. "Your birthday! Of course! Oh, I wonder what he's planning. Do you think it's a trip? You totally deserve it, and if your parents can't take Rocco you know I will." I was so happy for her that she had such an awesome guy.

"I don't know yet, but I'm excited anyway. And I haven't told you the best part—he gave his landlord his notice so, as of next month, Nate will officially be living with us!" she announced.

I squeed. "Oh my God! I'm so happy for you guys." I reached across the table and hugged her. "I feel like we should order a bottle of champagne or something, but then we can't drive." My smile turned into a pout.

She waved me off. "Another time."

I looked at my best friend and she was glowing with contentment. "Laney, I can't think of anybody who deserves happiness more than you."

She'd smiled at me and then grabbed my hand across the table. "I can."

Aaand with that I'd switched the subject to planning Jake's party while we'd finished our meals.

It was now past dark and I'd been getting ready for bed when Laney's call had come through.

"No, I didn't find the cologne. This is better!" she taunted.

"Sweet Jesus, Nate's taking you to Paris! I love that man!"

Laney laughed. "No, it's about Mark."

Visions of springtime in Paris were replaced with those of me enjoying late night reality TV with my buddies Ben and Jerry. Kim would probably be invited too, but unless she figured out how to pair deliciously with ice cream she'd have to wait her turn.

"Hello?" I heard.

"I'm ignoring you." I tucked the phone between my ear and shoulder and opened the toothpaste.

"It's good news—I promise," she pleaded.

"Fine. Go on, if you must."

"So when I got home, Nate and I were talking and I very casually asked him about Mark's dating habits and—"

"YOU WHAT?!" The toothbrush fell into the sink and I braced my hands on the counter. *Deep breaths, Fiona.*

"Shut up and pay attention! I was a total ninja—he had no idea why I was asking."

I huffed at that.

She ignored me. "Anyway, he said Mark always makes it clear to anybody he's with that he only does casual one-nighters—"

I stood up straight. "*This* is your good news? What do you have planned for tomorrow? Are you going to buy me a pony and then say 'just kidding'?"

"If you don't shut up and let me finish I may do just that!" She was using the tone she reserves for Rocco when he's done something super inappropriate, like the time he asked Nate's mom if she liked having a big butt to sit on.

In other words, my choices were to listen while she finished or hang up and incur her wrath. I chose to listen.

"Fine." I didn't say I would be nice about it.

"As I was *saying*," she stressed the word pointedly, "according to Nate, Mark always—*always*—makes sure he and his 'partner' are on the same page *before* the deed is done. And—listen carefully—he never sleeps with girls he hangs out with." She sounded like she'd just delivered some kind of awesome news and was waiting for accolades. Um, thanks for the news that the guy I boffed is a totally indiscriminate manwhore?

"I don't understand," was all I could say. At this point, I dropped to the bathroom floor on my butt with my back pressed against the wall. I felt weird.

"Fiona, it means he went totally off-script with you. He never gets to know a girl first. He never hangs out with her casually or as friends. He never dates. Until you!"

"What do you mean? We're not dating. He hasn't even called me in two days!"

She sighed. "Answer me this: what was the last thing he said to you before you parted ways the other night?"

I thought back to the scene on the sidewalk where I'd been feeling all kinds of confused. I'd been tempted and scared at the same time, and when he'd tried to find a way up to my condo I had brushed him off with excuses of being tired.

And then that kiss! Gah!

"Um, I believe he didn't actually use words—more like just his tongue," I muttered into the phone.

"Ha! I knew it. He's totally into you!"

"Then why hasn't he called, dammit?!" I hollered before I could think better of it. "I mean, wait. No. I don't want to date him. I just want hot sex with him, Laney," I may have whined.

"Keep telling yourself that, girlie, but you're the only one buying it. And he hasn't called because he's obviously giving you a little space. I guarantee he will call you within the next twenty-four hours. And, besides, Nate said he's been working late trying to catch up. And then there's the whole thing with his dad—they're all arguing over who is going to tell him about the money. Cut your new boyfriend some slack." She snickered.

Bitch!

"He is not my boyfriend!"

"We'll see. Anyway, I just wanted to tell you the good news. And, like I said, don't worry, I was a total ninja so Mark will never know I was snooping."

I had too much else to think about to remind Laney that she was about as subtle as Lady Gaga. I hung up the phone and sat there for a few more minutes before picking my ass up and finally brushing my teeth.

Boyfriend?

No.

Absolutely not.

## Chapter Twenty-Six

# LOOK AT ME BEING ALL SENSITIVE AND SHIT

# MARK

**Nate:** *Heads up, man.*

**Mark:** *About what?*

**Nate:** *Laney was quizzing me about you. Fiona's flipping the fuck out.*

**Mark:** *Shit.*

**Nate:** *What are you going to do?*

**Mark:** *I'll figure something out. I've been so swamped I've hardly come up for air.*

**Nate:** *I know—that's why I'm sending the heads up. You'd best get your ass in gear if you want a chance with her. "If" being the question.*

**Mark:** *Okay, thanks, man. Prepare all your jokes and insults now. I'm going all in.*

**Nate:** *You just made my day, you pussy-whipped little douchebag! Wow, that felt good. Later.*

I deserved it so I figured I'd better be prepared for all the payback coming my way. Who was the fuckmuppet now?

It was ten at night on Thursday and I was exhausted. I'd taken work home with me the last couple nights and was playing catch up. It wouldn't have been so bad except while I had been in Atlantic City we'd had an order fall through on one of my jobs, and the client on another one was threatening to fire the architect, which would push our start date way out and screw up our whole schedule.

And, as if that wasn't enough, Jake, Mom, and I were in a stalemate over who was going to go see the old man and break the news to him that his money was all gone and his disregard for everyone's safety had earned him exactly what he deserved—a huge hospital bill and no prospects.

Thankfully, it now seemed our fears of our mom wanting to get back together with the asshole could be put to rest. She was as fired up as we were, if not more so. I know Jake and I both relished the thought of finally sticking it to him in person, but our mom was insistent that she be the one and only person he spoke to. I think she was afraid he'd hurt our feelings or something, but she just kept saying that he didn't deserve to see how well we'd turned out and she didn't like the thought of us in the same room as the asshole. Well, she'd said "loser" but I'm sure she'd meant "ass-hole." We had to decide soon, though, because he'd been expecting her to show up by now, money in hand.

Given all of that, coupled with the frightened rabbit impression Fiona had pulled again on Tuesday, I was letting that whole situation stew for a few days. But it looked like my time was up. I didn't want her flipping out and dismissing me—I'd only meant to give her time to miss me a bit and get comfortable with the notion of having me around. Apparently, my plan had flaws. Now I had to figure out a new one. Fast.

*Mark: Hey Shortcake. You awake?*

*Fiona: I am now, thanks to this annoying guy who just texted me.*

*Mark: Aw, I love it when you get all sweet and charming.*

*Fiona: Haha. Is there a point to this?*

*Mark: You bet. Been swamped since we got back but I wanted to know if you were free for dinner tomorrow night. Sorry for the short notice.*

I was proud of myself for being all sensitive and shit and not allowing her to bait me.

*Mark: Fiona? You still awake?*

Perhaps my idea of sensitive and hers were slightly different.

*Fiona: Sorry—just checking my schedule and it turns out I need to wash my hair tomorrow night.*

What a little smartass.

*Mark: Look, I'm sorry it took me so long to contact you. If it helps, I've been thinking about that thing you did in the shower…*

Honestly, I just wanted to tell her I hadn't stopped thinking about her at all—and not just the sex, although that was part of it. I *am* a guy. But if I told her I missed her or got overly attentive, I would definitely scare her away.

*Fiona: Well I should hope so—that was some of my best work.*

*Mark: Yes, ma'am. So dinner?*

*Fiona: You seriously want to go out on a date?*

*Mark: Yeah.*

Nothing.

*Mark: Shortcake, I've already seen you naked and shared several meals with you. I think you can handle it.*

*Fiona: Fine. What time and how should I dress?*

I was tempted to suggest getting take-out, but that wouldn't go well with my new strategy. It would just turn into naked dinner and the plan was to woo her instead of just jumping her.

*I know. I'm just as surprised as you.*

**Mark:** *7:15 and wear whatever you want—we're going to The Marshall Free House.*

**Fiona:** *Okay. I'm going back to sleep now.*

I wanted to tell her I wished I were there.

**Mark:** *Sweet dreams, Shortcake.*

That would have to do for now.

"I was gonna park and come up to get you!" I shouted out my window as I rolled up in front of Fiona's building. She looked up, startled, as if she hadn't been expecting me. There she was on the sidewalk, phone in hand, with her brow furrowed—though it loosened when she saw me. Huh, that felt pretty damn good. Then she smirked at me and the sass was back.

"Hey there, He-Man. Thought I'd just meet you down here," she said as she started toward the truck, tucking her phone back in her purse.

She looked like a magazine ad—her hair was pulled back into some messy knot which I'm sure was intended to look casual but in fact required tons of time and precision. And she was wearing these pants that hung daringly low on her hips. The only words I possess in my vocabulary to describe them are M.C. Hammer pants —but totally kick-ass in a girlie kind of way.

Okay, I'm just going to stop now because it's beyond obvious I don't know the first thing about fashion. And I am totally comfortable with that.

Suffice it to say, my future girlfriend was all kinds of hot. She officially had permission to stick her nose into my business anytime she liked.

I did wonder, though, if she had "people" or something to prepare her whenever she exited her condo and went out into the world. I've heard of that before, but I'm pretty sure that's only for rich people who live in New York and L.A., not the great metropolis that is Greensboro, North Carolina. I was sensing I had a lot to learn.

I stopped staring at her like an idiot long enough to shift into park and hop out to help her with her door. The Hammer pants looked just as good from behind. I shut her door and soon we were pulling away from the curb for the short drive to the restaurant.

She opened her mouth to speak but I beat her to the punch, wanting to set the tone for the evening. "You look beautiful."

Her jaw snapped shut, stifling whatever she'd been about to say. Her cheeks turned a little pink and she finally said, "Thanks. You don't look so bad yourself."

I regarded my cargo pants and plain cotton button-down. If she said so. "Thanks," I replied.

Just then her phone rang from inside her purse and I swear she growled at it.

"You need to get that?" I asked.

"Absolutely not."

"Okay, then." There really was no other possible reply.

The ringing stopped as the call presumably went to voicemail and then a few seconds later it started again.

This time, Fiona threw her purse on the floor of the passenger side only to change her mind and pick it up a couple seconds later, rifling through it for the offending device. She stabbed at the phone and put it to her ear.

"I'm only answering to tell you that I'm turning my phone off so you may as well stop calling. I will not be answering for the rest of the night and I felt it only fair to tell you that because I don't want you to jump to some insane conclusion that the reason your calls are going unanswered is because I'm languishing on the side of the road somewhere grasping in vain for my phone in one final attempt to speak with my beloved mother before I die under the heap of mangled steel that was once a car. I don't need you and Dad trolling the sides of I-40 all night looking for my body. I'm not dying, I'm not answering my phone, and I'm not talking about this. Goodnight and I love you." She started to pull the phone away from her face but brought it back up one more time. "Tell Dad I love him too."

She stabbed the end button, threw the phone back in her purse and let out a giant sigh. Then she turned to me. "Do you think Kelly would adopt me?"

"Shortcake, given that we're currently on a date and I've seen every inch of your naked body, I'd say that question is a tad inappropriate."

Her mouth twisted to the side. "Hmm. Yeah, I guess you're right."

"I would ask if everything is okay but I think even the people in the next town over know it's not."

"Ugh. It's my mother." She shook her head.

"I gathered that."

She rolled her eyes at me. "I told her I had a date."

"And?" I didn't see what the problem was. I switched my turn signal on and made my way toward Battleground Avenue.

"I don't exactly date much," she confessed.

"Me neither." I glanced over and grinned—in a way I hoped came off as conspiratorial as opposed to, say, lascivious.

"Yes, I know," she muttered under her breath. Crap, somebody had been hearing stories about me. I knew it would happen but I had to nip this in the bud.

"Until you," I said, flat out. I looked over again to gauge her response.

She squirmed in her seat. "This is a bad idea," was all she said.

"Why would you say that?"

"It just is," she sighed. Well, that wasn't going to cut it.

"Give me one valid reason," I challenged.

She looked out the passenger window and I thought for a moment that she wasn't going to answer me. Then she said, "It's complicated."

It was my turn to roll my eyes. "Quit dancing around it and give me something solid, Shortcake."

She twisted her body toward me. "Fine. I don't want our friends to have to choose sides when this is over. That right there is a damn good reason!"

Yeah, she was still under the impression that this was going to be some kind of temporary friends-with-benefits thing. Granted, if we dated like I wanted to and then for some unforeseen reason did indeed break up down the road, her point would be valid. But who wants to dwell on that kind of depressing thought? So, I went with the best response I could come up with.

"Fine. If things between us end, you can have them. Except Jake—that one would be a bit awkward at holidays and family reunions," I attempted to joke.

She scoffed. "Not 'if,' '*when*' things end."

"Are you psychic or something? You carry around a crystal ball I don't know about in one of your giant handbags?"

"You know, Mark, normally I'm a huge fan of sarcasm but I'm being totally serious and you're just making light of it."

I pulled into the parking lot of the restaurant and put the truck in park. Turning to her I said, "If I can promise you one thing, Fiona, it's that I'm not taking any of this lightly." And with that, I released my seatbelt and got out to retrieve my girl. Because she was—she just didn't know it yet.

## Chapter Twenty-Seven

# THE WORST KIND OF TROUBLE

**F**IONA

What the hell was that supposed to mean?! Whatever it meant, I was definitely in trouble—double-dog-doo trouble, otherwise known as *fucking* trouble. It seemed perhaps Laney had been right—Mark wanted to *date* date.

I didn't know how to do that!

I didn't want to do that!

I wasn't capable of doing that!

Pride cut in at this point. *"For the love of God, please don't hyperventilate and pass out in the parking lot of The Marshall Free House. We are getting those Scotch eggs if it's the last thing we do! Get your shit together!"*

I was beginning to really dislike her, but she did have a point— the one about the Scotch eggs, not the panicking and hyperventilating. That was completely justified.

Mark opened my door and put a hand out. I had no choice but to take it, noticing as always how warm and strong it was, but mine was shaking—although my breathing had miraculously calmed a bit.

The motherfucker just smiled at me as if he knew just how panicked I was and couldn't be happier about it.

Those Scotch eggs better be worth the heartache that awaited.

As we walked into the restaurant and the hostess led us to our table, I forced my mind away from the scary topic of dating. Unfortunately, that meant my brain decided to wander back to the phone conversation I'd had with my mother earlier in the evening.

I'd been having a perfectly lovely day and was looking forward to seeing Mark, even if it did make me all sorts of anxious. I hadn't messed up anything at work, an occurrence that had Jax and Ollie a bit flummoxed. They were already so used to me screwing stuff up that it was a wonder I hadn't been fired yet.

Ollie always assured me that Jax had seen my resume before he'd hired me, so he was aware of my job-hopping and knew there had to be a reason for it. Luckily Jax had been in such a bind when I'd sent my resume in, he'd had little choice but to at least interview me. That's where I shine, I've been told. Ollie said Jax was under my spell and offering me the job before he even knew what had happened. I guess I am pretty charming.

At any rate, I'd had a great day, and then my mom had called right after work.

She began talking before I even had a chance to greet her. "Sweetheart, I know it's really last minute, but is there any way you could pop over tonight and make an appearance at Barbara's dinner party? She adores you and she said her grandson wants to know more about the LLS Regatta. He's very involved in his sailing club and this could mean a big boost for the event. He'll be at the dinner tonight—it's at 8:00 so you have plenty of time. Is there any possible way you can make it? I'm sure he'd be much more interested in talking to you than all of us old folks."

"Hello, Mom," I said.

"Oh, I'm so sorry, sweetheart. I don't know where my head is. How are you?" I could perfectly picture her standing in the kitchen poring over paperwork and trying to organize a hundred things at once.

"I'm good," I said, dropping my purse and flopping down on the couch. "Work is going great and I got to do girls' night out with Laney last night."

"Oh, how is she? I still can't believe I haven't met the famous Nate yet! Although from the pictures she's posted I'd say she caught herself a live one." She chuckled.

"Nah, she keeps him in line," I joked. "And she's great—Nate is officially moving in next month."

"Aw. I'm so happy for her!"

"Yeah, me too."

Silence.

Crap. I knew she was thinking about how she wished the exact same thing for me.

I took a deep breath and, for some godforsaken reason, decided to share. "So, listen. About tonight, I actually have a date so I won't be able to make it."

More silence.

"Mom?"

"You have a date," she stated more than asked.

"Yes. I have a date."

"With a man." Again, more statement than question.

"No, with a small child. Of course with a man!"

"I...I don't...you really have a date?" This time it was a definite question.

"Yes, Mother. You make it sound as if I have a giant goiter or an issue with body odor. I've actually been told I'm kind of adorable, you know. It's not outside the realm of possibility that a man would want to take me out and share a meal."

"Of course not! I was just so surprised. I mean, not surprised, just taken off guard. Of course someone would want to take you out—what man in his right mind wouldn't find you wonderful and precious?"

Oh lord, here we go.

"All right. You don't have to oversell it. Besides, it's just dinner. It's not a big deal."

At this point, I actually heard her whimper a little in her attempt to hold back her hopefulness. I had to cut this thing off—now.

"Anyway, I'm sorry I won't be able to make it, but tell Mrs. Rogers I'd be happy to talk to her grandson any other time about the regatta."

"Oh, right. Of course, the regatta. Don't worry yourself over it one bit. You focus on your evening out."

God, I hoped she wasn't drawing blood with how firmly she was biting her tongue. The call simply had to end before she injured herself.

"I'm going to run to the store and then get ready for dinner, but have a nice time tonight and I'll talk to you later, okay?"

"Okay, sweetheart. Have fun! I love you!"

"Love you too. Bye."

I was willing to wager she didn't even set the phone down before dialing my dad.

After my quick run to the drug store for my prescriptions, and a short but fruitful detour to a tiny boutique on the way home, I carefully chose an outfit for the night. Mark had said to dress however

I wanted so I decided to go for casual to communicate that I wasn't trying too hard. I went with my D&G harem pants, a cotton tank, and my favorite True Religion denim jacket since it was a bit cooler tonight. I left my make-up as it was, threw my hair up into a top-knot and brushed my teeth.

Now, if you're not in the habit of saying a daily prayer, then might I suggest taking advantage of teeth-brushing time for any necessary spiritual connection. You are unable to engage in anything but free thought or self-contemplation, therefore making it a great time to chat with the man upstairs.

*Hey God, how's it going? I'm feeling pretty okay but I'm a bit confused about the sexy man who seems to want to claim me or something. Also, my hair is weird this week—what's up with that? Oh, thanks for that awesome parking spot yesterday. And, lastly, as always, please let me live. Thanks, God!*

Spit and rinse.

I know it's a bit untraditional but we all have to make it work any way we can, right?

Anyway, it didn't take me long to get ready so by the time 7:00 rolled around I was super restless and decided to throw on my wedges and meet Mark downstairs. I was just locking my door when my phone rang again.

"Hey, Mom, did you forget something?" I asked.

"No, not exactly," my mother replied. "It just occurred to me that you never said who this date was with."

Good God.

"That's because you don't know him. Did you think I was making up an imaginary date?" I decided teasing might do the trick and get her to stop snooping.

"Don't be silly." She forced a casual laugh. "So, it's not someone we know?"

I rolled my eyes as the elevator doors opened. "No, Mom, it's just this guy named Mark and, like I said, it's just a date—no big deal. I'm getting on the elevator now so I'm going to lose my signal. Have a great night!" I hung up the phone as the doors closed, freeing me from the painfully awkward conversation.

As I stepped from the building to wait on the sidewalk, my damn phone rang *again*. Dammit, woman, I love you dearly but stop calling me! I checked just to make sure it was indeed the woman who'd given birth to me whom I was sending to voicemail —and not, say, some friendly customer service rep from India— when I heard Mark's voice calling from his truck.

At the time, I'd been so relieved to have a distraction from Miss All-up-in-my-business that I'd let my guard down for a moment and had literally *gazed* at him. Luckily, I'd quickly remembered my mission to keep this shit casual and brought out the smirky face I reserve specifically for Mark.

Not that it had done any good. Here I was sitting across the table from the mouth-watering man who'd just thrown down and announced his "intentions" or something.

Eek!

I opened my mouth to say … something, when he beat me to it again.

"Okay with you if we order the Scotch eggs as an appetizer?" he asked.

Pride chimed in again, telling me what I already knew. "*Fiona, girl, you are in* fucking *trouble.*"

Dinner was awesome, as was the whole freaking date if I'm being honest. In addition to the perfection of the aforementioned Scotch eggs, Mark was an outstanding dinner companion. Not only did he look hot in his casual button-down, but he was funny and smart and considerate without laying it on thick at all. He maintained the same sarcastic charm that was quickly catching me up in his web, and I almost forgot I was supposed to be resisting this dating thing.

Thinking about it, I was shocked to realize that not only had I never had a boyfriend, but I don't think I'd had an actual date—the kind that hadn't been planned as merely the precursor to a scheduled tumble in the sheets—since high school. This dinner with Mark was my first actual adult date, a fact that suddenly made me a bit sad.

*"Don't be sad! We can still turn this around into great after-dinner sex!"* said Vagina, who was then echoed by her pervy cohorts.

I needed Guilt back to remind me why having a boyfriend was a terrible idea and was totally unfair to a guy like Mark—a guy who, I was coming to realize, was quite wonderful.

But this kind of thinking was getting me nowhere, so I had to back this truck up and get back into the good time I'd been having. And what better way to accomplish this than to talk about his double-crossing dad who was about to get bitch-slapped by Karma? I don't know why everybody assumes I'm so sweet.

"So tomorrow's the day, huh?" I asked as I scooped up the last forkful of chocolate cake. He even let me have the last bite—what in the hell is a girl supposed to do with that?!

"Yeah," he said, scratching the little bit of scruff on his chin. "I think Jake and I are going to have to admit defeat and let my mom go in by herself. But we will definitely be listening outside that door in case he goes off on her."

"I think that's smart to let her go in alone."

"Oh you do, do you? What a surprise." He grinned at me. I wanted to kiss that grin right off his face.

"Yes, I do. She needs to finish this on her own terms," I said in all seriousness.

"Well, I'm so glad you approve, Shortcake." He gave a little bow.

"You sound so sincere," I responded with a tilt of my head.

"Then I didn't say it right." He flagged the waiter for our check with that damn grin still planted on his stupid hot face.

"Oh shut up." That was my brilliant come-back. Awesome. "What do you think he'll do?"

"There's not a whole lot he can do. That's the beauty of it."

"Well, I'm glad you'll be there to back your mom up in case there's trouble."

"I'd never let her get hurt." His tone was quiet and serious.

I had no response.

## Chapter Twenty-Eight

## CLEANUP IN ROOM 437

**M**ARK

I was a little disappointed I let dinner end on such a sober note because up to that point it had been damn fun. Fiona loved her food, something I'd already known from her cooking and road trip binging, but it was great seeing her in her element. She fought me for the last egg and moaned her way through her main course so I had little option but to let her eat most of the dessert while I watched and tried not to get hard. What I didn't understand was how the girl stayed so tiny with the way she ate. I guess she somehow burned it off by running her mouth like she does—something I was now finding to be mostly charming as opposed to irritating, as I'd first thought.

I held her hand on the way outside and kept a firm grip when she tried to pry hers apart. After a huff and an accompanying eye roll, she relented and didn't try to pull away again until I helped her into the truck. She fidgeted for the entirety of the short ride back to her place.

"Shortcake, I can actually *hear* you thinking, you're doing it so hard," I said as I pulled into a parking spot a block away from her building.

She scoffed and released her seatbelt. "For your information, I was thinking about my mother," she lied—poorly.

"Oh?"

"Yes, as a matter of fact."

I let that sit for a minute while I went around and helped her out of the truck. Her hand wasn't shaking as it had been when we'd gotten to the restaurant, but she was definitely flustered.

"So, were you thinking about how to tell your mother about the guy you're about to invite up to your bed?"

That earned me an indignant gasp and an arm punch. Totally worth it.

While she was busy assaulting me, I cut in with, "Because if that's the case, you won't have much to say. You can, however, tell her about the guy who took you to dinner because he likes you and enjoys your company. The same guy who is going to walk you to your door and kiss you goodnight—and then, tomorrow, he'll call and ask for another date. That guy, you can tell her about."

I don't know that I've ever actually seen a person sputter, but that is the best way to describe the sounds that came out of Fiona's mouth at that moment. I may have done the impossible and rendered her speechless. I pulled her along the sidewalk while she tried to recover. This time she didn't even attempt pulling away.

I was as good as my word and after a hot fucking kiss that began to stray into groping territory, I unlocked her condo door and gently pushed her inside while she stared up at me with lust-glazed eyes. I'm sure mine were a mirror image.

Now I was headed home but figured a call to Jake was in order.

"Yo, dickhead!" he greeted as usual.

"Hey, shit-for-brains. I'm calling about tomorrow. You come to any conclusions?"

He sighed. "I don't know. Part of me wants to storm in there and let him have it and the other part of me would be happy to never lay eyes on him again. The only conclusion I've been able to come to is that we need to make sure Mom comes out of it unscathed."

"Ditto. I think we're gonna have to let her go in like she wants. But no matter what she says, you and I will be right outside the door, not waiting in the car like a pair of douchebags."

"Damn straight. You want to tell her or do you want me to?"

"You go ahead. I'm headed home and I need some shut-eye. What time are we going over?"

"I think she said 10:30."

"Sounds good. I'll meet you two there unless I hear differently before then."

"Sure thing. Later."

"Later."

The next morning, I rolled up to the medical building and parked my truck in the space next to my mom's car. My nerves were tight and I couldn't wait to get this over with. I'd had a hard time sleeping, despite my level of exhaustion from the week's activities. My mind had kept wandering to the various possible outcomes today could have held had we not recovered the money. My gut burned with fury over my father's intended plan to take the money and let my mom fall prey to whatever the goons had in mind.

The only thing that cheered me was knowing that even if he had gotten the money, his idiotic plan involved handing it right over to another group of con artists. In other words, he'd be eyeballs deep in shit regardless. I believe that was the thought that had finally let me drift off around two this morning.

I found Jake and our mom in the main lobby and I had to do a double-take. Was she wearing makeup? I took her in from head to toe and realized that not only had she done her face up, but she was wearing a stylish outfit that looked new and fit her perfectly. The blouse was a deep blue, and the black skirt hit just above the knee, showing off her legs and—holy shit, she was wearing heels. Not Shortcake-height heels, but heels nonetheless. What had happened to my mother?

She spotted me and gave me a nervous smile and a little wave. Jake was pacing beside her and only spared me a quick glance as I approached.

"You look pretty," I told my mother as I bent to kiss her cheek. "You ready for this? Jake and I can always—" I began, but she cut me off.

"Absolutely not. I'm as ready as I'll ever be."

"Let's get this over with then," grumbled Jake, and we all headed for the elevator with him leading the way.

Outside room 437, my mom gave our hands one last squeeze and then she slipped through the door. This was really happening. Finally.

The sound of her heels clicking toward the far side of the room reverberated in my skull and I stopped breathing for a moment so I could hear everything.

"Jim." Okay, good strong voice—confident.

"Thank God! It's about time. I was starting to get—wow, look at you!" He sounded completely surprised. Ha! Eat your heart out, old man!

"I have some news." She plowed right on through.

"Please tell me you got the money." His voice came out weak and a bit whiney.

"I did," she replied.

"Thank God." I could hear his relieved exhale all the way out in the hallway. I glanced around to see if anybody else was paying attention to us. The hall was empty.

"I did…" she repeated, drawing out the words, "but then there was an unfortunate run-in with the guys you borrowed it from. They weren't too keen on me keeping it."

"What the fuck?! That's why I told you to come earlier this week before they had a chance to come to the house and take it!"

I moved to enter the room, but Jake held me back. "Give her another minute." Where he'd suddenly found his calm was beyond me. I was on fucking fire.

"Is that so?" my mother asked, as smooth as can be. "What made you think they were coming to my house? According to our last conversation they didn't even know about me."

"I don't know…they didn't!" he tried to cover. "Fuck! The fucking money! Did they take it all?"

"They took the money before it even made it across the state line, not at my house! And I'm afraid I have nothing to give you, so you'll just have to figure out something else."

"B…but," he began again, "what about your money—the money you're investing?"

"Oh, that? Well, I think I've changed my mind. I'm not too fond of the kind of people you associate with," she responded breezily.

"Well what in the fucking hell am I supposed to do now?!" the asshole shouted.

Jake had to hold me back again.

"I haven't the first idea, Jim. But I can tell you what you're *not* going to do." Her voice had suddenly turned icy, her words cutting the air in a tone I'd never heard from her before. "You are *not* going to contact me ever again, and you are *not* going to set foot in this city again.

"Then you are going to *forget* that you ever had a wife and two sons, something that should be habit by now anyway. And lastly, when you get served with divorce papers later today, you are going to sign those damn things as fast as possible so I can get on with *my life,*" she practically hissed at him.

What the fuck? I looked to Jake only to find that he was just as surprised as I was. He shook his head at me and we kept eaves-dropping.

"Well then, I think I've said everything I need to say so I'm heading out. And if you want one more piece of advice, you should figure out how to walk soon because I know more than a few people who want you gone even more than I do. And a couple of them could bench press you with one hand tied behind their backs."

The sound of her clicking heels resumed, followed by our father's pathetic pleading.

"Kelly, wait! You can't just ditch me here!" This was followed by a thump and a cry of pain, but the heels never faltered.

Our mom came strutting out of the room and right past us toward the elevators. We were both struck stupid and it took us a moment to get our feet in gear. Still ahead of us, she passed by a nurse.

"You may want to check on the man in 437. I think he might have fallen out of bed." The nurse hurried by us and our mother turned around. "You coming or what?"

Who was this woman and what the hell had she done with my mother?

"Shit, my favorite part was when she said Lou and Terry weren't 'keen' on letting her keep the money," Jake said, slapping the table.

Our mom chuckled and I laughed before taking another pull on my beer. "I highly doubt that word has ever come from either of their mouths," I responded.

"Thankfully, I never met them so I'll just have to take your word for it." My mom tucked her hair behind her ear and took a sip of her champagne. "I can't believe you boys have me drinking champagne at one in the afternoon."

"I can't believe you managed to rip the old man to shreds without even technically lying. It's like you were a morally upstanding version of Nurse Ratched. God, I wish we'd recorded that." Jake sighed. Mom and I snickered.

"I don't mean this to come out wrong," I said, "but I didn't know you had that in you. You eviscerated him and stayed as cool as shit."

"I didn't know I did either." She gave me a small smile. "And watch your language." She smacked my hand. "Now, you boys may not have anything to do today but I've got a long to-do list and I'm working tonight." She stood from the table and took her glass to the sink.

Jake and I both stood and gave her hugs goodbye.

"Next time someone at works steps out of line I'm sending you in," I joked. "You were amazing."

And that was no joke.

## Chapter Twenty-Nine

# A CRASH COURSE IN GYM ETIQUETTE

**F**IONA

"This isn't exactly what I had in mind when you said 'date.'" I looked up a bit pitifully into Mark's handsome face.

"What do you mean? I love this place." He blinked those ridiculous lashes.

I watched him take a satisfied perusal of his surroundings. "I'm aware." I gestured to his biceps. "Although I should have known when you told me to wear a t-shirt and 'those stretchy pants.' For some reason, I just thought you wanted a better look at my ass."

"Well that's just a plus," he said with a naughty grin followed by a smack to said ass. "Come on, Shortcake, enough stalling."

I should have guessed our destination moments after he'd picked me up from my condo after work and handed me a Belk bag. The level of excitement that had subsequently coursed through my veins at the gesture was more than a little over the top. But when a man like him—one whose entire being screams that he is not now and never will be a shopper—gives you a department store bag, what's a girl to do other than swoon? I snatched the bag and kissed him on the cheek. My Spidey senses should have anticipated a bribe of some sort.

"I asked the sales lady to pick something that a girl with only heels in her closet would wear. This is what she came up with. I hope you like it."

He looked nervous so I tore into the bag to end his misery. Inside were a small pair of pristine white socks and a shoe box with "Madden Girl" on the lid. A shoe box! Dear sweet lord, remind me why I wasn't keeping this man forever? I lifted the lid and tissue paper to reveal the most sparkly sneakers I'd ever seen. They actually shimmered in the sunlight streaming through the truck window. I felt like crying, but I held myself in check as I turned to face Mark.

"I love them!" I said as I threw myself across the seat and onto his lap.

One PG make-out session and a quick drive later, we'd arrived at our destination where my enthusiasm had begun to wane a bit— but only for the location, not for the first pair of adult athletic shoes I'd ever owned (sparkles or not).

"Fine," I huffed and stepped up to the strange contraption that had been promised to provide me with tone and definition in my upper arms.

Mark ran his fingers deliberately down the entire length of my arms before moving my hands to grasp the handles of the machine. I shivered.

I wished I could blame it on this godforsaken den of torture he had lured me into. Known to some people as a gym, the establishment was loud and smelly and filled with sweaty people and machines that looked like robots on the precipice of taking over the earth. But, no, this horrid place was not the cause of my shiver.

It was the delectable man standing behind me. The very same one who had been slowly torturing me for the last two weeks with flirty touches, passionate kisses, and nights ending in complete sexual frustration.

The entire gaggle of bitches in my head and nether regions were all up in my face insisting I find some way to pin the sexy beast down and screw the living hell out of him. I suspected even Guilt was secretly booking some alone time with her vibrator at this point. We were all strung as tight as one of Mark's t-shirts and I was bound and determined to get this show on the road.

Unfortunately, the current environment was less than ideal for seduction. So "triceps pushdowns" it was. Ugh.

"Now, I've set it at the lowest weight since this is your first time and I don't want you to overdo it." He stepped back from the stack of black weights in the center of the machine and faced me, apparently assessing my position or something.

"Oh come on," I argued, totally offended. "You can add a little more. I *have* exercised before, you know." I didn't mention that the last time had been high school gym class.

He put his hands up in a defensive position. "All right, Short-cake. Point taken—just trying to look out for you." He added another couple weights.

Honestly, how hard could it be?

Hands on the bar, I slowly pushed downward.

Nothing.

Evidently, I'd have to invest a little effort. No big deal.

I pushed down with what I considered a generous amount of strength.

The goddamn bar didn't budge.

Was that snickering I heard? My gaze flashed to Mark who was unsuccessfully attempting to smother his laugh.

I cleared my throat in reproach and he assumed a neutral expression.

No more fooling around, I was going to rule this damn triceps thingy!

I pushed down with every ounce of effort I possessed and let out a very unladylike grunt as the bar descended and I felt the entirety of my upper body scream in protest. Once it reached its lowest position, I triumphantly released the bar and prepared to woot-woot in victory.

That was, until the weights crashed back down on their stack with a staggeringly loud boom and every single face in the entire sweaty, smelly, robot-filled joint swung in our direction.

Mark covered his eyes and shook his head slowly in what I assumed was either shame or disbelief.

I just did what twenty-four years of humiliating myself had taught me to do. I met the disapproving gazes, smiled, and shrugged my shoulders. "Oops."

After the weight machine debacle Mark decided cardio was the way to go, so he set me up on an elliptical machine and then he proceeded to run an entire marathon on a treadmill.

Surprising myself, I actually had fun. This particular robot was sort of like a self-powered carnival ride. I could go forward or backward and the thing was wired up to a TV which I could program to any channel. I ended up getting exercise while not even noticing because I was so engrossed in watching Ina Garten prepare the loveliest picnic for Jeffrey—although I always think to myself that a more apt spelling would be Geoffrey. Right?

Anyway, once Ina signed off, I was ready to do the same so I hopped off the elliptical, nearly falling on my face in the process. They should really post a warning to use caution when exiting the

252 • SYLVIE STEWART

ride. I signaled to Mark that I was heading for the locker room and he nodded and smiled in return.

However, I did not go directly to the locker room. It seemed my feet had been nailed to the rubber coated floor. In the process of completing his world-record marathon, Mark had taken the liberty of removing his shirt, much to the delight of the female occupants of the room. But, damn, I could not blame them one bit.

Sweat glistened on his chest, face, and arms while his legs pumped furiously on the treadmill's speeding belt. There was not one jiggle in sight, just firm hard-earned muscle and gleaming skin. He noticed my pause and his eyes stayed glued to mine, his feet never missing a beat. When I still didn't move, his smile transitioned into shit-eating territory.

He knew exactly what he was doing to me. Damn that man.

I forced my body to turn and get a move on.

In addition to being frustrating, the last two weeks had also been thrilling, fun, and, dare I say *romantic*? Mark challenged me in all the right ways while also making me feel like I was the most beautiful woman on earth, something I knew for a fact wasn't true. That honor belongs to Penelope Cruz and no one will ever convince me otherwise.

The only thing missing was the actual sex, although all the making out we'd been doing was pretty stellar if I do say so myself. Still, I was acutely aware that this arrangement was like no other I'd ever had. Mark was kind of my boyfriend.

Eek!

One piece of evidence pointing me toward that conclusion was Mark's reaction to a situation the previous weekend.

On that Friday, my mother had called, but this time it had not been to grill me about my mystery man. I was still trying to keep Mark under wraps lest I unleash the mothership and she descend to take his tuxedo measurements. The purpose of the call was actually to tell me that Chandler Rogers, Barbara Rogers' grandson, was going to be in Greensboro the next day and would like to take me to lunch to talk about the fundraising regatta for leukemia research. This was the kind of thing I did all the time and I didn't think twice before agreeing.

Well, let me just say that someone else had some real specific second thoughts about that idea.

"You're going out on a date with this guy?" Mark asked in disbelief when I told him why I couldn't hang out on Saturday.

"It's not a date." I laughed, but inside I felt a pang of satisfaction at his jealousy.

"Then what would you call it? A man who is not related to you is taking you to lunch alone." I could *hear* his scowl over the phone.

"It's just a lunch meeting to talk about some fundraising for my parents' pet cause." I was very careful not to get too specific.

*Go ahead and get your judgy pants on.* I had not told Mark a single thing about my leukemia or any of its implications. He was supposed to be my fuck buddy and fuck buddies did not talk about cancer. The fact that we were not actually fucking did cast a bit of doubt on that reasoning, however.

"Don't you find it kind of odd that your parents are constantly calling *you* to help out with *their* charity?"

I inhaled sharply, ready to let him have it, but what could I really say without revealing too much?

He continued, "I mean, don't get me wrong. I think you're a very generous person for volunteering your free time, and I feel the same about your parents. But why are you better qualified than they are to inform this guy about some fundraising event? Especially when it sounds exactly like a date?"

Gah!

*Well, Mark, the fact is I am the proverbial poster child for this charity, seeing as the entire reason for its existence is the woman you are currently not fucking. I am often brought out like a show pony to be admired and serve as an example of the possibilities that lie ahead. I'm actually quite similar to Harry Potter, but instead of being "The Boy Who Lived," I'm "The Girl Who Lived"—but the amount of staring and attention is pretty much the same. Sorry I haven't mentioned I'm a leukemia survivor, but if I told you then I'd have to tell you everything and you would treat me like a fragile piece of china and then I'd have no choice but to punch you in the dick.*

No, I couldn't really say that.

"We're just…we're just really close, and they count on me. They've always helped me out so much, so I help them when I can." Oh, and because Guilt won't let me say no. "Look, it's just lunch. Then you and I can do something afterward." I tried to appease him.

He exhaled. "Fine."

"Good."

"Not 'good,' fine."

That made me grin. "We can go see a movie and I'll even let you choose," I tempted.

"You know I'm not seeing anybody else, right?" Mark said out of nowhere, or at least that's how it felt. We were not talking about this.

"Hmm," was all I could make myself say.

I heard a reluctant little chuckle from the other end of the line. "You're killing me, smalls. I'll see you tomorrow. You'd better be up for some hard-core action because I have plans for you, Shortcake."

Ooh! This sounded promising. Thank God he was finally coming to his senses. And I had the best La Perla thong for the occasion! The lady bits started to cheer, but then his voice cut in and all our sexy-time hopes were snuffed out like the slutty girl in every horror movie ever made.

"The new Bruce Willis movie opened today." His chuckle had intensified and become downright self-satisfied—and dare I say a bit mean-spirited. Jerk-face.

As I made my way into the locker room and away from his tempting bod, I recalled that smug, jerk-faced chuckle and cursed him for once again making me all hot and bothered while refusing to deliver.

I was in need of a cold shower, but since I had no fresh clothes to change into, I just used the facilities and splashed my face with water while I waited for Mark. I was reaching for a paper towel when a sugary sweet voice came from behind me.

"Don't get your hopes up, sweetie. He doesn't take call-backs so you'd best enjoy tonight. You may want to think about a shower, though."

I looked around, face dripping, and saw Sports Bra Barbie standing behind me, designer water bottle in hand and boobs hailing an enthusiastic salute. I may have stared. Okay, I totally stared. How did she fit those things in that bra? With the distraction presented by her mammary display, it took a moment for her words to register.

Wait.

What the fuck?

I pointed stupidly at myself. "Um, are you talking to me?"

She rolled her eyes and shifted to one hip. "Duh."

What were we, five?

*"Who does this bitch think she is?"* asked Vagina, who was already on edge from the particularly tough couple weeks.

I took a moment to wipe my face and calm everyone down, and then it suddenly occurred to me. This girl was one of Mark's one-nighters. And evidence suggested she was seeing all shades of green and did not like the sight of the competition on her turf.

I lifted myself to my full height—damn that sweet man for buying me athletic shoes that only afforded an extra inch! "And you are?" I asked, attempting a tone of complete confidence.

"Aubrey," she answered and inspected her flawless nails. "I'm just trying to look out for you, honey," she said with the utmost *in*sincerity, conveniently leaving off the unspoken portion that was most likely something along the lines of, "as I help you over this scenic cliff and down to the rocky waters below. Whoops, my bad."

I gave her a fake-ass smile in return. "Thanks, *sugar*, but I think I've got it covered." I started for the exit.

Her hands came up in defense. "Fine, but don't come crying to me when he forgets your number."

I continued on by at a measured pace, resisting the urge to throw an insult at her, and walked into the main gym area in search of Mark. Our minds must have been in sync because I practically ran straight into him. He grabbed my upper arms before I collided with his sweaty bare chest.

"Hey, Shortcake. You ready to head out?"

"Definitely," I said, upset with myself that I'd allowed Sports Bra Barbie to get under my skin.

And, speak of the devil. "Hi, Mark." I heard her voice come from behind me again. I was going to have to rename her Ambush Barbie.

I looked up at Mark and saw his eyes drift over my head to the big-boobed model behind me. Who was I kidding? I couldn't compare to her. I didn't even want to. I was only in this thing for the sex anyway and once I finally got that a few more times he would move on to another version of Aubrey.

"Oh, hi," Mark paused and I saw a flash of panic cross his face. Interesting. "Aubrey," he practically shouted.

He'd forgotten her name.

Is it bad that I wanted to laugh my ass off?

After that, the girl couldn't get away fast enough. Mark popped into the men's locker room for a quick shower and then we were off.

"Well," Mark said as we exited the wretched gym and made our way to his truck. "That didn't really go exactly as I'd envisioned."

Not sure if he was talking about my less-than-stellar athletic prowess or the run-in with Aubrey, I decided to assume the former. "Hmm, then it seems you're not quite as bright as I thought you were. I will say, though, I did have some fun on that elliptical thing —it really has some potential."

"You were a great sport," he said, grabbing my hand and lifting it to his mouth for a quick kiss.

"I'm glad you think so. We'll see how you do when I take you shopping."

Was it my imagination or did his face pale a bit?

*Chapter Thirty*

# DOG SWEATERS AND PANIC ATTACKS

**F**IONA

The following night was Jake's long-awaited welcome home dinner. And as far as I knew, I was still the only one aware that he was considering a permanent move.

As promised, I'd set up the meeting with Jax and by the laughing and clear camaraderie I'd witnessed, I assumed the meeting had gone exceptionally well. What would happen next was anyone's guess.

My main focus was still on getting Mark back into bed, hussy that I am, and the previous night had not born fruit as I had hoped. He'd, once again, extricated himself from the nice steamy clutch we'd had going on and had left me practically panting in his wake. Clit was no longer speaking to me, and all the other girls were beginning to curse Mark's name. He was now known universally by my nether regions as "That Fucking Clit Tease" and "Future Bloodstain on Karma's Highway." What in God's name was he waiting for?!

Happy to have a distraction, I spent the morning grocery shopping with Laney and fielding phone calls from Kelly on what to bring, what to wear, what time to come over and about ten other things. I'd heard all about her stellar performance at the rehab center and was so looking forward to seeing her again and giving her a giant hug. I was so flipping proud of her.

Nate and Gavin agreed to take Rocco out for the afternoon so Laney and I could prepare for the dinner party. Well, it was really so Laney could frantically clean the house and I could prepare for the dinner party. I love that girl like a sister, but one of these days I may have to call an intervention. Although I did have to admit the house was much tidier in general since Nate appeared on the scene. Still, Laney had more junk drawers than anyone I'd ever met—yet I was constantly uncovering odd bits of things in every imaginable spot in her house. It was not unusual to pick up a throw pillow and find a pack of paperclips and a bottle of cough syrup hiding underneath. True story.

Anyway, while she stashed things away, I washed and cut various ingredients and prepared dips and bread dough. When I had done everything I could, I retrieved three large cardboard sheets from their hiding spot in the garage. I was just unwrapping them when Laney reappeared.

"Oh my God! I can't believe we actually did this!" She covered her mouth.

I ripped the first sheet of wrapping and uncovered a giant poster-sized image of a young Jake and Mark—the very one that had sent us into fits of laughter at our first lunch with Kelly. Mark's skinny little ass faced the camera and Jake's very naughty smile beamed as he held his brother in a headlock. See? I'd known he was trouble from the beginning.

Impatient to see the rest, Laney ripped open the next two—one taken on Jake's sixteenth birthday, and another of both brothers where Jake was acting like a jackass and Mark was smiling shyly at the camera.

Sweet Mark.

Gah!

We ran around like crazy people trying to finish all the last-minute preparations while leaving ourselves time to get pretty before everyone arrived. I had chosen a gold metallic flared dress with wedge booties, and I had invested considerable effort into convincing Laney to wear a halter style pin-up dress in a vibrant red. She was stunning and I just knew Nate would choke on his tongue. I was putting the finishing touches on Laney's make-up when the doorbell rang.

"I know we're early but I just figured you could use the help so I dragged Jake out the door and we hit the road—oh dear lord!" Kelly stopped in her tracks on the way into the main living area. Laney, having just answered the door, trailed behind her with Jake bringing up the rear. Kelly covered her face and I couldn't tell if she was holding back laughter or tears at the sight of the huge photos of her boys. I didn't have to wait long to find out because she began fanning her face. "Oh, you girls are gonna make me cry! Just look at my sweethearts."

But my eyes didn't go to the photos. Instead, they traveled down Kelly's body, taking in her slim frame and the lovely floral wrap dress covering it. I also marveled at her styled hair (a layered bob!) and carefully applied makeup. This was one beautiful babe!

"Kelly, holy shit, you look hot!"

"Completely," echoed Laney.

Kelly colored slightly and drew her eyes away from the photos and down to her dress. "You think?" she asked hesitantly.

"I *know*. Damn, woman," I said, and all three of us girls giggled a bit.

"Jesus Christ, what the hell is that?!" Jake was now gaping at the photos, having just noticed them.

"Um, surprise?" said Laney as I simultaneously shouted, "Welcome home!"

By the time guests started arriving, Jake was pretty much over the shock and had actually started throwing out some self-deprecating jokes. Nate's parents arrived, bickering about something I couldn't quite hear, and soon after, Rocco burst through the door from the garage and practically sprinted into Riordan's arms. He was subsequently rewarded with a bear hug and a swing onto the older man's back. Erin, Nate's mom, smothered Rocco with kisses as he pretended to be offended. "Nana, I'm practically six!"

Moving at a more human pace, Gavin sauntered in and headed straight for the kitchen counter, stealing some mushroom crostini and a scallop skewer. I moved to smack him on the back of his stupid head when I heard a thump from the direction of the garage.

Turning around, I caught sight of Nate rubbing absently at the back of his head where the door had obviously just smacked him. He stood still in the doorway and his eyes were laser-focused on Laney, who was chatting with Erin. Laney hadn't seen him yet but Nate had apparently seen all he needed to because in the next moment he opened his mouth and said loudly, "Marry me."

Everyone, except Rocco of course, stood in stunned silence as Laney finally turned to Nate. "W...what?" She brought her right hand up to her cheek.

Nate drew himself up and said it again, just as loudly. "Marry me."

"Oh, dear sweet baby Jesus," Erin stage whispered and clutched her chest.

Laney took a hesitant step toward Nate. "Are you serious?" I could see her hands trembling as they held both of her cheeks.

"I've never been more serious in my entire life." Nate stepped toward her until only a foot separated them. "Well, what's your answer? Don't leave me hanging." Nate smiled his devastatingly handsome smile accompanied by his equally devastating dimple. How could a girl ever say no to that face?

"I may be mistaken but I don't think you even asked me a question. It sounded more like a demand," Laney said with a sassy little grin as her hands dropped to her hips.

Nate rolled his eyes and then took her hands in his and asked with appropriate sincerity, "Laney, will you please marry me?"

"Hell yes!" Laney exclaimed and threw her arms around him.

"Mommy said 'hell'!" yelled Rocco.

Fifteen minutes and a billion hugs later, I stood gazing at my best friend whose face was literally glowing with happiness. Or maybe it was just the reflection off the gorgeous diamond that now adorned her hand. It turned out Nate had not been planning a trip to Paris, he'd been planning a proposal instead. When he'd caught sight of her in that dress, though, instead of choking on his tongue he'd spontaneously proposed.

I was still admiring the ring when I suddenly felt a tingle run up my spine and I knew, I just knew, the cause of it. As unbelievable as it sounds, I actually felt his presence in the room. What the hell? At that moment, no force known to man—not even an invitation to cobble shoes with Jimmy Choo himself—could have kept me from turning to face Mark. My belly took a supersonic nosedive while my heart suddenly rocked out to heavy metal and I stared.

He was sheer perfection—black dress slacks, pressed moss green button-down with just the right number of buttons undone, clean-shaven face, and a look weighted in ... *something*, directed firmly at me.

My mouth forgot how to produce saliva and my forehead suddenly felt damp, as did pretty much my entire body. I opened my mouth but had no words, and he was all the way across the room anyway, so it wasn't as if he could hear me. A very unfamiliar sensation swept over me, and in that moment I recognized I had real *feelings* for this man. Feelings that had little to do with my schemes to get him into bed or my admiration of his hot bod. These feelings made me want to keep him for myself—damn the consequences.

My face must have been an open book because Mark's eyes swept over every inch of it and then he visibly exhaled and dipped his head, shoving his hands in his pockets. He seemed...relieved.

Wishing simultaneously that I could run away or I could pull him off to another room and figure this crazy thing out, I chose neither and focused on hostess and cooking duties instead. I withdrew to the kitchen, excusing myself from my conversation and ensuring a small bit of privacy for the panic attack I would be experiencing momentarily.

I gripped the counter, still feeling confused and hot. I didn't understand this emotion that rushed through me at the sight and thought of Mark. I took a few calming breaths and then let it settle in.

Maybe this was kind of how a dog feels when presented with her first doggie sweater. It's strange and foreign and a bit intimidating at first, and she thinks, *no, not for me, I'm good.* Then once it's on and she wears it around for a while she starts to feel the warm cuddliness of it, not to mention the awesome zebra print— *just deal with it because even if it's imaginary, no dog of mine is going to dress in anything less than designer wear.*

I took stock of my emotions and general state of mind when I was with Mark or when I thought of him, which I couldn't seem to stop doing lately. Yeah, it definitely felt like I was wrapped up in something warm and soft. It was a damn nice sweater and it felt really freaking comfy. I was thinking this sweater might be for me after all.

So, I guess I was the dog and my feelings were the sweater? Or Mark was the sweater and I was still the dog? Wait, that's not a very flattering analogy. Whatever. This was too confusing.

I vowed to put the thoughts aside for the moment and directed my attention to the soup simmering away in a large pot. Time to get down to business and ignore the giant elephant in the room— the one that may have been wearing a zebra-print sweater.

## Chapter Thirty-One

# ME AND MY BIG FAT FUCKING MOUTH

*M*ARK

    I stood next to Jake as he gave me shit about the ridiculous photos that someone, *ahem*, had decided to blow up in a clear effort to add just the right tone of humiliation to the evening. One point to the ladies. Well done.

I took my lumps and didn't even attempt to dish any back. I was too distracted by the thought of Fiona and that look she'd given me when I'd walked in tonight. There was no way I had misread it. She may have tried to hide it, but it was right there on her face before she fled to the kitchen.

She was falling for me.

Thank fuck.

No, seriously, this bullshit plan of mine to withhold sex until I was sure she was in just as deep as I was (Christ, even my choice of words was sexually driven)? Worst plan ever. My balls were so blue it was a wonder I could still walk.

Now that I had some confirmation of Fiona's feelings, it was *on.* This party couldn't be over fast enough. Shortcake had better watch out because I was coming for her. (Goddammit, I did it again—I really needed to get laid.)

I decided to give her a little space since it wasn't as if I could have my dirty way with her on Laney's kitchen counter. And besides, she was full-on deer-in-headlights, so it was only fair to give her a minute. Not to mention, the smells coming from the kitchen were nothing short of fan-fucking-tastic, so I wasn't about to mess that up either.

A strong hand gripped my shoulder and turned me around.

"Did you hear the good news?" Nate asked, a huge-ass grin on his face.

"What news? I just got here."

Laney popped up between us and shoved her hand in my face. For a second, I thought she was going to back-hand me—I'm sure I deserved it for something—but then I noticed the diamond that was about to jab a hole in my eye. Holy shit, he'd actually pulled it off!

"No shit?" I looked to Nate.

"No shit," he replied, still grinning like an idiot.

I wrapped Laney up in a hug. "You know, darlin', you could do better but I'm happy for you anyway."

She pulled back and punched my arm, but her grin was just as big as Nate's. "Thanks, I think."

I held out my hand to shake Nate's. "So you worked up the balls to do it, huh? Congrats, man." And I found I was genuinely happy and excited for them. Look at me being all mature.

"Thanks," he replied and then looked around. "Where's Bay? I thought you were picking her up on your way."

"She couldn't make it after all, but you should definitely call her with the good news—I know she'll be upset she missed it."

My plan had indeed been to pick Bailey up on my way, but when I'd gotten to her place I could tell something was up. If I didn't know better, I'd have sworn she'd been crying.

"Can you just make something up?" she'd asked when she'd opened her door and poked her head out.

"Like what? Why don't you want to go all of a sudden?"

"What's the big deal? I've never even met your brother," she'd countered, suddenly defensive.

I'd reluctantly agreed to drop it, knowing I was already running late, but I was still determined to get to the bottom of this. Just not right now. No, I had some awesome food to eat, some hands to shake, and my girl to take home. Not bad for a Saturday night.

"Have you ever thought about being a chef?" I asked a few hours later when we were on our way to my place. I was making my intentions crystal clear by not even asking if my place was okay. Fiona would have to speak up on her own if she wanted to call it a night. She'd willingly left her car at Laney's so I wasn't expecting any surprises.

"No way," Fiona said, shaking her head emphatically.

"Shortcake, everything you've cooked has tasted incredible. You'd kill it as a chef." I was genuinely puzzled at the vehemence of her dismissal. "What was that soup again?"

She smiled in my direction. "Zucchini with crème fraîche and cilantro."

"See! I don't even like zucchini and I had seconds—that's how good your food is. And don't even get me started on the chicken." I grabbed her hand and held it on my thigh.

She continued to grin at me. "Well, I'm glad you enjoyed it, and I really do love to cook. But I would never make it as a chef."

"Why the hell not?" I was feeling defensive on her behalf and I got that feeling again that there was something I was missing. Somebody had made her see herself negatively. I was hoping I wasn't going to have to kick anybody's ass.

She sighed. "Well, first of all, I don't have a degree. Second, being a chef takes lots of smarts and the ability to remain calm under pressure. Does that sound like me?"

I thought about it for a moment. Had she asked me that question a month ago, I probably would have laughed, but now I had seen first-hand how good she was at maneuvering her way through tough situations. And she was so far from the dumb blonde I'd pegged her as in the beginning. "I think you're selling yourself short."

"I believe that detail is pretty obvious, big man." She laughed at my unintentional joke.

"Let me ask you this. Do you like the job you have now as much as you like cooking?"

She squeezed my hand. "It's a lot more complicated than that, Mark. Trust me."

I could tell the subject was closed for the night but I wasn't going to give up. My girl deserved to be happy in every way, and damn anybody and anything that stood in the way.

"So, now that you have me here, what are you going to do with me?" Fiona sat perched on my couch with one slim leg crossed over the other, her gold dress riding up her thighs and showcasing some short leather boots that belonged behind my back.

"I'm going to ask you a question." I stood a few feet away from her with my hands on my hips.

Her saucy smile fell a little. "Oh."

"You want to be with me?"

Her brow furrowed. "Of course. I would think that was obvious. I've been trying to get you back into bed for weeks—you're the one who keeps pulling away."

"You know that's not what I meant." I should have expected she'd deliberately misunderstand.

She uncrossed her legs and shifted forward on the couch, hands clasped on her lap. "Mark, you know I really like you, and I find you incredibly attractive. I also like spending time with you. But I'm not cut out to be anybody's girlfriend if that's what you're asking."

"That *is* what I'm asking and you know it." I kept my tone gentle. "I think you're scared and you're making excuses. What are you scared of?" I sat down next to her and grabbed one of her hands, rubbing the back of it with my thumb. "Shortcake, what's scaring you about this?"

She groaned and dropped her forehead to our connected hands on her lap. "Ugh. This is so hard. I don't know anymore."

"What is your gut telling you right now?" I asked, hoping like hell I'd get the answer I wanted.

"Honestly?" She pulled her head back up and looked at me.

"Honestly."

"It's telling me I can trust you."

"You can."

"It's also telling me that I am so horny I might actually cause you bodily harm if I get another brush-off, Mark."

I laughed. "No more brush-offs. I promise." It seemed Q & A time was over so I leaned in and met her lips with mine.

Things quickly became intense—we were both so keyed up from the last few weeks I was starting to wonder if I'd even last long enough to let her come first. Knowing I had to keep myself in check I decided to change up my game plan. I pulled away for a moment when I realized she had already gotten my belt undone and was working on my button with one hand while her other gripped the back of my neck.

"Come on, Shortcake, we're taking this to the bedroom." Before she could protest, I flipped her over my shoulder in a fireman's hold and strode down the hall. She shrieked and smacked my ass, threatening to put her heel somewhere unpleasant if I didn't let her down. It was cute.

I plopped her down unceremoniously on the bed.

"Why do you do that to me?!"

"Because I can." I shrugged my shoulders and then knelt on the bed.

She huffed and pulled her dress down.

"Oh, no you don't." I pushed it right back up and kept going until it was gathered in a golden swath under her breasts. "Damn." I'd missed seeing her like this, silky bare skin and lacey panties.

My hands parted her legs at the knees and I leaned in for a kiss on both of her inner thighs. Goosebumps rose on her skin and she gave a little gasp, so I buried my nose in the lace of her panties, feeling her heat and reveling in her scent. "Your panties are already damp," I said.

She panted a little. "No shit. You've had me so hot and bothered I've never done so much laundry in my life." She grabbed onto my head, as if I had any intentions of moving from my favorite spot in the world.

My fingers hooked in the sides of her panties and pulled them down and off. I brought my hands back up to part her folds and then swiped my tongue up, circling it around her clit.

"Oh God," she moaned.

Loving the taste of her, I continued my exploration with my tongue and then added my index finger, slowly making my way inside. She was soaked. I was hard as a rock and hoping like hell I could hang in there.

"Mark," she moaned as I found the perfect spot. "I want you inside me."

Not wanting to ignore the lady's request, I took one for the team and decided to comply. I quickly applied a condom from my nightstand and settled over her with my elbows on the bed and my hands framing her face.

"God, you're incredible," I murmured as she squirmed under me. I pushed her hair from her face and traced her lips with my thumb. She opened her mouth and bit it.

Okay, that was it. The combination of the squirming, biting, and lingering taste of her on my tongue propelled me to action and I pressed into her center, pulling back only once before thrusting completely inside. I groaned and she mewled like a cat, with her nails in my back to make the comparison particularly apt.

"Don't stop," she said, and I continued a slow rhythm while we both worked to remove her dress the rest of the way. Her flimsy bra was next and then my teeth tugged at her pebbled nipples while she groaned her approval and gripped the back of my head.

Wanting desperately to see her ride me, I easily flipped us over, without losing our connection, and thrust up into her. She cried out and found her rhythm, one hand to my chest and the other to her own breast.

Shit, that was hot.

I gripped her hip with one hand and grasped her ass with the other as she rode me. She picked up speed and began whimpering as I thrust up to meet her each time.

"Holy shit, Mark," she gasped.

"Shortcake," I responded through clenched teeth. "I need you to come."

She was moving even faster now and I couldn't understand the words coming out of her mouth. The only thing I knew was that nothing in my life had ever felt better and I was about to come in the next few seconds. I brought my thumb down to her clit and circled it a couple times.

That did the trick. She exploded around me, writhing and squeezing my cock with her inner walls as she climaxed. Needless to say, I was right behind her.

She collapsed in a sweaty heap on my chest with my cock still inside her. I couldn't have moved if I'd tried. To be honest, I wanted to stay just like this for the rest of my life with Fiona on top of me sated, happy, and relaxed.

Once I worked up the energy I brought my hand up to stroke her hair. "Are you still alive?"

"Barely," she mumbled. "Actually, I might be dead after all. I'm not sure yet. I'll get back to you."

I chuckled and the movement of my chest caused her to move with it.

"Hey, some people are trying to sleep here so knock it off," she said.

"I hate to break it to you, but there is the matter of the condom to take care of at some point." I continued to stroke her hair and had as little enthusiasm to break our contact as she did.

"Bah," was all she said.

"Are you a sheep now?"

"Shhh, not a sheep, asleep." She sounded drunk.

I couldn't help but laugh again, finally causing her to roll off me and collapse on the bed.

"I'll be right back." I leaned over and kissed her lips before pulling myself up to go take care of the condom.

When I got back to bed she was in the same exact position, gloriously naked and resting on her back with her hands above her head. I climbed over her again, dropping kisses on her belly, breasts, chin, and lips. My eyes roamed her face and she opened her drowsy eyes and gave me a smile so sweet it practically knocked the wind out of me.

Without any thought, I went ahead and did the dumbest thing in the world. I opened my big fucking mouth and said the one thing sure to ruin everything.

"I'm falling in love with you, Shortcake."

## Chapter Thirty-Two

# SCENT OF A MAN (AL PACINO WILL NOT BE APPEARING IN THIS FEATURE)

IONA

*No No No No No!*

Why did he have to say that? I was basking so blissfully in my afterglow and mentally writing my Dear Diary entry on the best sex of my life. I was even going to include classic phrases like "swollen staff" and "glistening portal of womanhood" and "fiery culmination," and he had to go and ruin it by saying the most fucking wonderful thing anybody could say to another person.

Dammit!

I proceeded to flip the fuck out by squeaking—yes, I actually squeaked—and then retreating as quickly as possible to the bathroom.

I'd been in Mark's house a couple times before, but never for long lest I use my womanly wiles to lure him into the bedroom at a time that conflicted with his "trick Fiona into buying the cow" plan. Up until this evening, I had only seen the main living space and the kitchen. The house was nestled in a quiet street in an older neighborhood with beautiful mature trees and winding sidewalks. Mark kept the place very tidy and the furnishings were classic but simple—nothing fussy in the least, yet a step up from "single twenties guy" decor.

What I'd seen of the bedroom on my upside-down ride there seemed to be much of the same, and now I was getting my first look at his bathroom. It, too, was tidy, but that wasn't the first thing I noticed. As soon as I slammed the door behind me and leaned against it, that scent surrounded me. It was a little different—a little more sterile—than when it was combined with Mark's own personal scent, but this was definitely it.

Happy to focus on something other than the horrible/wonderful thing he had just said, I let my nose lead the way and bloodhounded it over to the bar of soap sitting unceremoniously in a plain soap dish next to the faucet.

Soap? Not possible.

Soap did not make you want to consume an entire person in one bite. Soap did not make butterflies invade your belly and have a rave. Soap did not make you want to throw caution to the wind and risk absolute heartbreak. Soap did not make you fall for a guy.

No! This was not happening!

I turned right around and flung the door open. Mark was standing directly in front of me with his hands braced on either side of the door. I jerked back, a bit startled, and then darted under one of his arms and raced for the living room, grabbing my dress off the floor in the process. Panties be damned.

Buck-ass naked, I found my purse and scrambled wildly for my phone. One quick emergency text to Laney and I was throwing my dress over my head, knowing that Mark wouldn't just let me walk out—and I couldn't have this conversation naked.

Seemingly in no hurry, Mark finally emerged from the

bedroom in only a pair of boxer briefs. He folded his arms and leaned against the far wall while I tried to occupy my hands with tidying my dress and fussing with my purse.

He still didn't speak.

I really didn't want to do this.

Still no speaking.

Shit.

"How many times have I told you this is a bad idea?" I finally said, facing him with an entire room, an entire world, between us.

"I already agreed you can have our friends if things don't work out for some unforeseeable reason. I don't really even like Nate that much."

He was making fucking jokes?

"This isn't a joke, Mark."

"I know it's not. Do you know how many times in my life I've told a woman I have feelings for her? Once. You." He maintained his calm and his pose.

"This will not end well." My whole being begged him to just accept it.

"So you've said, but before this discussion circles around *yet again*, I just have to ask, did somebody hurt you? Did some guy treat you badly? Break your heart? Or worse?"

What? Where in the hell had that come from?

"What?! Why in the hell would you think that?"

His calm faded a bit. "Look at it from my perspective. You like me, you like spending time with me, you're attracted to me, the sex is great, we have fun together." He checked things off on his fingers. "There has to be a reason you don't even want to try!"

"There is!" I knew he had a point and I also knew I would have to tell him everything.

"Then tell me so I can fix it."

"Gah! That's the exact opposite of what I want!"

"Then what do you want?" His hand scrubbed over his hair in clear frustration.

*I* was doing this to him.

"I want my life to be simple, manageable," I started.

"Boring? Lonely?" he countered. He was hurt.

"Normal."

"What's more normal than having a boyfriend?"

"You don't understand." Jesus, I was a broken record.

"Then help me. For the love of God, Fiona, help me understand. What am I missing here?" He gesticulated with open hands.

"It can't last, Mark."

"Why? And I want the truth this time," he demanded.

I stood my ground but I knew my eyes turned tender. "Because good things are taken away all the time. I may trust you, but I don't trust a good thing and there's nothing you can do to change that."

"What was taken away from you? Tell me." He pushed off of the wall and his voice was gentle again as he stepped toward me.

"My childhood, my future," I whispered.

"What does that mean?"

I swallowed the lump in my throat, wishing with all my might that I could just erase everything.

But I couldn't. So, I let it all out.

"When I was nine, I was diagnosed with leukemia. We fought it for a long time using a lot of drugs that eventually got the leukemia but did other kinds of damage. I can't have kids. I have a good chance of developing other cancers. My brain doesn't work right. I am twenty-four years old and I have a cardiologist and a pulmonologist. My bones are weak. I constantly feel stupid and

278 • SYLVIE STEWART

inadequate and I can't even hold down a job answering phones and making coffee. I am going to be a burden on everyone who loves me and I can't take on one more heart that will eventually break because of me."

He had stopped in his tracks at the word "leukemia."

"Shortcake. Fiona. W...what...why didn't you tell me? Are you sick? I mean, are you sick now? Shit, have I been hurting you? I can't believe I threw you around like that. And I made you lift weights!"

"This is exactly why I didn't tell you," I said, my voice choked with tears that were on their way.

"What do you mean?"

"The way you're looking at me right now. That's why I didn't tell you. I wanted to be sexy, fun, silly Fiona—not damaged, sick, breakable Fiona. I've always been that."

He closed the distance between us and grabbed my hands. "You're not damaged! You're beautiful and you *are* sexy and fun and absolutely nuts and I love that about you! But I can't just ignore what you're going through—what you've been through."

I tried to pull my hands away but he held on. "Look, Mark, you deserve a girl who is funny and smart and sexy and *healthy*. Not somebody you will probably have to take care of, who can't give you everything you want in life."

"What if *you're* what I want in life? What if I *want* to take care of you? Don't I get any choice in the matter?"

"No. You don't. I'm going to go. I texted Laney already and she's probably outside waiting by now."

"Don't do this, Shortcake." His eyes were wet.

"I have to." I pulled at my hands again and this time he let them go.

"You don't."

"You'll thank me later."

"I promise you I won't."

A horn honked outside and I kissed his cheek quickly, one last time. "Goodbye, Mark," I whispered and then, before I could change my mind, I dashed out the door.

## Chapter Thirty-Three

# LESSONS FROM KARMA AND HER MINIONS

MARK

"Well, this is even more pathetic than I imagined."

Maybe if I opened just one eye it wouldn't be so bad.

Nope, didn't work. Bailey stood at the end of my couch with her hands on her hips and a look on her face that suggested she'd just tasted something rotten.

"If you're not here to bring me more liquor then you can go away now," I mumbled.

"I mean, I knew it wasn't good when you didn't show up for work, but you haven't even been to the gym—this is serious."

The song playing on my phone ended and then started once again.

"Are you shitting me? You have this song on repeat? How many times have you listened to it?"

"I lost count after Sunday morning. Did you know Fiona lives on the fourteenth floor? That has to mean something, right?"

"Fuck. I'm going to need reinforcements. Hang in there, Buffy, I'll be right back."

She left the room for God knows where and I couldn't have cared less. All I wanted was to be left in peace to get drunk and listen to that fucking song. Too bad I was out of booze.

Every word of "Kiss Me Slowly" was burned into my brain, and with each verse and chorus I remembered every single moment with Fiona, even the ones where I'd wanted to murder her and hide the body. Her smile, her sexy-ass little outfits, her smart mouth, her laugh, her eyes, the way she fought me on everything, the way she felt in my arms, the way she changed everything.

It was official.

I had grown a vagina.

The irony was not lost on me. Fiona had ditched me immediately following mind-blowing sex that would never be repeated. How many times had I left a girl's bed happy in the knowledge I would never sleep with her again?

Karma had planted her boot firmly up my ass.

"Okay," Bailey began, once again interrupting my mental breakdown. "I am woman enough to admit that I'm not capable of handling this shit on my own. Help is on the way."

"I don't want help. Just go away." I put my arm over my eyes.

"Just go away," she mocked me using the tone of a nine-year-old. Resuming her normal voice, a.k.a. her jerk voice, she continued, "Not happening. Seeing you wallowing in misery seems like it would hold a lot of appeal, but in reality, it just makes me a bit ill." She fake gagged.

Why in the hell had I given her a key? I don't have a pet. I don't have plants. I could just have my mail held by the post office when I leave town. Idiot.

"So, first off, you need to put clothes on. I may be immune to you but the rest of the world's female population seems to find you pleasant-looking for some reason. At least put on a pair of pants—those boxer briefs are bordering on indecent and I can only avert my eyes so much."

I thought about just removing them entirely in an attempt to scare her off, but then I remembered we had to work together—and there is really no going back once your coworker and almost-sister sees your dick.

"Exactly who is coming over here?"

"Jennifer Lawrence. Who the fuck do you think? Laney."

"What the fuck?! Shit, get me some pants, will you?"

She stalked by me on her way to my bedroom and flicked my ear with her finger.

"Ow! Don't you have anybody else to torture?"

Her voice came from down the hall, "I do have a list, but you won today's drawing, asshat."

She came back with a pair of track pants and a blue t-shirt. I guess it was time to sit up. Ouch. I pushed past the head spins and got dressed.

Bailey turned my music off.

"Hey! I was listening to that!"

"No you weren't. You were torturing both of us with that."

"I like that song. It's really good."

"Oh my God. Are you pouting? I am half tempted to look inside those pants and make sure you still have your balls."

"You don't understand." I laid back on the couch and ignored her comment because it hit a little too close to home.

"Then tell me."

I lifted my head a bit and caught her eye. "Why do I always have to tell you stuff and you keep your shit tight as a duck's ass?"

"Because I'm not the one who hasn't showered in two days and who missed work so he could cuddle up with a sappy fucking song and a bottle of Jack."

She did have a point.

"Fine. Fiona dumped me."

"Duh. I already know all about that—leukemia, shitty fallout, thinks she's a bad bet—what else?"

I sat up. "Wait, how do you know that when I just found out—wait, what day is today?"

She moved my legs over, somewhat violently in my opinion, and sat down on the couch where she proceeded to flick my other ear. "Monday!"

"Ow! Stop doing that shit!" If she were a guy I could hit her back. This woman perfectly embodied the utter unfairness of a double standard.

"Oh, don't get your twat in a knot. I just found out last night. Emergency girls' night at Fiona's. I barely survived." Her head dropped back.

"So what am I supposed to do? I can't *make* her be with me."

The doorbell rang and Bailey put a finger up signaling me to wait while she let Laney in.

"Damn, he's worse than she is," said Laney when she saw me.

"This is nothing," said Bailey. "You missed the Thunder Down Under show I caught earlier. It was obscene."

Laney set her purse down and went to the kitchen before coming back with a sports drink and some ibuprofen she'd unearthed from her bag. She handed both to me and shrugged. "I'm a mom."

I took them from her and then couldn't resist asking, "How is she?"

"A fucking mess, just like you," said Bailey before Laney could answer. "I was just trying to get his drunken recollection of events. I feel like Derek Waters—but at least that dude gets to drink along."

"Well, I'm all out of booze, thank you very much, so you're shit out of luck," I said in what was probably a petulant tone. "But, like I said, I can't *make* her be with me so there is nothing you can do."

"I hate this so much for both of you," said Laney, the nice one. "She *wants* to be with you but you have to understand, all this stuff she's telling herself is so deeply ingrained in her mind she can't see past it. I'm her best friend and even I have to tread lightly where all of this is concerned."

"Well, if you want my two cents, I know one place you could start," said Bailey.

Was it possible she could actually have helpful input? Ha!

"You need to stop treating all the women in your life like they'll break if you don't constantly hover over them." She pointed accusingly.

What a crock.

"What are you talking about? I don't treat *you* that way," I protested.

"That's just because you think I'm half dude. I don't count."

"I don't treat Laney that way," I countered.

"That's because she and Nate would both kick your ass."

Laney stepped in. "I have to say I agree, Mark." She hesitated for a moment and went on, "Take your mom—I think it's really sweet you care about her so much, but have you seen her lately? For the first time in her life, she is kicking ass and taking names all on her own."

I stared at her.

It's always been my job to take care of my mom. She needs me.

Right?

Shit.

"Fiona did that," I finally said.

They both nodded.

"That's why she didn't tell me, isn't it? About the health stuff, I mean."

"I'm sure that's part of it," responded Laney. "But I think the bigger part is, despite all outward appearances, *she* sees herself as weak, and nothing we can do will change that."

I popped the ibuprofen in my mouth and chased them with the entire bottle of sports drink. "Well, ladies, if you can help me, I'd like to just see about that."

## Chapter Thirty-Four

# AND NOW, "THE AMAZING DISAPPEARING MAN!" PARTS ONE AND TWO

FIONA

"Thank you so much," I said as I forced my gazillionth smile of the evening. "Your support is truly appreciated."

The couple finished shaking my hand and filtered back into the crowd of attendees and donors. My mother leaned over to whisper in my ear.

"Are you sure you're okay, sweetheart? You seem pale. Are you coming down with something?"

I shook my head and shrugged my shoulders. "I'm fine—just a rough week."

It was Friday night and I was back at another function, but this time we were just guests, thank goodness. That didn't mean we could relax and fall back on our duties, though. Anytime we were in the presence of big money, we had a job to do.

*"Well poor little you,"* Guilt chastised. *"I'm sorry to trouble you with all the kids out there who still need help."*

Okay, okay. She was totally right, but sometimes a girl just wants to take a night or ten to wallow in sadness when she gets her heart broken. Even if she's the one who broke it.

I vowed to do better and wallow tomorrow instead. I had been a complete zombie all week, and at this point Jax was probably ready to fire me. If it weren't for Ollie picking up the slack, I'm sure I would have gotten the ax already.

But tomorrow was Saturday and I had no commitments, so I planned on taking full advantage. I had Tina and Amy cued up, Kim waiting on the counter, and good old Ben and Jerry on standby. This time they would work in shifts, though. Fool me once, shame on you; fool me twice…

Shame on me.

Indeed.

I had done this to myself. What idiot turns down a guy who gets a look under the hood and still wants to be with you?

*"It's for his own good and you know it,"* Guilt chimed in again.

*You know, if you're going to make me take this damn high road the least you could do is pitch in for the wine!*

This week had probably been the worst of my entire adult life.

When Laney had picked me up from Mark's, she'd behaved like the model best friend. I'm ashamed I ever considered trading her in for Rocco. She asked zero questions and drove like a bat out of hell to get me away from Mark's house. Once we were back at her place she gave me a huge comfy t-shirt, a blanket, and a bag of Cheetos. Then she settled us in on the couch and put her arms around me in a giant snuggle. I cried into her enormous boobs and she stroked my hair. Neither one of us had spoken a single word.

After my sobbing had subsided to the occasional hiccup, she released me and looked into my face. "Do you want to talk about it?"

I shook my head and hiccupped again.

"Okay, I'm going to change my shirt so I don't look like I'm competing in a wet t-shirt contest and then we're going to watch some crazy bitches on TV." She stood up but then looked back down at me. "But tomorrow we're talking, Fee."

An hour later we both fell asleep on the couch with orange fingers and the TV still on. It was only later that it dawned on me I had hijacked my best friend's engagement night with my own drama and neither she nor Nate had said a word about it. Damn, I have extraordinary friends.

The next day I still felt wretched, but I dragged myself home after promising Laney we'd have a girl gabfest at my place that night. She took it upon herself to invite Bailey and Charlotte, her neighbor, thinking that the more women we involved the better our chances of solving whatever problem had sent me into a tailspin. At that point, I was beyond caring who knew my business. I just needed this giant knot in my chest to go away. And, besides, Charlotte was Texas born and bred and tended to throw out wacky Southern phrases and call people "Sugar" and "Honey Pie." I figured that on its own might help.

So, I spent the evening spilling my guts and drinking wine with these awesome women. They were understandably a bit shocked by the breadth of my personal history share—Charlotte and Bailey hadn't even known about the leukemia, much less the rest of the shitstorm.

They all tried to reassure me that Mark was a grown man and could make his own decisions about what he did and didn't want. And I had to endure the lectures about how I deserved to be happy and I needed to stop worrying so much.

Still, at the end of the night I was right back where I started—broken heart and aching chest. But at least I had people to share it with. The problem was that as hard as they tried, they couldn't know what it was like to stand in my shoes, even if they were kick-ass Manolos.

The rest of the week was the same. Laney called and texted constantly and sometimes tried offering more advice, but we both knew it wasn't making a dent. I was useless at work, and on Thursday morning, when I absentmindedly poured a bag of sugar into the coffee filter, Jax finally told me to just go home and rest.

But resting meant lying around thinking about Mark, so that was the last thing I wanted to do. I decided to go shopping and take myself out to lunch instead. Going with the fake-it-'til-you-make-it theory, I dressed up to the nines and headed for Friendly Center where a girl could always find good fashion, food, and hopefully some perspective.

I stopped at a couple cute boutiques and picked up some good-ies. I was about to head into Soma for some sexy underthings when I remembered there was nobody to see such things, so I quickly moved on with only the briefest sniffle.

In need of distraction and caffeine, I headed to Caribou and pulled open the glass door—only to run smack into the last person on earth I expected to see.

"Terrence?!"

His face brightened at the sight of me, and out came that perfectly imperfect smile. It immediately warmed me, but not in the same way it once had.

"Fiona! Holy crap!" He wrapped me up in a hug while balancing two takeaway cups. I hugged him back tightly. "It's so good to see you," he said to the top of my head. Why was every-body so freaking tall?

He pulled back and we stepped out of the doorway to keep from blocking traffic. "You're looking beautiful as always," he said with a smile.

I had to laugh. "You're not looking too bad yourself. What are you doing here? I thought you were based out of Raleigh now?"

He looked a little sheepish. "Well, I am, but my…my girlfriend is here in Greensboro."

I didn't know what reaction he'd expected, but despite the miserable state of my own love life I was so pleased for him. "Really?" I put a hand to my chest and drawled dramatically.

That relaxed him immediately and he smiled again. "Yeah. She's an intern at the hospital." He gestured down the road. "I'm actually on my way to bring her a caffeine fix," he said, raising one of the cups in his hands. "You know, I'm happy I ran into you. I've been meaning to call."

Huh? "Oh?"

"Do you have a minute?" He set the cups down on the nearest table and indicated I should sit.

"Sure," I responded, completely *un*sure.

We settled and he dove right in. "So, I feel like I owe you an apology."

I jerked my head back. "Why in the world would you think that? I'm the one who went all Hulk on you when you told me you wanted a relationship."

He looked suddenly uncomfortable. "Yeah, about that…I have a confession."

In the history of mankind, nothing good has ever followed that opening. I braced.

"Remember that time when I was in town and you had to run over to pick Rocco up?"

"Yeeaahh…" Where was this going?

"Well, you'd left some papers on the counter. Some medical paperwork."

Shit.

"I know it was a total invasion of your privacy, but I saw the first page and once I read that I couldn't seem to stop. I read the whole damn packet—your entire medical history was summarized."

I knew exactly what packet he was talking about and I suddenly remembered that weekend like it was yesterday. "That was the weekend you had to leave early."

He looked right into my eyes. "I didn't have to leave early. I panicked."

"But the next time you came to town you told me your feelings had evolved into something more and you wanted a relationship."

"Yeah," he said, shifting in his seat. "This is why I owe you an apology. I invaded your privacy, then lied to you and bolted. Once I got home, I felt like such an asshole for ditching you and for running like a scared kid when I found out the girl I was hanging out with had baggage."

"Why do you think I only wanted casual in the first place? I mean, yeah, it was kind of douchey to read my private stuff, but I don't blame you for running. What I don't understand is why you came back and why you suddenly wanted more." I was completely perplexed.

"This is where I owe you another apology," he said and then took a deep breath. "I felt so guilty about what I'd done and I thought about how you needed someone to take care of you, not ditch you. So, I told myself I should man up and be that someone."

What. The. Fuck?

"So, let me get this straight. You felt guilty. Then you pitied me so much you decided to take one for the team?! That's…that's… awful…crazy…and really fucking embarrassing, Terrence!"

"I know!" He covered his eyes with his hand.

I was getting pissed. "Why exactly did you feel you had to

share this with me? Especially now that it's in the past? You never struck me as the type who would need to get something off your chest knowing it would only hurt the other person." I started gathering my things so I could get the hell out of there.

"No—that's not why I had to tell you," he said imploringly. "Please, just give me one more minute."

I dropped my bags and crossed my arms. "Then why?"

"Because when I met Carly—I don't know. When I met her it hit me like a lightning bolt and I knew right then I had been a fool to be content with always keeping women at arm's length." He ran a hand over his face, clearly frustrated.

"You and I are similar, Fiona, whether you can see it or not. I was afraid of letting anyone in, and I assumed my career that had me absent half the time was unfair to put on someone else."

He put his hands on the table. "Look, I understand that your situation is definitely more serious, but I think the fear is the same. You're afraid to pursue your future. And you're afraid to let someone in because you don't want to hurt them. But, honey, *nobody's* future is guaranteed—I don't care if they're on their deathbed or healthy as a horse. When opportunity comes, you have to grab onto it, and when love comes, you have to hold tight and just take it one fucking day at a time."

He grabbed my hand and squeezed it. "Fiona, I know you and I weren't meant to be together, but I'll never regret having you in my life. I just really want you to get out of your own way and be happy."

Well, shit. Now I'd gone and lost my mad.

I couldn't really say anything. This was too much information to process all at once.

Terrence stood. "I'm sorry I ambushed you, so feel free to call me later and yell at me," he teased. "I have to run, but I mean it—

THE SPARK • 293

call me anytime." He dropped a kiss on the top of my head. "One day at a time, honey. I promise it works." And he was gone.

He'd been like a strange messenger of shock and awe, here one minute, gone the next. After that, I'd had to upgrade my order to a grande and ask if they happened to carry any liquor behind the counter.

That had been yesterday and I still hadn't fully processed everything Terrence had said, but I had a niggling feeling it was important. Putting those thoughts aside and re-focusing on the party, I smoothed my dress—my *black* dress—and attempted a reassuring smile for my mother. But she wasn't looking at me.

"Fiona?"

Holy baby Jesus and all his baby friends—I knew that voice.

"I don't believe we've met," my mother spoke up as I attempted to hide in open space. "I'm Johanna Pierce," she greeted the only man on earth capable of simultaneously breaking me into little pieces and making me whole. Fuck!

"Mark Beckett." I heard him say and then I couldn't keep my eyes averted any longer.

I may have whimpered.

His voice addressed my mother but his brown eyes never left me for a second. He stood there in a perfectly tailored dark gray suit and an *orange* tie—the leukemia awareness color—and I thought I might faint. If I'd thought he looked good in cargo pants and a henley, that had nothing on this man in a suit. It was on par with naked Mark, and that was saying something.

"Oh my," I heard my mother whisper.

Oh my, indeed. Was it really fucking hot in here all of a sudden?

I could not make my mouth function properly so I proceeded to speak in tongues and let out a combination of about ten words at once. "WhButIwhoHoMy." Then I tried to end the awkwardness for all of us by clamping my hand over my stupid mouth.

I saw one corner of Mark's lips twitch. "Good to see you too, Shortcake."

There was no ignoring the intense stare coming from my mom, so I had to remove my hand and get my shit together. "Um...so... Mom, this is my friend Mark." His eyebrows rose at that and I ignored it. "Mark, this is my mother, Johanna."

"Yes, we've just met, Fiona," my mother said deliberately. Turning to Mark she said, "It's lovely to meet you, Mark. It's not often we get to meet Fiona's *friends*." Her glance shifted back to me oh-so-subtly.

"Um, what are you doing here?" I asked, trying not to sound panicked or rude or absolutely fucking crazy.

"Just came to make a donation and to give you this." He held out his hand, palm up, revealing a small pink flash drive with rhinestones on it.

I couldn't help the smile that came to my lips as I plucked the little device from his outstretched hand with trembling fingers. "How very secure you must be in your masculinity," I teased. What the hell was I doing?! "What is this?"

"Just something I wanted you to see," he said, telling me absolutely nothing helpful. Then he turned back to my mom with an outstretched hand and said, "It was a pleasure to meet you, Mrs. Pierce." To me, he just said, "Shortcake, I'll be seeing you." And then he was gone.

What was it with men dropping bombs on me and then disappearing in a puff of smoke?

Good grief.

*Chapter Thirty-Five*

# FYI – THE APOCALYPSE IS NIGH

**F**IONA
I shut the door to my old bedroom, my dad's laptop tucked under my arm. I had no earthly idea what was on that flash drive but there was no way I was going to let my parents see it.

The rest of the event had flown by, mostly because I'd been so completely and utterly distracted. As I'd known she would, my mother pulled me aside and grilled me about our mystery visitor. I finally had to admit to her that he was, in fact, *the* Mark I'd been seeing, but I made certain she knew things were finished.

"Well it didn't seem like *he* was finished," she felt the need to point out.

"Mom, we have friends in common. We'll have to see each other on occasion but, trust me, it's not going to work out."

"I don't understand. Don't you like him?" She smoothed her flawless hair which was arranged in a side bun this evening. She looked beautiful.

I more than liked him. I was afraid I might be in love with him. "It's not that."

"Then what? He seemed nice and even I could see that he's a hottie." She smiled wickedly.

"Ew—just ew. That is more than I needed to know. I'm going to run to the restroom." I had to avoid having the exact same conversation I'd been having with everyone for the last week. I didn't need my mother repeating the "give love a chance" mantra, so I managed to avoid her until the drive back to their place. And even my mother had known better than to bring this subject up in front of my dad. I was relatively certain that my mom's level of desire to marry me off was rivaled only by my dad's level of desire to shoot the balls off any man who came near his innocent baby girl.

Now safely ensconced in my bedroom, I'd reached the moment of truth. I pushed the power button and waited for the computer to start up. Meanwhile, I changed into one of my silk nighties and brushed my teeth.

*Hey, God. It's me again. So, as you probably know, I've had quite a week. Any idea if the next one will be better? Mark came to the fundraiser tonight. I realize you already know that—you didn't have anything to do with that, did you? Please make him happy—you did a good job with him and he deserves it. Okay, that's about it. Oh, wait, one more thing. The peep-toe sling-backs I tried to buy were on backorder—I don't suppose you could...never mind. Thanks for letting me live. Later.*

Rinse and spit.

It was time. I took the laptop to my bed and laid down on my stomach before inserting the flash drive. A video file popped up. It was titled, "Dear Fiona." I took a deep breath and double-clicked.

I almost gasped when Mark's handsome face appeared on the screen, although I don't know what else I expected to pop up. I could see his living room in the background.

"Hey Shortcake," he said with a sad smile. I wanted to reach out and touch him. "So, I know you probably don't want to hear from me but I've got a few things to say and then a couple other people want to talk to you."

Say what?

"I think I understand a little better now, and I don't blame you, but you still need to know something." He took a deep breath and peered intensely into the camera. "You, Fiona Pierce, are the strongest person I've ever met in my life. Yeah, you're tiny and you have the muscle mass of a two-year-old." He smiled and that about undid me. "But you have strength where it counts. Your character, your determination, your independence, your drive to help people, your willingness to go it alone without putting your problems on other people. All of that and more." My eyes began to tear up but I willed them to stop so my view of his perfect face wouldn't be impaired.

"And that isn't even counting the kind of strength you bring out in everyone around you. You single-handedly let my mom see just how strong she could be—I've been taking care of her for years and you come along and she suddenly has 'lady balls' as you so eloquently put it." He covered his eyes with his hand for a moment at that comment. "The point is, she always had it in her, but you brought it out. *You* did that, Shortcake." He pointed at me through the screen.

"Then there's me. Before you came along, I was kind of an asshole. Shocking, I know." He grinned and my heart flipped over in my chest. I released a sputtering laugh against my will.

"I'm sure you're having a good laugh over that."

How did he know that?

"I know now that I was scared of opening up to anyone. I figured that caring about another person only made you a target—it was easier just to be by myself. But you changed that—you made me brave enough to risk it. And even if things never work out between us, I'll never regret it. You changed me for the better." He was going to make me cry for sure.

"Now, before I officially lose my man card and get in touch with too many emotions, I need to ask you a question." He shifted and I felt like his eyes were burning into me. "What if I got into a terrible car accident and was paralyzed or injured in some traumatic way? Would you wish I had let you go before anything like that could happen? Think about it and stay tuned." The screen turned black.

I sat there in shock, but had no time to process what he'd asked.

The screen suddenly lit again with Laney's face. To say her smile was strained was an understatement.

"Hi, Fee. Don't kill me. Damn that man—he is so convincing when he's determined. Sorry." She shrugged her shoulders. "But since I'm here I do have something to say and I'm kind of happy I'm talking to a camera so you can't change the subject."

Grrr.

"You know I couldn't love you more if you were my own sister, but I haven't been the friend I should have been. I guess I didn't realize how much of your own pain and guilt you were holding back until we really started talking about it this week. You were always my fearless and crazy and lovable Fiona." She smiled, but there were tears in her eyes.

And mine too.

"I hate that you put on a brave face when you're hurting inside." She swiped a finger under one eye and let out a breath.

"So, here's the deal. You gave me the courage to give Nate a chance and now look at us—we're getting married." She couldn't help but smile and I did as well. "So I am going to do the same for you because I want you to be as happy as I am—and it's not because I think I'm Marcia. I'm happy to be Jan as long as you get to be happy too, whatever that means.

"Having said that, though, I will kick Mark's ass so hard he won't be able to do butt presses—or whatever the hell he does—if he hurts you even a little. I love you, Fee. And give the guy a chance—I don't think I've ever seen anybody so pathetic." She giggled and gave me a little wave before shutting off the camera.

Next up was Jake of all people. "Hey, future wife. I don't know why Mark asked me to talk to you since any woman given the choice between the two of us would obviously pick me, but that's his mistake." He laughed a bit maniacally.

"I do want to thank you, though, for your help on my little project." He winked into the camera, his naughty smile on full display. "Things are shaping up really well, thanks to you. And, if I'm being completely honest, I'll admit my little brother is a pretty good bet, faults and all. The one thing I can tell you is that he's never let me down a single time in my life, which is more than I can say for myself. Looking forward to the next dinner! See ya."

Short and sweet. The exact *opposite* of how I'd describe Jake.

Before I could do more than smile over Jake's little speech, Jax appeared on the screen.

WTF?

His spiky blond hair was its usual mess and his wicked grin lit up the computer.

"I thought it would be funny to start this video by telling you

you're fired, but your man here didn't agree." He laughed at his own joke and then got on with it. "So, I'll be quick."

He took on a serious tone I didn't see very often. "Miss Fiona, do you know why I hired you?" He paused as if I could actually answer him. "I hired you because from the moment you opened your mouth during your interview you made me fucking happy. When you left that day, I was so damn cheerful Ollie was about to call a doctor.

"And that's what you do for every customer you talk to. I should have shown you this before now, but do you see this?" He held the camera up to his computer screen. I could make out a little but not much. "All these customer reviews mention you. Sure, they love me because I'm brilliant and I treat them right, but every review since you started working here raves about how awesome you are too."

He brought the camera back around to himself. "So I don't give two shits if you misfile a document, break the copier, or pour cocaine into the coffee maker. You are fucking brilliant at your job and don't ever doubt that. So, that's all I've got for now but I'll see you Monday." He reached for the button to shut the video off and then paused and brought the wicked grin back. "Oh, and I'll make the coffee."

The screen switched and my heart flipped in my chest again. It was Mark.

"So, it's me again. I'll let you go and you can decide what to do next. But I can tell you with one hundred percent certainty that I want to be with you, and I want us to take care of *each other*. Hopefully, that will mean bringing out the best in one another and being happy, but even if it doesn't and bad shit happens, it's still what I want. Later, Shortcake." He winked and shut off the camera. The video ended.

I was in a bit of shock.

I was equal parts embarrassed, confused, and bowled over by the outpouring of affection from the people in my life and the effort Mark had gone to in order to fight for me.

I bawled my eyes out and fell asleep knowing that I would look like Sloth from *The Goonies* when I woke in the morning.

"Rise and shine, beautiful." I heard my father's voice beside me. I opened my eyes a crack and saw him standing at the side of my bed dressed in his navy-blue robe. It was still dark out.

"Sorry to wake you so early, sweetheart, but I couldn't sleep—I had too much on my mind," he said.

"What time is it?" I managed to mumble. My face was tight and my eyes were practically swollen shut from all the crying I'd done last night.

"Six-thirty—I know, it's early, but I want to talk to you."

What was this, confession time before the apocalypse? Since when did everybody have so fucking much to say to me?!

"Dad," I whined, "I need sleep. You can talk to me later."

"I want to talk before your mother wakes up."

That got my attention. He never kept anything from her. I made myself sit up and piled the covers around me. He took the opening.

"Your friend called me."

I was wide awake now. "Laney? When? Is something wrong?"

He shook his head. "Not Laney—Mark. He called me earlier this week."

"You're joking." It wasn't enough that he had rallied my friends to give me motivational speeches—he had to enlist my dad as well? Couldn't they all find a celebrity charity to focus on instead? I'm sure there are plenty of homeless cats in need of a good catnip supplier.

"Before you jump to any conclusions I want to tell you why he called."

"I know why he called. I broke up with him and he's using extortion to get me back for some unknown reason!" I huffed.

"He called to ask me about your health, not about anything having to do with a relationship. That's between the two of you."

Ha! If only. "But my health is open to public discussion?"

He gave me the "Dad" look. I guess when half of Raleigh knows all about your medical history it's kind of public already.

"What did you tell him?"

"Nothing at first," he said and then settled on the edge of my bed. "But then the more I talked to him the more I realized how much he cares for you and how worried he is."

I didn't know what to say.

"Fiona, why is it that this young man you've only known for a short while had to be the one to tell me that my baby girl is living scared?"

"He had no right—" I began, but my dad cut me off.

"Maybe not, but *I* have the right. Your *mother* has the right. You've always been such a cheerful, positive young woman. Your smile brightens the room—you take everything in stride. How is it I didn't know you've been living each day waiting for the other shoe to drop?"

Well, he had me there. I looked at my dad and was reminded again of my reasons. But I guess the jig was up.

"I didn't want you to worry about me anymore. I saw what a toll the leukemia took on you guys and I wanted you to think my life was perfect again."

"But clearly it hasn't been."

"Not so much," I admitted with a pathetic little shrug.

He pulled me in for a hug. "Baby girl," he whispered, and I cried a little into his shirt. At this rate, I was approaching the dehydration level of a stick of beef jerky dressed in cute pajamas. Lovely. No wonder Mark was so hot for me.

Following our conversation, my dad made pancakes while I sat at the kitchen island and drank a regimen of juice, water, and coffee while holding a cool cloth over my eyes so I could hopefully regain my full vision one day. He set my plate in front of me and then went to wake my mother so we could have a family meeting.

Yay. Cue sarcasm.

But it actually didn't turn out to be so bad. Knowing my love of lists, my father proceeded to line the island with list after list. First came the statistics on someone in my situation developing another cancer. Then came lists regarding the health of my heart, lungs, and bones. And lastly, he produced a list of therapists, and both of my parents encouraged me to focus on that list in particular.

Our little meeting ended and lots of hugs and promises to check in with each other followed before I gathered my things and headed back to Greensboro. At the last moment, though, my dad pulled me aside and reminded me exactly who he was. "By the way, in the event you do decide to date this Mark guy, please remind him that I know where to find him if I ever have cause to."

Good God.

My brain buzzed on overload the whole way home—I had a lot of thinking to do.

But first, I owed somebody a response.

*Fiona: Thanks for the video. I think.*

*Mark: Yeah, I figured it could go either way.*

*Fiona: Can I have some time to think?*

*Mark: As much as you need, Shortcake. You know where to find me.*

# M ARK
*Six Weeks Later*

"For the one-hundredth time, yes, I am coming to the engagement party."

"Don't bite *my* head off. *I'm* just the messenger. Laney was afraid to call you again. Wimp," Bailey said on the other end of the line.

"I'm a grown-ass man. I can be in the same room as Fiona and not lose my shit. And, besides, I'm actually looking forward to seeing her," I admitted as I leaned back in my desk chair.

"So you're still holding out hope? Pardon me for saying this, but you're a glutton for punishment, Beckett."

"I think that's the first time I've ever heard you say something in a remotely polite way," I baited her.

"Shove it up your ass, Romeo," she growled.

"And, yes, I'm still holding out. She's gonna come around —you'll see."

"Well, I hope for all our sakes she does because I don't know if I can handle any more of these GNOs she keeps organizing. I mean, it's bad enough with all the wedding stuff."

"What in the fuck is a GNO? It sounds like a lady-doctor problem."

"I know—they actually have an acronym for it. It's supposed to stand for 'Girls' Night Out' but I secretly refer to it as 'Got No Orgasms.' It's just a bunch of girls drinking and talking shit about guys. I mean, sometimes I guess it's not so bad, but with all the girly wedding crap? I'm maxing out on all things 'girl.'" She made a lovely gagging sound. "Laney's going to make me wear a dress to the wedding," she whined.

"Bailey, you're one of her bridesmaids. Of course you have to wear a dress. In fact, I think you're required to wear the exact same dress as the rest of the bridesmaids."

"What? That's just idiotic."

"I don't make the rules. Anyway, I gotta run but I'll see you tonight. And don't wear jeans and a t-shirt! This party is the kind you dress up for." I stood from my chair.

"Motherf—" She began, but I hung up, laughing to myself.

I grabbed my hard hat and headed toward the trailer door to go check in with the crew. Before I got there, however, there was a knock on the door. I turned the knob and swung it open, expecting to see one of the guys. Instead, Fiona stood on the top step looking like a fucking dream. Hell, maybe she was.

"Hi, Mark," she said quietly.

Nope, not a dream.

"Hey, Shortcake," I responded and couldn't help the dopey smile I'm sure was plastered across my face. Her returning smile told me it looked as stupid as it felt.

"I'm sorry to barge in on you like this but I finally worked up the courage so I just had to go with it." She looked down at her designer-shod feet before bringing her eyes back to mine and scrunching her face up in the cutest fucking way.

"You can barge in on me anytime you want—you know that." I was starting to get a bit nervous. For all the waiting and forced confidence I'd had, now that the moment was here I was afraid she was going to end things once and for all. "Come on in," I stepped aside and held the door for her. If I was going to get dumped at least I could ensure a little privacy.

She stepped in and walked toward my desk before turning around. "You've been so patient and I really wanted to thank you for that. Um...a lot has happened." She ran her hands down the skirt of her sexy little sundress. Girls don't wear sexy outfits when they're going to dump a guy, do they? Oh, who was I kidding—she looked sexy in anything so it was a moot point.

"Oh?" was all I could manage.

"Yeah," she began again. "I've started seeing a therapist my oncologist recommended. It's been helping me gain a new... perspective...on things. I'm taking a break from my parents' foundation—from all the charity stuff, really. My therapist thinks that in order for me to stop fearing the worst around every corner I need to shed the past as much as possible and focus more on the future."

"That sounds pretty smart," I said and then forced myself to ask, "So, which part do I fall in—the past or the future?"

She turned and plucked a stapler off the desk, playing with it to occupy her hands. "I'm also considering starting a small catering business—a *very* small one." It was as if she hadn't heard my question.

"That sounds like a great idea," I responded, genuinely pleased, but not understanding where she was going with this.

"Yeah, it's funny. Your mom was the one to come up with the idea."

Now that was a surprise. "My mom?"

She let out a small laugh. "Yeah. With all her waitressing experience she has a lot of great ideas. I don't know, it's just a kernel of an idea at this point."

"Wow. I never thought of that—of course she would be a huge help in that area." I scratched my chin.

"The future," she said suddenly, her eyes meeting mine in earnest.

My heart may have stopped. "What?"

"The answer is, you're part of the future—if you want to be, knowing what that could mean."

She'd hardly finished her sentence before I scooped her up and kissed the fucking hell out of her. She started laughing halfway through the kiss and that got me laughing too. "We sound like complete idiots," I managed to say between laughs and kisses.

"No, *I'm* the idiot. I almost let you go," she said, grabbing my face in her hands.

I pulled back and looked at her. "Nah, I never would have let that happen, Shortcake."

She scoffed. "Cocky bastard." But she was smiling.

"You know it," I replied and pulled her in again.

The party was in full swing by the time we got to the restaurant. A small detour to Fiona's condo ended up in a furious round of what I suppose qualified as make-up sex. Whatever it was, I was looking forward to a whole lot more of it.

"Oh, thank God you're here!" Laney accosted Fiona the

moment we walked into the private room. It took her a moment to realize Fiona and I had come in together. She pointed back and forth between us, her mouth agape. "You…you…really?" She was beaming at us. We both nodded our heads and then she Lost. Her. Shit.

There was squealing that I probably only heard part of—the rest being audible only to neighborhood dogs—and some weird references to the Brady Bunch. When the squealing started again, I managed to still Fiona long enough to kiss her quickly before I went in search of testosterone.

I found Nate, Gavin, and some of the other guys gathered near the makeshift bar in the corner. After a round of handshakes and some razzing about my date, Nate cut in.

"Hey, why am I just finding out now that your brother is moving back to Greensboro?"

I put my hands up defensively. "Don't ask me—I just found out the other day when he called to tell me." Truthfully, I'd missed Jake since he'd left a few weeks back, but I wasn't ever going to tell him that.

"What's that all about? I mean, not that I'm not happy to have him around, but I thought he loved Florida."

"Who the hell knows," I replied. "All he said was that he was sorting shit out and he'd be moving here within a couple months, hopefully. I don't know what he has in mind." I left out the part where he'd said he was moving back to steal Fiona. Why did I miss him again?

"Must have to do with his future wife's cooking," Gavin taunted, as if he'd read my mind.

"You'd best watch yourself, Junior, or you're gonna end up with a broken nose," I told the little douchebag. Okay, so maybe he wasn't little, but he was definitely a douchebag.

"Calm your tits, Beckett. All of you sappy lovesick assholes are such easy targets," he threw back at me and then wisely backed up a few steps. "I'll grab some beers."

I refocused my attention on Nate, considering that he and Laney were the actual guests of honor at this party. "Congrats, man. I'm really happy for you guys. Laney's got her work cut out for her, though." It was my job to give him a hard time.

"Speaking of," he replied. "I hope you don't mind that I volunteered your new girlfriend to save the day and get me off the hook."

I just looked at him quizzically.

"The chef was supposed to prepare some healthy shit for my dad, but now he's saying it's a set menu with no exceptions so Laney is panicked."

Nate's dad had a heart attack last summer and his mom had been vigilant about Riordan's diet ever since then. She'd gotten Laney on board as well so I knew this had the potential to mess with the evening. Let's just say Riordan was not one to acquiesce quietly. And neither was Erin.

"Well, if anyone can sweet talk her way into a professional kitchen it's Fiona," I said.

"My thoughts exactly," said Nate.

Gavin approached and handed us each a fresh beer—probably as an apology for being a douchebag. Or not.

"To crazy-ass women," Nate said, raising his beer.

"To the man brave enough to take on my crazy-ass sister," Gavin chimed in, raising his.

"To the ladies brave enough to take on…anything," I finished as we clinked bottles and took a healthy swallow of our beers.

Yeah, I was a total fuckmuppet.

*You got something to say about that?*

# EPILOGUE

## MARK
### *Three Months Later*

"Hurry up, Shortcake! The ceremony starts in fifteen minutes."

"I just had to make sure Kelly has everything under control!" she yelled as she rushed up the front steps of the church where I was waiting.

I held out my hand and she sighed dramatically before handing over her cell phone. She was adorable when she pouted. It also usually made me want to bite her bottom lip.

I turned the phone off and tucked it into the pocket of my tux. "You know everything is going to run perfectly. The two of you have been over this a hundred times, everything is already prepped, and you yourself said the recipes are simple."

She sighed again. "You're right. I don't know why I'm worrying about this. I should be focusing on Laney—I'm a terrible Maid of Honor."

"Ducking out to make one phone call does not make you terrible. You girls spent the entire morning together and she's all ready to go."

"I hate that Kelly can't be here, though," she said quietly as I opened the front door of the church and ushered her inside.

"We'll all see her at the reception, and Jake promised to take lots of pictures. Now kiss me quick because I have to go keep Nate from passing out."

She did, letting her lips linger a little too long for a church setting—not that I was complaining. Then she shot me her gorgeous bright smile and strutted off in her tan heels and blue dress, looking as stunning as ever. Oh, right—a few weeks ago I'd been scolded for using the words "tan" and "blue" and had been informed that the wedding colors were to be referred to only as the very elegant "parchment" and "pale cerulean." That had been the moment I'd decided Nate was more pussy-whipped than I was.

It was hard to believe Nate and Laney's wedding was already upon us. The last three months since their engagement party and the "official" beginning of Fiona and me as a couple had flown by.

In the beginning, I'd vowed to tread lightly and try not to over-whelm Fiona, but she'd put the kibosh on that pretty much imme-diately and we'd spent every night together since. Although we still maintained two residences, we were basically living together.

Fast? Hell yes.

Scary? A bit, especially when I got my first real look at her closet and realized that if we were ever to get a place together we'd have to dedicate an entire room to her wardrobe. The shoes could possibly require a small addition.

But we made sure to communicate openly with each other, and her therapist was helping her work through things and focus on her strengths. Her mantra was to take things one day at a time and I was totally on board with that.

And that kernel of an idea my mom had had about doing some catering had actually turned into a great little side business for the two of them. They were only doing small events, but word was getting out and I was sure the wedding reception today would result in new business.

Fiona hadn't wanted to do the reception at first because she wanted to be able to focus all her attention on Laney. But when Nate and Laney decided to just do hors d'oeuvres and drinks and save their money for a kick-ass honeymoon, Fiona had finally relented.

The business was doing wonders for her self-confidence, and she and my mom worked together like a dream. My mom never let Fiona freak out about forgetting things or losing track of her thoughts, and she was always the one in charge of any waitstaff and set-up. That allowed Fiona to delve into her favorite parts of the business, which included creating menus, cooking, and schmoozing with clients. It was a wonderful partnership, and I was relatively certain they could turn this into a full-time business and hire a manager if they wanted to. We'd just have to wait and see— one day at a time.

I made my way up the center aisle of the church, which was about half-full, and sought out Nate, hoping to find him still upright. He was exactly where I'd left him, standing with Gavin in the sacristy just off the altar. Gavin tucked a flask into the inside pocket of his tux jacket as I walked in, and Nate was looking a bit calmer but still kind of pale.

"Well, man, everything's under control. The moms, Bailey, and Fiona are with Laney; Rocco and Laney's dad are waiting to walk her down the aisle; and your dad is gonna walk the moms down in just a few. All you've got to do is hang in there a few more minutes, say your 'I do's, and we can all go have a drink." I had no idea how I'd gotten so involved in my friends' wedding, but there are certainly worse things than standing up with a good friend when he gets hitched to the right girl.

Nate took a breath. "Okay, I can do this."

"Did you remember to break the news to Fiona about the reception speech?" Gavin asked.

Shit.

"Shit. I forgot," I said and then gestured for him to bring the flask back out so I could partake.

I knew I'd forgotten something.

You see, back at the engagement party, Fiona had insisted on giving a little toast to the crowd where she had, in her traditional style, said something that really struck a chord. I believe the exact phrase that had sent the crowd sniggering was, "To Laney and Nate, as they enter into this union, may they only have happy endings." While it had certainly been a memorable toast, it was not one that Laney and Nate wanted repeated at their wedding reception. As the boyfriend, I had been tasked with breaking it to Fiona that there would only be Gavin's Best Man speech this evening, although I wasn't sure how that could possibly turn out much better. Their wedding, their rules, though.

"I'll catch her afterward and tell her."

Just then, the priest walked in and I quickly hid the flask behind my back.

He just laughed. "Son, you think Jesus didn't drink?" Then he turned to Nate. "You ready?"

Nate nodded once and then stiffly exited the small room to go meet his bride.

"I still don't understand why I'm not giving a speech. The food is all set and the servers and assistants have things covered. I'm just here to party," Fiona said, giving a little shimmy.

I pulled her to me and wrapped her up in my arms so I could feel her against me. "Then party away, Shortcake," I said into her ear before giving the lobe a little nip. She shivered and I smiled.

The small band Laney hired had just begun their first set, so I swayed with Fiona a little as we stood beside the dance floor. The newlyweds were about to have their first dance and I intended to spend the rest of the evening with my girl in my arms, both here and upstairs in the hotel room I'd booked for the night.

Nate and Laney had chosen to dance to "The One" by Kodaline, and as the song started even I had to admit they looked pretty damn perfect dancing out there with eyes only for each other. That was, until Rocco decided to join in. Nate bent down and easily hoisted him up to join in the dance.

"Awww," Fiona said into my shoulder and I could swear I heard her sniffle. Apart from Laney and Nate, I don't think there was a happier person in the room than my Shortcake. That's just who she is.

When the song was over and everyone clapped uproariously, the band's lead singer invited everyone to join the couple on the dance floor and enjoy the music. Fiona and Laney performed a shockingly sexy dance that had me almost sweeping Fiona away to our room that minute. I managed to resist, but I made sure every man in the room knew she was spoken for. I was less than subtle in my claim and caused Fiona to smack my chest at one point and call me a caveman.

I was just about to suggest we take a break and get another drink when the lead singer addressed the crowd again. "This one is a special request for Mark, one of tonight's groomsmen. Enjoy." I pulled my head back in confusion and then looked down at Fiona, sure she had to be the one behind this. But she looked just as clueless as I was.

Then the first chords of a song I knew better than any other in the world rang out over the room. I swiveled my head in search of the culprit and, sure enough, Bailey stood leaning into a high table across the room. She was wearing a strapless dress identical to Fiona's, and I had to admit the girl cleaned up good. When I caught her eye, she smiled her smartass smile and lifted her drink to me in a silent toast. I laughed out loud and ushered a confused Fiona back onto the floor where we proceeded to dance to "Kiss Me Slowly."

Fiona burrowed into me and then, partway through the song, she drew back and looked up at me, her eyes alight. "I live on the fourteenth floor! That's got to mean something!"

I smiled and said, "Yeah, I think it does."

The song was just winding down when I heard Nate's voice come from my right. "What in the hell does he think he's doing?"

I turned in his direction and Fiona and I moved closer. "Who?"

"Your asshole brother," he said, gesturing to the other side of the room with his chin.

I'm allowed to call Jake all sorts of filthy names because he's my brother and he usually deserves it, but I was taken aback by the uncharacteristic acid in Nate's tone. That was, until I looked over and saw that my brother was indeed the asshole who happened to be kissing Bailey in the corner of the room, his hand halfway up her thigh.

Fuck!

Laney and Fiona both gasped and then for some reason known only to the female population of this planet, they both sighed and said, "Aww."

"This shit is not happening," Nate spat out and started to remove his jacket.

"Whoa there, Mayweather, I got this. Stick with your bride and go cut some cake or something." I eyed both women and they ushered his ass away.

By the time I got across the room, the slutty little slutbags were nowhere to be seen. I made a token effort to search the adjoining hallway and the men's room (I wouldn't put much past Jake) but came up empty.

Back in the reception hall, I found the rest of the wedding party gathered together watching Rocco show off some hilarious dance moves.

"He totally gets that from me," Laney said, and I actually think she was being serious.

I put a hand on Nate's shoulder and gave him a thumbs-up when he turned to me. No use spoiling his big night. Bailey and Jake were both adults and nothing I could say would have made a difference anyway.

Rocco finished his performance by giving a little bow to hoots and cheers from his family, and then Gavin spoke up.

"Well, I guess it's about that time," he said and then walked toward the band to take the mic and start his Best Man speech. We all turned our attention to him and he ran a nervous hand through his messy brown hair.

"Um, hi everybody. For those of you who don't know me, I'm Gavin, Laney's brother. I wanted to say a few words to the happy couple." He gestured in our general direction and someone in the crowd hooted.

"Nate, I've never had a brother but I'm proud to call you one now. You make my big sis and the little dude happy, and that's what counts in my book."

Laney and Fiona both awwed again.

"Laney, you've been a great sister and a better friend than I probably deserve, and I'm really happy for you that you found the right guy to make your family complete."

Nate looked at his shoes and Laney tucked her arm around his waist while she beamed at her brother.

"Now, I was going to end my speech there, but I think something else needs to be said, so everyone please raise your glasses for a toast." We all obeyed and Gavin smiled. "To Laney and Nate, as they enter into this union, may they only have happy endings!"

Fiona squealed and fist pumped the air.

Laney buried her face in Nate's shoulder.

Nate dropped his head in defeat.

And I threw my head back and laughed my fucking ass off.

~THE END ~

*Continue the series with **The Lucky One**, Bailey and Jake's story.*
*Read on for an excerpt.*

*Stay up to date on Sylvie's upcoming books and projects by subscribing to her newsletter!* http://bit.ly/NewsSylvie

www.sylviestewartauthor.com

**BONUS SCENE and DOWNLOAD!**

Here are two exclusive extras for this latest edition of *The Spark*:

- Print and complete this fun word search based on *The Spark* for your chance to win a signed paperback! http://bit.ly/TheSparkWS
- Want to read what happens next for Kelly? Read the exclusive **Bonus Scene!** http://bit.ly/TheSparkBonus

# ABOUT THE AUTHOR

*USA Today* bestselling author Sylvie Stewart is addicted to Romantic Comedy and Contemporary Romance, and she's not looking for a cure. She hails from the great state of North Carolina, so it's no surprise that most of her books are set in the Tar Heel state. She's a wife to a hilarious dude and mommy to ten-year-old twin boys who tend to take after their father in every way. Sylvie often wonders if they're actually hers, but then she remembers being a human incubator for a gazillion months. Ah, good times.

Sylvie began publishing when her kids started elementary school, and she loves sharing her stories with readers and hopefully making them laugh and swoon a bit along the way. If she's not in her comfy green writing chair, she's probably camping or kayaking with her family or having a glass of wine while binge-watching Hulu. Or she's been kidnapped—so what are you doing just sitting there?!!

\*\*Winner of the 2017 National Indie Excellence Award for Romantic Comedy

\*\*Winner of the 2017 Readers' Favorite Silver Medal for Romantic Comedy

Thank you so much for reading *The Spark* – I hope you enjoyed it.

If you did, a **review** on your favorite book site is always appreciated!

*Want to stay updated on new releases, promotions and giveaways?*
Subscribe to my newsletter! http://bit.ly/NewsSylvie

*Want to hang out with me and my other readers?*
Join my reader group on Facebook: **Sylvie's Spot - for the Sexy, Sassy, and Smartassy!** http://facebook.com/groups/SylviesSpot

Thanks! XOXO,
*Sylvie*

*Keep up to date and keep in touch!*
www.sylviestewartauthor.com
sylvie@sylviestewartauthor.com
Follow me on BookBub for sales and new releases!

facebook.com/SylvieStewartAuthor

twitter.com/sylvie_stewart_

instagram.com/sylvie.stewart.romance

## AUTHOR'S NOTE

I would like to apologize to the great state of New Jersey. It's not me, it's Fiona. I swear.

Also, if you're wondering what makes Mark smell so good, it's Hudson Made *Worker's Soap*. Makes hard-working men smell yummy!

# EXCERPT FROM THE LUCKY ONE

## Carolina Connections Book 3

*Chapter One: Hello, My Name Is Satan*

**BAILEY**

"I swear his eyes are following me."

"It *is* a little creepy, I'm not gonna lie," said Mark, glancing over my shoulder.

A shiver ran down my spine and the hairs on the back of my neck stood at attention.

Mark took in my expression—which I'm sure was one of intense revulsion—and laughed right in my face, his straight white teeth not even attempting to bite his tongue. This was entirely unsurprising.

Mark's day is not complete unless he has tortured me in some way. He's the twin brother I never had and certainly never wanted. I already have an older brother, but Mark somehow worked his way into my life and I can't seem to get rid of him and his ridiculously bulky bod no matter how hard I try.

Still smiling at my pain, Mark shook his head and asked, "If he freaks you out so much, why the hell did you say yes?"

I glared at him, hands on my hips. "What in the hell was I supposed to do?! There were tears! Wet, sloppy tears!"

This did nothing to tame his smile. "You are such a fucking pushover," he whispered in my ear before skirting around me and approaching the creepy son-of-a-bitch.

"Ha!" I declared as I turned around, completely forgetting to keep my gaze averted. "Shows how much you know. I talked the kid down from a puppy!" I was actually quite proud of myself, despite my lack of forethought.

Turns out I can't stand lizards. Who knew? But the joyous expression on my nephew's face and the complete cessation of all waterworks was my prize to revel in.

Totally worth it.

I'm sure I broke every babysitting rule in the book, but desperate times call for desperate measures. It looked like my brother and his new wife just got themselves a pet gecko.

Whoops.

"Okay, little man. Everything is all set up," Mark said to a nearly-vibrating Rocco. "The light will keep him nice and warm, he's got a good place to hide in that log, and your Aunt Bailey will show you how to feed him the crickets." Mark's smile turned evil as his eyes found me again.

What in God's name had I been thinking? To be fair, I had assumed these crickets would be dead when the twelve-year-old sales associate had pushed his glasses up on his nose and mentioned we'd need to stock up. By the time I realized we would instead be bringing home a plastic container teeming with live insects, it was too late. Rocco, my adorable nephew, had fallen in love.

"Fist bump," Mark requested of Rocco, whose attention was completely captured by his new pet. Rocco extended his little fist without letting his eyes stray from the tank. "Thanks, Mark."

"Sure thing," Mark replied, ruffling the kid's dark hair. Then to me, "I gotta get back to Fiona."

"Is she feeling any better?" I asked, leaning against Rocco's dresser.

"Eh, hard to say."

Mark looked slightly distressed at the thought, and I marveled for the umpteenth time at the transformation my once-slutty friend had undergone since meeting his girlfriend, Fiona. Gone was the arrogant manwhore and in his place was an arrogant, pussy-whipped little douchebag. Ah, it warms the heart.

"I picked up an antibiotic for her, so hopefully that will start working soon," he said as he gathered his things.

I felt a sympathy pain in my throat just thinking about Fiona and her bout of strep throat. I cursed the damn virus for forcing me to step in and babysit Rocco while my brother, Nate, and his new wife, Laney, were off on their honeymoon. The same virus that, today, revealed just how ill-equipped I was to care for a child without becoming the biggest sucker known to man. "Well, tell her I hope she feels better and not to worry about Rocco—I got this."

Mark stopped in his tracks on his way to the door. He cocked his head, his eyebrows arching and his mouth sporting that damn smirk I wanted to knock off his stupid face. "Oh, I can see that."

I flipped him off, confident that Rocco's attention was elsewhere.

Mark's smug cackle echoed in the hallway outside Rocco's bedroom. "I'll let myself out!"

"You do that, Buffy!" Asshole.

Damn. It was just me and the kid again.

It's not that I don't like kids—I love my new nephew. I'm just not all that comfortable around tiny humans. I think I'm always waiting for them to judge me and find me inadequate somehow.

I'm the youngest of two kids, and I was never the babysitting type. My teen years had been spent sketching, reading, and plotting to get Nate in trouble whenever possible. And I'm a total daddy's girl, so I never pursued anything Riordan Murphy would consider "girly," much to my mom's disappointment. Babysitting, makeup lessons, and trips to the mall were eschewed in favor of hanging out at building sites with my dad and rocking out to heavy metal while painting and drawing. And, although my taste in music evolved as I reached adulthood, the rest pretty much stayed the same.

Everything I knew about taking care of a child consisted of lessons learned through trial and error over the last twenty-four hours.

I had been minding my own damn business last night, scarfing down cold pizza and channel surfing, when my phone had rung. I'd been ready to let it go to voicemail when I saw it was my brother. I hit the accept button; I should have let it go to voicemail.

Get your copy of *The Lucky One* today!

# ALSO BY SYLVIE STEWART

*The Carolina Connection Series:*

**The Fix** *(Carolina Connections, Book 1)*

**The Lucky One** *(Carolina Connections Book 3)*

**The Game** *(Carolina Connections Book 4)*

**The Way You Are** *(Carolina Connections Book 5)*

**The Nerd Next Door** *(Carolina Kisses, Book 1)*

**Then Again**

**Happy New You**

**Game Changer** *(July 2019)*

**About That**

**Full-On Clinger**

**Between a Rock and a Royal** *(Kings of Carolina, Book 1*

**Blue Bloods and Backroads** *(Kings of Carolina*, Book 2)

# THE FIX:

**My life is a friggin' fairytale—just not the kind any single girl would ever want to star in.**

**LANEY:**

Like any good heroine, I have challenges to face. Getting my son to wear pants is one; dealing with my snooze-fest of a job is another. Then there's the Beast, my freeloading brother who's worn a permanent dent in the couch at my new place. And no fairytale would be complete without a smoking hot prince, of course. Too bad he's a complete ass.

My instincts scream at me to steer clear of Nate Murphy. Because, if life has taught me anything, there is no such thing as happily ever after.

**NATE:**

I may not be a superhero, but I do my best to come to the rescue when I'm needed. And, hey, I just moved halfway across the country after a single phone call from my mom. But being back home and taking on the responsibilities involved makes me a bit cranky at times. Unfortunately, the one time I completely lose my cool is in front of the hottest girl I've ever met. I've got my work cut out for me if I'm going to fix this. But I *will* fix this.

I'll be anything Laney Monroe needs me to be … a superhero, a prince, or just a guy she might take a chance on.

Order your copy of *The Fix* today!

# THE LUCKY ONE:

**Luck is no lady… in fact, she can be a downright bitch.**

**BAILEY:**

Let's get one thing straight. I am not your typical girl. Sure, I've got all the parts, but I've been a stubborn, irreverent tomboy since the womb. Despite my Irish blood, bad luck makes a sport of messing with me, especially when it comes to men. But my shields are firmly in place now; nothing can touch me again. Except maybe Jake Beckett. He just might make this tomboy do the girliest thing in the world—fall head over heels in love.

**JAKE:**

I'm a pretty lucky guy. I have a phenomenal family, a career I love, and I'm building a brand-new life back in my hometown. And, not to be a jerk about it, but I do more than all right with the ladies. Everything's going according to plan—like I said, I'm a lucky guy. That is, until my luck runs out. Until I meet the girl I call "Irish." Irony can go kiss my ass.

Order your copy of *The Lucky One* today!

# THE GAME:

**They say opposites attract. Someone needs to tell that to Emerson Scott.**

**GAVIN:**

All I ever wanted was to play ball. When an act of sheer stupidity took that dream away, I thought I'd never bounce back. But now I have the opportunity to coach an up-and-coming phenom, and I'm giving it all I've got. The fact that I've been lusting after his smoking-hot sister only sweetens the deal. Emerson may be buttoned up like a school librarian, but I play my best when I'm under pressure ... and I *always* bring the heat.

**EMERSON:**

Never lose focus. Never lose control. Those are the first two rules in my carefully calculated plan for success. Finding myself thrown into the role of guardian for my little brother was *not* part of that plan. But I can adjust for Jay's sake; I'm not about to let one change make me lose sight of my goals. Too bad Jay's hot young baseball coach doesn't seem to give a fig about my plans. He has one of his own—and it includes me. Gavin Monroe may play like a pro, but that boy will never win this game.

Order your copy of *The Game* today!

## THEN AGAIN:

**It's been two years since the divorce papers slapped Jenna in the face, and it's high time to dive back in.**

Step one: find a romance-novel-worthy man for a hot summer fling.

How hard could it be?

But disastrously bad flirting, a failed honky-tonk hookup, and a mix-up with one of Sunview's finest have Jenna seriously doubting if this is all worth it. Maybe she's better off leaving the world of love and sex to others—or maybe she's just looking in the wrong place ...

Order your copy of *Then Again* today!

www.ingramcontent.com/pod-product-compliance
Lightning Source LLC
Chambersburg PA
CBHW072021110726
47910CB00005B/1825